Death Revokes the Offer

Catharine Bramkamp

A Few Little Books Press Cotati, California

First edition copyright 2008 Catharine Bramkamp

This is a work of fiction. Names, characters, some places and incidents are products of the author's fevered imagination or are used fictitiously and are not to be construed as real. Except for the advise on wine. Any resemblance to actual events, local organizations or persons, living or dead, is entirely coincidental.

It's not about you.

ISBN 13: 978-0-9816848-0-2

Published by A Few Little Books, Cotati, California

May 2008

Design and layout by A Few Little Books

Printed in the United States of America

A Few Little Books Press

Acknowledgements

To my Write Group: Laurel, Lori, Michele and Cyma, thank you for your feedback and encouragement. Thank you to the 3C's Writing group members; Cynthia and Carol for providing last minute answer. Thank you to Melissa Mower for her excellent copyediting. Thank you to members of my book club especially Stacey and Jenny who offered valuable feedback on the cover. Thank you to Century 21 Classic Properties for starting me out on such an interesting career.

Thank you to Trevor Hunt at istockphoto, and Morgen Benoit for the author's photograph.

and to you, the reader, for taking a chance on this book.

To Andrew

Chapter 1

The conceit to these stories is that I speak directly to you.

The first thing you should know about me is that I do not cut my own hair with nail scissors. Please. Robert would kill me if I even considered touching my hair with my own two hands.

I'm also not a doctor and I never know exactly why a body is dead. I only know that when you find a dead body in the kitchen, it makes it that much more difficult to sell the house, what with all the hysteria about full disclosure nowadays.

Difficult, but not impossible.

I am not a national park ranger. I do not do this in between caring for adorable children or difficult teens. In fact, I completely forgot to have children. I'm sure the word *children* was written on some long ago to-do list along with items like *white wedding at the Marin Country Club* and *lose 50 pounds by Christmas* penciled in just below that.

And I am not a sheriff for a small town in the Deep South.

I also know that some people will look to the author and say, "Oh, is that YOU?" Of course it's not her. I have twice the listings she does and better hair. I already own that Dooney & Bourke purple crocodile embossed bag she craves but can't afford. So I'm here to tell you, I am myself. For some people like my best friend, Carrie, that is enough. For others like my long-suffering broker on record, it's too much.

"Can't you just tone it down a little?" Inez asks on a weekly basis.

Nope is my answer.

Sometimes I think I should get a little dog. But I worry that it won't really go with the bag.

So, the body in the kitchen. You are probably wondering about that, like is it some kind of metaphor? No, it was Mr. Mortimer Maximilian Smith. He had two interesting first names to make up for the third and by the time I discovered him, he was dead on the floor of his rather pedestrian — in my opinion — home in southern Marin.

I wasn't really supposed to be there at all. I don't usually sell homes in Marin. My beat is the River's Bend area of Sonoma County, but my mother knew Mr. Smith from her exercise class. He told her that he wanted to sell his house quickly and needed someone he could trust.
I can appreciate his concern. Especially since, according to my mother, Mr. Smith's children don't exude trustworthiness (although she later admitted that she had not, in fact, met any of the Smith children, so you can see we began this project based strictly on cold hard facts). But since the children had apparently announced last week that they thought it was better for dad to move out of his huge home and into a more suitable location, Dad, in response to this new threat to his lifestyle, needed to counter fairly quickly.

I love old children. Suitable location? That meant some community far enough away from said children so they weren't obligated to weekly visits. From the sounds of it, the children were probably considering one of the active senior communities currently proliferating across the country.

And I love Baby Boomers. An Active Senior Community? Retirement home. I can hardly wait to see how Boomers manage to spin death. In Mr. Smith's case, he already knows.

Here's another fact: the children weren't planning to sell the house; that was Mr. Smith's idea. And it made no sense at all.

Enter me, Allison Little — a Little Goes a Long Way — with New Century Realty. I had a dead man on the Spanish tile floor, survivors who did not want to sell, and the police on the phone. Or was it the fire department? Whomever. I was personally hoping I was calling within the county limits, but there is no guarantee. I could be talking to some nice young thing in Sacramento or L.A., or Bangladesh.

"There's a dead body in the kitchen," I calmly announced.

"How dead?"

"Very. Can someone come out and, you know, get him?"

"There's no hurry, ma'am, if the body is already dead. Are you in a safe place?"

I hadn't even considered that. Really, I don't consider my own safety that often — overconfidence coupled with having read too many magazine articles with titles like "Take Back the Night" when I was a teenager. Anyway, who would want to take me on? Most desperate junkies weigh maybe a third of what I do. I could sit on them and crush them. It seems that enough junkies have spread the word to that effect. I'm never accosted when I'm in the City.

So anyway, safe place.

Actually, I was standing here in this semi-secure (and secluded, which is a great home feature unless you need help) location in the first place because of a phone call last week.

The call interrupted me just in time. I was languishing in one of those interminable information meetings that realtors must endure on a depressingly regular basis. Sometimes we attend the meeting because of peer pressure, sometimes because we need the credits to continue our license. My manager, Inez, made me attend. She was probably angry with me for something and this was her method of punishment. And sometimes we can acquire actual, useful information. This was not a meeting that covered the latter. This meeting was entirely devoted to beating the dead horse of 1031-exchange subject. We had been flaying the horse of exchanging properties to defer taxes since 9 a.m. I knew there was only forty-five days to identify the new property; I understood that before I came in.

It was two o'clock when the rescue call came in. The phone buzzed and danced across the Formica laminated table. I blinked, trying to focus on the phone. My eyeballs were about to fall out because they were so dry. I picked up my eyeballs (that was a metaphor) and escaped to the women's room murmuring something about a family emergency — the acoustics in the ladies' room are excellent.

It was my mother.

She had an idea that could only be discussed over lunch.

I'm all about a free lunch, so I agreed.

I think I'll name my first child Liz Pendens.

"Mr. Smith is such a nice man," my mother insisted. "He should be able to sell his own house if he wants."

We met at the country club because that's my mother's favorite place to eat, play, and relax. To help you picture my mother, she is sitting across from me. She sits perfectly straight in her soft chair at her favorite table at the club. Her back does not make contact with the chair back. She is clad in her "casual" uniform; pressed tan slacks and a pressed cashmere sweater. No, I do not know how her dry cleaner manages to press cashmere.

My mother always wears pearls. Even when she golfs.

She is sitting on the edge of her padded chair, daintily cutting her tiny side salad that she claims is enough for a full lunch. She eats the lettuce bite by bite.

She chews carefully.

I, too, chew carefully.

But I'm chewing a double-decker cheeseburger with a side order of fries. I don't know why I always crave something like a double cheeseburger with fries every time I eat with my mother, but I do. And the club chef does a passable job with burgers; I assume a better job is done with a dinner salad because Mom always orders that. And black coffee.

Mom likes to think she's younger, slimmer, and prettier than me, which for the most part is true, especially the thinner part. Mom is still embroiled in that ancient rivalry between wife and daughter for the love of the father/husband. And I was not clever enough to mitigate the competition by tossing a grandchild between us. My bad.

"So Mr. Smith is a nice man," I repeated between dainty bites of my burger.

She swallowed and took a sip of iced water. "A very nice man. He's been in the area for years. He loves modern art, is a patron to the arts both here and in San Francisco. I think he even donated a considerable amount of money to some organization down there. Anyway, he's lovely, and his kids want to move him out of the house and, I suppose, move in themselves."

"They don't want to sell?" I picked up three fries and daintily dragged the tips through the ketchup puddle sitting exactly an inch to the left of the burger.

"No, they don't. I think the daughter, Hillary, wants to keep the house, maybe buy her brothers out. She lives in Danville. But that's not the point," Mom waved her fork. "The point is Mortimer wants to sell the house before the kids take over."

"Well, Mom, they can't take over unless he's dead."

I'm so sorry I said that.

I looked down at the body of poor Mr. Smith. Over the phone he had announced that his house should list for $4.5 million, leading me to believe he had plenty of time to sell. I hadn't even seen the house, but there was nothing, nothing, to support a $4.5 asking price, but I put out some feelers anyway and Bam! A couple from L.A. with more money than common sense heard about the home and offered full price. All we had to do was the paperwork.

I had that paperwork in my hand. It's a lot of paper, in case you were wondering.

The sales commission would have taken care of me for six months; I was already planning a trip to Costa Rica.

But no. Mr. Smith wasn't able to accept the offer and now this lovely asking price offer was void, null and void. I don't suppose telling him now would really count, would it?

No, really, it would not. But I did think of it. Come on, $4.5 million? In a buyer's market? You'd think of it too.

"They loved the house sight unseen, which means that location can trump even that strangely shaped guest bath," I told him when I finally finished talking to the police dispatcher.

"Just nod your head. Twitch an eyelid. Tell Allison yes."

No luck.

Blood oozed from underneath his skinny, prone body. Which ruled out a heart attack, not that I'm a professional. We already established that.

The man was 80 if he was a day, and thin from all that exercise and healthy eating. And he died violently anyway. See?

That would mean, in the words of the dispatcher who had assured me someone would come out and pick up the body, (I know that in mystery books, the coroner picks up the body but we always do things differently in California. I was personally hoping for a couple of firemen because it's been my experience that firemen are very attractive and I haven't come across one yet who couldn't put out my fire, but I also know it wouldn't end up being that kind of day) that the murderer may still be in the house.

Oh, and I forgot a salient point. There was no front door.

This is a material fact and would require an addendum to the contract, signed by both parties, but since the offer couldn't be accepted in the first place, the lack of front doors was a moot point.

No front door.

Other than that, it's a typical, traditionally overblown Marin home: 4,000 square feet, view of the city, large yard that stretches to the Bay, front elevation screened from the road by a dry stacked stone wall. Mature trees, upgraded kitchen, blah, blah, blah. More important to the children, they'd inherit the current Prop. 13 property tax limitations. I could go to Costa Rica five times for what they will save yearly in property taxes.

But dad didn't want his children to inherit. And I had a voracious couple fresh from L.A. who heard about the price and the address and that magic word, waterfront, and that was that.

I love people from L.A., I really do.

Maybe the daughter Hillary would sell once she learns the listed price. Or I could help her with the sibling buyout. Maybe I could point out the problem of inheritance taxes and the fact that even though my mother expressed the situation in the most veiled language possible, I knew that for these three siblings, sharing the house was out of the question.

Did they all stab dear old dad? A la Agatha Christie? Do I want to turn the body over to discover if he harbored multiple wounds? I did not.

And I felt the murderer was away and gone. Possibly he took the door with him. Clues, should I look for clues?

I'm not good at clues. Oh sure, there was 3490 Coast Edge Ave., where I found the water line that reached to just under the hot tub deck and I had to practically shake the owner to make him admit that maybe, on occasion, the river rose past the first story of the house, but only during the winter, or when it rained really, really hard. Most buyers would consider that a potential problem and important to disclose, yes?

But that was my only triumph in the detection field. Okay, clues. No, no, I wasn't going to get that involved. The kids would have to decide what to do with the house, and they could use me or someone else. And hiring a real estate agent who was not as certain as I that a violent death had recently occurred in the house may be a more strategic choice. Of course, the kids would have to replace the doors.

I know what you're thinking; it was one of the kids. When it comes to money, inheritance, and taxes, it's always family. I know that.

I was planning to list the house today (even with an offer, you never know), I had my checklist, and the camera and a lockbox in the car. Well, the lockbox is fairly pointless since there is no door on which to hang it. I entered sans key, sans knocking, sans everything.

So who will pay for a new door?

I walked out to the front entryway, stood on the marble floor, and looked out. The hinges on the left side of the door frame were still attached; the right hinges had been pulled off with the door. This was not a careful job. The door frame was splintered. That would have to be replaced as well. The thieves must have used crowbars. Unscrewing the hinges would have been less destructive, but time seemed critical to this operation. From the inside, can't you just tap out the pins from the door hinges and steal the door that way?

I peeked around the edge of the door frame but I couldn't tell if the doors had been taken from the inside or the outside. And that, I thought, may well be an important distinction.

Crowbars. Who walks around with crowbars, and while we're at it, who the hell takes a door?

I couldn't just sit and wait for the police. And I certainly wasn't going to hang around a dead body. I skirted around poor Mr. Smith and checked out the property. I hadn't seen the house myself, I took the listing over the phone, per mother, the price pulled in the buyers, per greed. And here we are.

Good thing they didn't see the house first.

Don't get me wrong; it's a lovely mansion, big, grand, but somewhat ordinary, which means that after viewing countless homes in my line of business, most homes end up being either small rooms strung together, or really big rooms strung together. It pretty much takes an original Frank Lloyd Wright (I know, but I don't spend that much time in the Marin County Library. Did you know that when Wright designed the Marin Civic Center, he intended the roof to be gold?), to get me excited at all. But this home was made up of pretty standard features. It sported a nice curved stairway leading into the front foyer, which would make a very impressive photo on the Multiple Listing Service, from which all internet information comes, MLS and a good lead for the website. The front room was curved at the end, which is where the obligatory Tudor turret was located. When the very rich design their homes, a turret is a disturbingly typical addition. A little cash and suddenly previously reasonable men turn into Henry the Eighth.

I glanced back at Mr. Smith. Rejected lover? Hadn't considered that. Maybe mom knew something.

Ah hell, I'd have to tell Mom. I was not looking forward to that conversation.

She would think it's my fault. She'll say something along the lines of, "Oh Allison, if only you had arrived for your appointment EARLY, you could have saved Mr. Smith."

No, I am not kidding, she thinks that way. I have witnesses.

So we have the Tudor turret. We have the Gatsby swimming pool. I glanced up the stairs. We had more.

More and more. More of what, you ask, because you probably figured out that you can't just log onto Greaterhomes.com and check this place out. Sorry about that. You may not want to. Because what really set off Mr. Smith's big expensive house was an overwhelming collection of very, very big art.

Not big like important, big like huge, massive canvasses covering what were probably nice innocent white walls.

I love nice, clean white walls almost as much as I love curtain-less windows. We didn't have either in this home. Heavy curtains protected the big art from the sunshine. A dubious save.

I may not know much about art, but I know big and scary when I'm confronted by it. And the house was filled with it: big colorful, disturbing, scary art. There must be a museum or haunted house that would take these, um, priceless paintings, but I knew for certain that I could not sell this house with that stuff defacing the interior space.

Here's an example of what Mr. Mortimer Smith lived with on a daily basis: a huge mask with the dried grass for a beard that loomed over the living room couch, a large, unframed canvass covered in distorted images colored red and purple, dominated the opposite end of the living room. I spent a minute staring at that one. But even after a minute I couldn't figure out what the painting was suppose to depict, or say, or indicate. Nope, I do not even know what it's a picture of. And of course, what every kitchen needs — three scary devil masks over the stove. Maybe because it's hot in there.

All the works radiated with violence and I'd be hard-pressed to give you a specific reason why. But even the small, carved figure in the foyer looked menacing. That would have to go first, not the welcoming image we want for the home.

No door and Mr. Smith dead when I arrived. What is that called, DOA? Dead On Arrival? I don't watch enough real action TV to be conversant with the lingo. I do know that on TV the detectives are glamorous, have great hair, and a second after they discover the body, they get to have a drink at the local bar. I was not that lucky.

I could not get a drink; it was not that kind of day. I had to call Hillary, the oldest Smith child and tell her that her father was dead. Who else would do it? Call the daughter, that is, not murder the father. Please stay with me here.

It was the kind of day where I had to call the buyers and tell them the deal was off, for now, and I'd see what I could do.

"Yes," I reassured them. "You are in first place, I have the dated offer with me. I'll see what I can do."

But I knew what they would do. They were looking at a place on Bainbridge Island, listed for only $2.5 million and included a back deck that hung over the water. They will make an offer on that property and I'm going to assume that seller is still alive to accept. Oh well, I'll get a referral fee. Enough money for shoes, not enough for a vacation. At least not the kind of vacation I had in mind.

It was the kind of day where, when the two police officers arrived, they treated me as a suspect.

"How long have you known the deceased?" The female officer asked. Her uniform looked a little tight as if she had gained a few pounds but wasn't ready to acknowledge it by getting a larger size. Not yet, maybe she was giving herself a couple more weeks to take the weight off before splurging on a larger uniform.

I understood. I smiled my best smile.

"I don't know the deceased at all." I pulled out my business card and handed one to her and one to him.

Another van pulled up. Damn, no firefighters.

My phone chirped the opening bars to "I'm in the mood for love." I looked down, one of my mortgage brokers. I pressed a couple of buttons, slid the ringer onto vibrate and turned my attention back to the officers.

"I'm Allison Little. I'm a real estate agent; I just arrived here to present an offer to Mr. Smith. And I found him here. Or rather, over there." I pointed to the kitchen where Mr. Smith's foot was just visible.

The male officer, Tom, shook my hand. "Nice to meet you, Ms. Little."

"There's no sign." The female officer looked at me coldly.

"What?"

"There's no sign." She took in my Anne Klein suit and Jimmy Choo shoes and wrinkled her nose. Hey, if she had wanted to make more money she should have visited a different job booth during Career Day.

"You said you have an offer, but there is no sign outside," she repeated, as though I were under suspicion.

"And there may not be," I muttered.

To her I said, "No, there wasn't time, I had an offer almost as soon as I posted the listing."

"You can do that?" asked Tom, the other officer.

"Sell before the property is on the market? Of course you can," I replied.

She sniffed and scribbled in her black covered notebook. "Doesn't seem fair."

"It's real estate," I said succinctly. The second set of police officers carefully wheeled out the black body bag that was my former client. Fair indeed. But she was the police, I was a civilian. I did not belabor the point.

Aha, you say, this is where Allison becomes involved and solves the murder. Well sure, but I didn't do it on purpose. Really I had other listings, places to go, another Louis Vuitton purse to purchase. Shoes to acquire. An unopened carton of Ben & Jerry's calling to me. Plus I needed to berate my mother for getting me into this because these are her people, not mine.

Honestly. When I was growing up in Marin, absolutely nothing happened, and now this. I'm not suited for the unexpected. My last big crisis was poorly applied acrylic tips.

"Here is the daughter's number." I scribbled Hillary's number, per mom, onto the back of another one of my cards. "She lives in Danville, but she'll probably have to come in and identify the body or something."

Nancy, her name tag said, nodded, and took my card. All I could think was *please don't ever call me*. But I could always refer Nancy to a realtor I didn't particularly like.

Buy why murder him? Especially when the kids could just do it slowly and legally simply by following the plan already in place: shut Dad away in a strange environment away from everything he loves and acquired over his lifetime and watch him die of loneliness and boredom. It wouldn't have taken long.

Don't look at me like that; I will never have the chance. Mom will live with one of my perfect brothers, who will love and cherish her all the days of her life because that's what you do when you are the perfect child. I, however, am not the perfect child. I'd put her in a home. In a minute.

I think she knows that.

Maybe it wasn't one of his children.

I was sent away because after an hour of traipsing around the house, the police declared that it was a crime scene and I had to leave. I left peaceably. But not before I keyed in my lockbox and slipped the key to the side garage door Mom gave me, into it. I attached it to the garden hose spigot to the right of the front door area. You just never know, and now I did have to list the house — because that was the initial wish of the client. I can always take it off, but I wasn't about to let any opportunity slip by.

I drove carefully out of Tiburon and back north toward my old house. Once in the country club area I passed by three signs for Mark Smith — DA. It was a little early for political signs, but who was I to complain about advertising.

My parents live in Country Club Estates in the most northern part of Marin, which, when I was a child, wasn't much to brag about, but is now terribly chic and populated by people who, in my opinion, are far too impressed with themselves. But the golf course was green and pristine; the crepe myrtle was full and brilliant pink. And it's always about 10 degrees warmer here than up in River's Bend (we have the ocean breeze), so it felt like summer as I cruised toward my old house. Should have brought my bathing suit. But I also knew this wouldn't be a relaxing visit. When I drop by the family home, it's not about sitting around the pool and relaxing; it's about listening to my mother talk.

"What do you mean he's dead? I just saw him yesterday!" My mother actually looked panicked, even concerned. Well, well.

For a minute I sympathized, it was shocking and I didn't really give her much time to warm up to the idea, so to speak.

"I'm sorry, Mom. But I have even more bad news."

"Heart attack? He was so careful about cholesterol and he jogged as well as attended our class."

I wasn't going to point out the futility of jogging, low-fat, and the benefits of eschewing all cholesterol at a time like this, but I was thinking about all those hours, days, and weeks Mr. Smith wasted to "stay healthy." You were thinking that too, so don't lie to me; enough people will do that in the next few weeks. So stay with me. Be friendly.

"He jogged, he kept healthy," Mom chanted as she carefully walked out to the back patio and sank down under one of the five umbrellas that dotted the small area.

"He liked art," Mom continued.

I chose one of the few seats in the sun. Ah, okay, as much as I like my own weather system (California Coast, home of the extreme micro-climate), sometimes it's too windy and foggy on the coast.

"Anything else? Why didn't he want the kids to have the house?" I lifted my face to the sun.

"It's a lovely house," Mom said absently. "He just got those new doors, Gilberto doors, his have the glass inserts, and they are just lovely. You'll ruin your skin if you keep doing that

"I know. Tell me more about the doors." I closed my eyes and saw only bright red. Just like those damn paintings in Mr. Smith's living room.

"Well, everyone has Gilberto doors because they are so unique. Mine are on order. They're made in Columbia so the native population doesn't have to sell drugs, they can make doors instead. We paid quite a premium — don't tell your father. But Mary Jane says they are so worth it, updates the entry and the front, so the house looks practically new."

I looked at her, not with dawning horror that she probably spent three months of mortgage payments on one set of doors and not because I had t never heard of Gilberto doors and obviously was behind on an upcoming trend. No, I am horrified and thus morbidly fascinated by my mother and her friends. I'm convinced that Marin is what happens when too much money and too much time collide: new political parties with green and freedom in their name are formed; large public art installations are approved sight unseen. (Which means the city was suddenly host to an installation in the public park that looks like a large single breast (think Woody Allen's "All You Ever Wanted to Know About Sex ...") and is filled with real silicone implants. The long explanation by the artist was that the breast represented the disproportionate numbers of breast cancer cases in the county. The photos, taken by every paper in the country, made the art look like, well, a large breast. At least it was bigger than mine.) Anyway, that's what happens in Marin.

"So these were new doors?" I did not share that the famous doors were missing.

"Oh yes, he spent a good, what?" She thought about it for a moment. "Well, ours cost $10,000 and our house is smaller than his, so he probably spent about $15,000."

"On doors." I did not even dare open my eyes. Did Dad know? Probably, and he also probably didn't care.

"Gilberto doors," Mom corrected.

"You'll never get that back out in a sale," I pointed out. "Bathroom remodels yes, front doors, no."

"It enhances the feel of the entryway," Mom repeated diligently.

"Okay, unique doors," I conceded. I had to remember to whom I was speaking. Mom once booked a tour of France that was specifically focused on shopping in Provence for those colorful yellow, blue, and red patterned tablecloths and napkins. The stores also carried quilted purses, head scarves, full-quilted skirts, tea cozies, and large travel bags in which to carry it all home. Mom insists to this day that she saved money by traveling to France to get her Thanksgiving tablecloth set. But here's the kicker: everyone in her tee club went, they all bought the same linens, and so, they all match. Scattered across the country club are homes filled to the brim with Provence napkins and soft jackets.

And now, I suspected, every home in the country club now sported Gilberto doors.

"And who or what is this Gilberto?" I finally asked. I opened my eyes to a slit against the sun. Mom sat perfectly composed under the shade of the umbrella, not a drop of perspiration marred her almost smooth brow.

Mom shrugged. "We order them through Doors and More down in San Rafael. They are the exclusive importer."

"Well," I said brightly. "That's great! Except there are no doors on Mr. Smith's property. They are gone."

I waited, but she didn't really react.

"So you need to call his daughter and tell her she needs doors," I prompted.

"You call her, you're the agent," Mom replied back.

I shook my head and stood my ground, or rather, continued to sit where I was and not lunge for my phone.

"My client's dead," I pointed out, a little brutally I know, but sometimes my mother needs help cutting through the trivial. "I don't have a client. As a close friend of the deceased, you may want to call the daughter."

"I'll call her," Mom said huffily. But she delivered her special look that said: you are not off the hook yet. "But maybe they want to sell?"

"They can sell if they inherited the house. It will be a while before it all gets cleared up," I replied easily, since it still wasn't my problem. My problems were up north in another county in another town where people do not spend ten grand on front doors. In fact, most people don't spend ten grand unless it's for a car. In fact, some people (clients, I'm not telling you their names) did just that, while in escrow and they are about to lose the house they want. Their loan officer is wild-eyed about it and calls me every other hour to confirm it's true and to also confirm that these people are really that stupid.

Well, of course people, are really that stupid.

"Do you know anything else about him besides his cholesterol levels?" Okay, maybe the sun was a little warm. I moved into the shade of a nearby umbrella. But no closer to my phone, thank you.

"He's originally from New York. His first wife passed away about ten years ago and he just lost the second last year."

"Children are from the first marriage?"

"Yes."

"Children from the blended family?"

"I'm not sure. He doesn't talk much about the second wife, but he was devastated when she passed away. I met him right after her death, so I don't know much about that part of his life."

"So the children get everything," I summarized. "Did he donate money?"

"Yes he did. You know, I can't remember what he said he used to do. Most of us are retired. Our old careers don't seem to matter anymore," Mom mused.

Well, it wouldn't hurt to see if there was a CRT to be negotiated or a sale on behalf of the children.

"I'll call the daughter about the door," I said finally.

Mom beamed, and for about five minutes, I was the favorite child.

"What a dump," Hillary Smith-Rodriguez marched into her father's house, hands on hips, righteous anger in her eyes.

I had hoped, as we scheduled this meeting for the very next morning, for the devastated daughter, the sad-eyed child, the distracted newly made orphan. It would have made my life easier if the children were distracted with grief, sometimes they want to sell the family home, just because they can't bear to see the place anymore. Sometimes the children are just sad. Hell, I'm 35 and I don't know what I'd do if I lost my own parents this early (I would miss my dad).

Hillary looked like the kind of woman for whom no meeting is too early, no event is too difficult. Hillary was older than me by about seven to ten years. Don't get me wrong, she didn't look seven to ten years older; she looked quite lovely, so smooth and even that it was clear she had lots of work done. I'd say she had her breasts hoisted back up to prepubescent levels a couple years ago. If mine were lifted that high, I'd suffocate.

So Hillary was not one of those women who denied her own comforts for the good of the family. Or maybe in her family, there was plenty of comfort to go around. In any case, I couldn't remember if Mom mentioned Hillary's husband, perfect children, anything like that. Did Mortimer Smith not keep a thick album of grandchildren on his person like some grandparents we could mention?

Instead of children, Hillary marched into the house trailing the latest look. She was dressed in tiny yellow slides, white Capri slacks, and a tight yellow tube top that displayed her latest investment to full advantage. I braced myself for the invariable look that thin, well-molded women give me when we meet, the look that says: you are a food slut and obviously can't control yourself and I am all about control and extreme sports, and I am superior to you in every possible way.

I got the look, I returned it with my best dumb blonde look, because if anything, I do spend a considerable amount of cash on my hair, so I feel justified appropriating the persona. I am a salon blonde. Smart enough to pay for the look myself, smart enough not to let on that I am smart.

And we were off.

"I can't believe Dad let this place go. What's in the kitchen?" She teetered past the devil mask collection, intent on more practical concerns. "Whirlpool? Not even a Sub-Zero refrigerator? Honestly, how did he expect he could ever sell it?" She opened the refrigerator and sighed. "Look at this, five cartons of Cooper ice cream. He promised he was on a low-cholesterol diet!" She shook her head and closed the door. "He was always sneaking around like that."

Yes, but it wasn't the ice cream that killed him in the end was it? To my credit, I did not say that out loud. But it was kind of funny. Mom mentioned his healthy habits as well; how he ate low-fat, exercised, and in public, ordered the low-calorie, alternative dishes. Made me wonder if my own mother wasn't snarfing down raw cookie dough in the middle of the night. No, if she did, she'd have hips like mine.

Instead I said, "I have buyers. Are you still interested in selling?"

She shook her head. "No, tell them to go away. We're keeping the house."

Damn, double damn.

"I see," I said as smoothly as I could. "And you plan to buyout your brothers?"

She continued to prowl around the house. After finding the ice cream, she abandoned the kitchen cabinets and moved on to search around the rest of the first floor. She peeked into the hall closet, examined the hardwood floors, lifted the edge of each Indian rug scattered around the cavernous great room (the one with the view of the City, just so you can keep this all straight). The rugs matched — to a certain degree — the wild reds in the big painting on the far wall.

"No. Yes," She kicked the rug back with her tiny, French pedicured foot. "I will be able to buy them out. But not yet."

"What about this art? Are you going to divide that up?" I asked.

She laughed, short and brittle, as if her vocal chords had some work done as well and were tightened to make them look younger.

"Keep the art? Dad would have never approved of that. These," she gestured to the devil masks, the living room art, and possibly everything else upstairs, "Are here to keep them out of the public eye. He thought the wrong art was bad for people, can you believe that? Even my stepmother thought so, helped him hunt down some of this crap. Damn, if she were alive, she could take care of this, but nooo." She contemplated the rug. "We'll sell the damn art. One more thing for me to do. The rugs might be worth something."

"Okay, well good," I nodded. "Then you don't need me. I'll just get out of here." I carefully placed about three of my business cards on the table in the foyer, reproduction French; it didn't fit the décor at all.

Hillary continued to peek behind the paintings in the living room and tried to look behind the large cabinet.

I couldn't stand it. "I'm sorry, but are you looking for something?"

She cautiously lifted herself up from the floor where she had been peering under the green couch. "No, no, not looking for anything." She daintily swiped at the knees of her Capri pants.

I wasn't getting very far with her, which is unusual. I usually have to ask people to stop blurting out details about their personal life, like when the waitress told me all about her second marriage, or the woman at the dress shop who told me all about her husband's virility problems and how long Viagra lasts. Too long, apparently.

But Hillary? No. She was a woman of few words. She moved into the kitchen and began opening cupboards again. "Oreo cookies? Oh, Dad," I heard her mutter to herself.

I hesitated, but then decided to exit. Her father was dead and there was a murder investigation, but after twenty-four hours, the police had no leads and I was exonerated because the time of death was two hours before I arrived and I had made a number of phone calls while I was sitting in traffic, so I had proof that I was nowhere near the body at the time of death.

There you go, case closed. And maybe the prowling Hillary was looking for her father. People deal with these shocks differently.

But of course, there was something wrong. For some reason I liked Mr. Smith. I liked that he sneaked food on the side. I liked that his children, at least this one, probably deserved to be screwed out of the house and their inheritance. Hillary clearly didn't like the art, so she wouldn't take care of it. And would the art have gone with the house? I looked at the 3-foot figure crouched in the hallway; it looked like a badly formed gremlin. If it were my listing, the statue would definitely not go with the house. It may not even make it through the first open house.

I left Hillary to her own devises and passed the Doors and More van on my way out.

Here's what I hate: tiny, petite women who don't eat. My best friend Carrie is a tiny, petite woman who eats nothing.

We lunch together on a regular basis. In my life, it's all about lunch, the one trait I did inherit from my mother.

"Order the fries," I perused the menu; maybe I'd have a salad like Carrie and my mother. A big salad. Ranch dressing. Extra bacon.

"Again?"

"Come on," I purred. "Who loves you?"

Carrie sighed and dutifully ordered her salad. And a side of fries. The waiter was well trained, enough so he didn't make much of a face. I demurely ordered a Cobb salad.

"So your customer is dead and you're out a beautiful commission," Carrie summed up.

"I'm doomed. I only have seven other listings, but they're all in the half million range, I so could have used the hit from that Marin house. She nodded with sincere sympathy. Which is why I love her so much.

The salads arrived along with a gleaming, golden, crispy plate of perfectly cut and fried potatoes. Never underestimate the glory of fried food. Carrie set the plate between us and began to pick at her salad.

I quickly demolished the fries to take the edge off my hunger then regarded the salad. I hate salads.

The waiter swooped by, took a look at the empty plate of fries, looked at Carrie who is about a size 4 soaking wet, raised his eyebrow just a little and whisked off the empty plate.

"They think I'm some kind of freak," she whispered.

"At least with you they have to wonder; me, it's pretty clear," I whispered back.

"So what are you going to do?"

The paper had mentioned my name, just as the listing agent for the house, and unfortunately, that I discovered the body. The paper also revealed the man had been shot. Shot. I had five messages I needed to return. Apparently that old adage for media that if your name is spelled correctly — it's all good — is correct.

"Work."

"Maybe you'll get another $4.5 million listing," she suggested.

That's what I love about Carrie; she's an optimist. Women as beautiful as she usually are.

Buoyed by my friend's optimism and anesthetized into a happier state by the fries, I was ready to face my evening alone.

No, I do not live in a trailer park and my house is not filled with depressingly dark antiques or hand-me-downs. I own a lovely home in the hills of River's Bend. I bought low. The house is 3,000 square feet and I have it all for myself. No, I do not own a cat.

Carrie volunteers for Forgotten Felines. Of course she volunteers to save abandoned kittens. One good look at Carrie and you would say,

"Now there's a girl who rescues cute little kittens." I myself am working on compiling a cookbook featuring recipes for baking, frying, and skewering the endangered California Tiger Salamander. That's mostly because saving the silly things has ballooned into a hugely annoying and suffocating project, development-wise. As you can see, Carrie and I probably should belong to different and completely separate nonprofit organizations.

I thought about Hillary stomping through her father's house, complaining about the caliber of kitchen appliances. Should I have a Sub-Zero refrigerator? A Wolf range? Would those things make me happier? Since the only things in my freezer are five cartons of Ben & Jerry's, for emergency purposes only, and three cartons of Cooper's ice cream — for guests, a Sub-Zero freezer seems a bit like overkill.

Overkill.

Since salad is never enough, I was already hungry. I pulled out a carton of Phish Food and thought about the murder. Why? Why would anyone shoot Mr. Smith and then just walk away? Well, they walked away so they wouldn't be caught. I know that. But nothing had been taken or even disturbed. Hillary did more disturbing just in her brief search around the house. And what was she looking for?

And why not let the children inherit? Why sell? I mean Hillary wasn't all that lovely and nice, but that's no reason to cheat the kids from a considerable tax break. Well, okay, maybe that was a good enough reason.

Mr. Smith had no other assets. Had he given it all away? Had he been blackmailed over those paintings? Had the blackmailer killed him when he couldn't pay? No, that sounded like a badly plotted movie and blackmailers don't kill; I know that from TV. They want the cash flow to continue.

The Ben & Jerry's finished, I fixed some dinner.

Like you've never gone through a whole carton of Phish Food in one sitting, or in my case, standing.

Chapter 2

But the next morning it still nagged at me. The questions, not the ice cream. So I called around.

I called my favorite mortgage broker. Not the one strung out over the car purchase; for that deal, the less we spoke, the better for us both.

"Hey baby," Kathy Jo greeted me.

"Hey baby, yourself," I answered. We have a very professional relationship. Being good friends and drinking buddies can be very beneficial to a working partnership. I have a lot of dirt on her; she had a lot on me. We will never part. We've been together longer than some marriages. "Can you look up Mortimer Smith?" I gave her more details. "I need to know what he's worth."

"Isn't he dead?" she asked.

"How do you know that?"

"Honey, I read the papers. You should try it someday."

"Too depressing. What did they say about Mr. Smith?"

"Died suddenly."

"That would be about right."

I was impressed that Hillary was able to suppress the story. Maybe there was more to this woman than I thought. Except for a willful disregard for her father's life and lifestyle. Then again, you've already heard my rant about my own mother. It's difficult to imagine parents as full-blown individuals; they mostly spring into our consciousness fully grown and devoted to our welfare. That's because when we meet, they are fully grown and we did just spring from them (spring, according to my mother, is not the right word at all) so what do we know as children of the parents?

Damn little.

And I, personally, would like to keep it that way. We may have a great deal in common, Hillary and me. Except she's a bitch and I'm not.

Armed with the information from Kathy Jo, I called Emily at North Country Title, and she ran a search as well.

"Major remodel about ten years ago," Emily reported. "Gave him another half-million in value, appraised at three. He took out a second on the house a couple of weeks ago. It should be posted about now, but those amounts sometimes take some time. Why are you asking?"

Three. Well at least I wouldn't have to explain low appraisal to an overheated buyer.

"How much on the second?"

"He could have taken up to a million, almost the full amount of his equity," Emily replied.

"A million dollars," I mused. "What would he do with that?"

"Car? Boat? Strippers? Use your imagination , woman."

"Thanks, Emily."

"My pleasure."

Three days and a cancelled escrow later, I got a call from Hillary Smith-Rodriguez.

"Uh, hello, Allison?"

"Yes."

"We'd like to sell the house after all. Can you help us?"

Her voice at least sounded more contrite than when we met, and that warmed my heart. A little.

"Sure, I can," I assured her. "Would you like to meet at the house?"

"Do you still have the buyers?"

"No, they moved on, but we can talk about the listing and the price and I'm sure I'll find some other buyers."

The commission was still enough to cover that Costa Rica trip, perhaps not in style, but still, I'd be covered. But my happy visions were countered with the prospect of working with Hillary and her siblings who, I did not imagine, were any more generous or kind than their sister. And I was pretty sure they were not aware how little equity there was left in the house.

A few hours later, I found out for myself. Hillary wanted to convene at the family home. Family home. Her father's home. They were all too old to have lived there. The three siblings trooped into their father's house without looking around and aligned themselves around the dining room table, one empty chair in between each sibling. Hillary positioned herself at the head of the table. I positioned myself at the foot with the two brothers on each side.

The older brother was the same Mark Smith who had scattered early campaign billboards around Marin. The in-person Mark possessed the same face I had seen on the billboard. He was just as broad and bland as his 10-foot photo turned to the morning traffic. It was an effective demeanor for an inscrutable politician or a lawyer, neither being members of my favorite category. But, I reminded myself as he gripped my hand in a great-to-meet-you-vote-for-me-because-I -have-a-powerful-handshake shake, it is not my job to worry about how clients make their money. It is not my job to worry about their new monthly payments and it's not my job to wonder how the paltry amount of cash this sale will engender will be distributed.

I am just the salesperson. Innocent. On the fringe, not involved.

"It's nice to meet you," I lied.

"It's nice to meet you too," he lied back. Strangely, his lie makes me feel better about him.

"I'm Stephen," said the second brother, leaning over the thick corner of the dining table to shake my hand. He was more sincere, but looked enough like his older siblings to make me think that he probably couldn't be trusted either.

We sat down.

"We cleaned," Hillary pointed out unnecessarily. She folded her hands on the table — the left one held down the right as if she was keeping them still so they wouldn't accidentally dance around and emphasize her words, or embarrass her.

"New doors," Stephen said, patting his head carefully. He sat up straight; his back did not touch the back of the chair.

"With a double bolt and lock," Mark pointed out, "So now the house is secure."

There is no such thing as secure, but I didn't need to go into that with them.

"We want a quick sale," Hillary said, still holding her hands.

"Why now?" I asked. "Are you selling because this is what your father wanted?"

It was part sarcasm by me and part necessary information. People like me want to know why someone is selling. For fun? For profit? Or was the house inadvertently built on an Indian burial ground, or maybe the neighbors held strange rituals well into the early hours of the morning.

Selling for reasons like company transfers, divorce, or a sudden inheritance work best for me. Those reasons are easier to explain to the buyers. If the sellers are hightailing it out of California in favor of a move to the mythical land of Oregon that with every passing year becomes more and more idyllic in the imagination of beleaguered Californians is not something I mention to potential buyers. I don't want any buyer to feel like a sucker for staying in my home state and paying outrageous prices for the privilege of doing so.

So why is a good question. I waited to hear that Mr. Smith had decided to haunt the place, the children had heard funny noises, or that the blood on the kitchen floor was reappearing regularly at midnight despite repeated cleanings, that kind of thing.

I also like to make sure that a seller is serious about selling and not just checking out the market to "see what they're offered." Because more often than not, after I've worked myself into a frenzy, fronted thousands of dollars in advertising, signs, open homes, contests, and giveaways, the sellers after three months change their minds and pull the house off the market.

I truly work to avoid that. I'd rather deal with reappearing bloodstains than work with a seller who's not on the up and up.

Hillary's hands trembled; the brothers shifted slightly in their seats.

"We think," Stephen said, clearing his throat, "that one of us taking on the burden of the house would be too much."

Mark glanced at Hillary, who nodded. Mark nodded too.

"I agree that a house this size is quite a project," I said as kindly as I could. "Have you decided on how to divide up the furniture? Or can we keep the house furnished while we sell?"

"Does that make a difference?" Hillary looked around at the inadequate tables and chairs in the kitchen, at the over-adequate dining room table that seats fourteen even before pulling out the extension leaves, and part of the two-story foyer because that's all she could see from where she sat.

"Yes, it does," I said smoothly. "Once we sell the house, then we can move the furniture out and you can put this in your own house."

She shuddered at the very thought. "I don't have room. My home is already furnished. No room at all." She looked at her smooth-faced brother, but he shook his head. "We're all modern. This monstrosity, for instance, would never go with my Bauhaus furniture."

I kept my expression neutral and realized I should not have opened this discussion this early in the game. The furniture stays for the showing, always good. I don't care what happens to it after the sale. But I know from experience, the sellers do.

"Nope," said Stephen, patting his head — oh, he had new hair plugs, well, good for him. "I can't take it. Candy would have a fit."

"How about if we offer to leave the dining room table with the house?" I suggested. "It may be a good selling point."

"How much should we increase the price?" Hillary immediately asked.

"We should reduce it if they take it," Mark pointed out. I smiled at him gratefully.

"No, we don't want to give anything away," Stephen countered.

"But we want a quick sale," Hillary reminded him.

"But I don't want to devalue the home," Stephen argued back.

I leaned back and let them debate. A decision to sell something this big, for a price in the millions, can be derailed by a mere few thousand dollars. I didn't feel I needed to intervene just yet. They were just warming up.

"And what about this art?" Hillary fired the next shot.

"What about it? We sell it," Mark said.

"Dad would have hated that. It was here so people wouldn't see it," Stephen said, his hair plugs pointing out.

"Since when did you become the defender of the public sensibilities?" his brother snarled.

"I'm not," he backed off. "I'm just saying that selling would be directly against Dad's wishes."

"Good," Hillary said.

Mark sighed and looked at me again. "Dad," he explained, "was funny about art."

"Funny? He loved collecting his paintings more than he loved us," Hillary said, her hands straining against her own version of decorum. One didn't smack one's brothers in front of a stranger. Well, I certainly could relate to that. I've probably been saved many times by that unwritten rule. My own brothers have never hit me in public. Mom credited them with self-restraint; I credited them with being smart enough not to get caught.

"When we were kids," Mark explained. "Dad dragged us to all these shows and museums and that counted as time with Dad."

"It wasn't really, but that's what he counted it as," Stephen added.

"Maybe that was the best he could do," I pointed out, always generous with the failings of other people's parents.

"Yeah, sure. He avoided the draft, you know. He enrolled in school out here, must have been the only boy in the place," Mark mused. "I always wondered about that, but we didn't find anything unusual. He must have had a disability."

"Dad was in perfect health," Stephen countered. "He always watched his weight and heart and cholesterol levels. Samantha was always watching over him. Remember that Christmas? She brought that tofu salad."

Hillary snorted but surprisingly, said nothing.

"We're not talking about Samantha," Mark said. He turned to me and in a more civil tone explained, "She was Dad's second wife after mom died. Thank god, she didn't have children."

"She passed away?" I asked.

"Thank god, yes," Hillary put in. And that was the end of that marriage. Perhaps they could finally express the fear that the second wife would get everything, leaving the children in the cold. Well, it's a legitimate fear.

"He liked me best," said Stephen, "and I didn't even care about art."

"None of us did," Hillary snapped.

"Dad," Mark turned his whole body toward me, freezing out his sister and ignoring his brother. "Dad had a theory that primitive people believed that when they don a mask, like a lion or a tiger…"

"Or a monster," Hillary chimed in.

He ignored the interruption. "They take on the attributes of that mask. Little children manifest it best during Halloween when they put on a devil mask or a superhero mask; they become that character."

"Oh, please," Hillary shot back. "Dad just thought this kind of art was evil and a bad influence on the tiny, soft minds of the public. And he and Samantha were these heroes for taking the art away and saving children or some crap like that."

"But not you?" I asked as innocently as I could.

She looked at me, her face looking a little too much like the third devil mask over the stove for my own comfort.

"I cannot imagine being influenced by art," she retorted.

"I think $3 million would be sufficient," Stephen worked to derail his sister. He was successful. Discussing hard cash return distracted her from conceptual art and she calmed down a bit.

Mark agreed with his brother.

"Okay," I said brightly. "Let's sign the listing agreement and the exclusive right to sell agreement and the TDS and you all can be on your way!"

TDS stands for Transfer Disclosure Statement, I think a more accurate interpretation is Tediously Discussing Stuff. I not only have the official form but an additional check list I use, just to cover some of the extras, like a pool, spa, horse paddock, that kind of thing. I instruct the client to check off the items on the list, then the client/seller signs. Sounds easy, yes?

Here's what it sounds like:

"Stove top or cooktop?"

"Stove top," says the husband.

"Cooktop," counters the wife.

"Don't we have gas?" he'll ask innocently.

"No, we have electric. I ask you over and over to get the gas. Even Mary Beth has a Wolf range, but we don't even have a range. Is range one of the options?"

I have to concede it is.

"See, we don't even have a range. Will that reduce the value of the home?"

That's an average conversation. Until the couple gets to the line item — swimming pool. The swimming pool always brings up hard feelings, either because they don't have one, or because one partner does all the work while the other had decided two years ago she was allergic to water.

Surprisingly, my group, after disclosing everything — and acknowledging the part about the violent murder, important, especially in the Bay Area; Asian Americans won't touch the place, I already knew that. The siblings ended up turning docile and signed the papers, here and here, right at the little sticky arrows, one of my favorite inventions. Three million.

I assured them I would do my best marketing work starting tonight and would be in touch by e-mail. In other words, they could all leave town and I wouldn't really have to talk to them. It's far more efficient that way, and better for my nerves.

We never did get back to what to do with the paintings.

Back to my personal life. Carrie called and asked me to attend the Rolling in Clover Gala on Saturday night. Because she needed a date.

"But I just want to sit down and read," I protested. Not even a mock protest, like, no I couldn't eat another bite, because a person can always eat anther bite. We do it all the time; this was a real protest. I had my first open house with the million-dollar mansion Sunday and I did not want to party the night before.

Not that the atmosphere of a formal gala invites partying per se. But that's beside the point. Spending $150 for chicken, pilaf, and a wad of green leaves that passes as an exotic salad because the busboy scattered pecans over the top is not my idea of value.

"There will be a band and a silent auction and it's for the Boys and Girls Clubs. I know you support the Boys and Girls Clubs," Carrie argued.

"Who is going that you want to meet?" I asked, cutting to the heart of the matter. Carrie didn't give a rat's ass for the silent auction, Boys and Girls Clubs or random acts of good causes; she doesn't have the cash to be a dilettante. Her pet project is kittens. Kittens or nothing. And since she's a receptionist for a local nonprofit (not the Forgotten Felines, it doesn't have enough cash for even its own phone, this is a larger organization) she too has eaten enough dry chicken breast covered with a tablespoon of mango chutney to take care of her for life. So something was up.

"No reason, I just thought it would be nice to go."

"Nice," I echoed. "Okay. Is that all? Nice?" I moved around my house clutching a damp kitchen towel and swiping at various table and bookcase surfaces. My version of speed housekeeping.

"Well, there are rumors that Patrick Sullivan will be there." Her voice altered just a tad over the phone.

"And who is Patrick Sullivan?"

I could hear her eyes roll. "He's the new president of Cooper Milk. The grandson, he just took over the company."

"And he's gorgeous," I put in. Cooper Milk, which sounds like an odd name for a milk company, is one of the largest dairy companies in the county. Becoming the largest dairy in town is not difficult to do; dairy is very localized and we have a lot of cows out in West County, happy cows by the way. Our cows look exactly like the cows in the commercials. In fact, I think I've recognized a couple of our own local talent on national TV.

Cooper Milk started out as a co-op in the 1960s. Its motto was to "do good in the community, and the community would reciprocate." It was right. The milk is excellent. Company donations to the community are stupendous. Oh, and you can see how co-op morphed into coop and then cooper because it's just easier to pronounce. The family owners, being pragmatic, just adopted a big chicken as the company mascot and called it good. There is a group of teenagers on call who routinely dresses up as the Cooper Chicken and for $12 an hour march around at cancer rallies, fairs, school openings, and any local event that attracts more than five people. But it works. And now there is a new, eligible president. He will not last. As head of the company, he'll probably do fine. But he probably won't stay single longer than fifteen minutes.

"And you want to meet him," I tossed the towel up into the corner of the hallway, hoping to knock down the spider web that I noticed last week.

Carrie took a deep breath. "Yes."

"You are so transparent." The towel came down, its mission incomplete, and the spider web ruled.

"Well he's single, I'm single."

"You just build from there, right?" I caught the towel and glanced down at my nails, They needed to be done. If I did attend something like this, I'd have to look my best. I had just enough time to get the nails done, the roots touched up, and I had a beaded dress I purchased special for last month's real estate awards and dinner.A beaded dress is not a garment to be taken lightly. I was determined to wear something spectacular to my company dinner event and I didn't really care how appropriate it was. Mom was safely in another county at the time, so I was free from her disapproving stare, I just got one from Rosemary -- the arbitrator of all that is tasteful in our office. Maybe that's why I did it. Anyway, I wore this dress and thus had the dubious distinction of being the most overdressed person in the room. But the sight of small jet beads covering a size 18 dress was enough to stun most people into silence, so I had a lovely time chatting and marching up to receive my well-deserved awards. In my company, if you enjoyed a good, productive year, you are rewarded. New Century hands out these gold-colored statues for the top producers. I know, the idea of getting a statue for just doing your job is pretty trite, even silly.

I have five statues. Count 'em. Five.

So that's how I came to the Rolling in Clover Gala. Me in my beaded dress, newly filled nails and Carrie in a little red number that screamed — Diana, the huntress. But only the women knew that; the men and her quarry would not notice — the huntress part they noticed Carrie right away. I wish my breasts would stay up by themselves the way hers did. But that's the beauty of being just 30 instead of on the way to 40 using the commute lane. Maybe I should get the name of Hillary's doctor.

We walked into the ballroom together. Carrie paused for just a second and I stepped in ahead of her.

"There she is," Carrie whispered.

"Who?" I stepped back to stay next to Carrie.

"Beverly Weiss," Carrie breathed. She sounded like she had just spotted a movie star, but I had never heard of Beverly Weiss.

"She's beautiful, donates hundreds of thousands to the community," Carrie explained, still in that breathless, worshiping tone. It was a little annoying.

"She's just a person." I craned my neck to try to see this paragon, but Carrie couldn't exactly point her out, so we indulged in the routine of: See that man to the left? Look over his right shoulder, second woman on the right, in the gold lamé dress. "That's her," Carrie confirmed.

Beverly Weiss was fashionably thin and her gold dress clashed with her red hair.

"I wouldn't worry," I said.

"Really?"

I watched Beverly. She tossed her head back in an exaggerated laugh and placed her hand on another man's arm to make a point. I couldn't see if she sported a big diamond or wedding ring on her left hand. Didn't matter.

"You can take her," I said.

"You think?" Carrie stammered a bit.

I nudged her toward the group standing to Beverly Weiss's right. "You are twice the woman she is. Now go."

"I want to be her when I grow up," Carrie breathed.

"No, you don't," I assured her. "Go."

I launched Carrie toward her goal, the delectable Patrick Sullivan, and entertained myself by wandering aimlessly around the hotel ballroom.

There are two choices for large parties in town. You can book the Hilton or the Hyatt. I'm sure to the staff at the Hilton or the Hyatt, the hotels are completely unique and special. But to the average citizen of River's Bend and parts north, the hotels are remarkably interchangeable. Often people show up at the wrong hotel, sometimes even staying at the wrong party for quite some time before noticing that event is sponsored by the Downtown Rotary Club and not the River's Bend Chamber of Commerce. And as a Chamber board member, some people should have recognized that right away. But some people took a bit longer, and drank some very nice complimentary wine before realizing her mistake.

Or so I've heard.

So there was little of interest to me, once I carefully read each list for the silent auction, reviewed the offerings for the live auction and said hello to half a dozen people, all of whom already knew my profession, had my card, and had already referred me to someone else. No new leads. Okay, now it was a waste of time.

I needed new blood, so I continued to prowl. I know what you're thinking, Allison would not have taken me, the patient reader (so far), to this excruciatingly predictable and can we say it — boring event —

if it didn't provide some insight that will move the plot along? Normally I wouldn't. But I live in Sonoma County, not Marin. And my dead man had been found in Marin. So it was really the Marin silent auctions and chamber events that I'd have to penetrate in order to gain more useful knowledge. And that wasn't likely; I can't afford to attend Marin fundraisers, not even to support world peace.

I idly bent over a silent auction list just to see if anyone was in a bidding war with anyone else.

"Well, I would love to have an unexpected million dropped on me," a rather pained voice said.

"Who wouldn't? Do you know who the donor is?"

"Well, of course not, Fischer wouldn't say, the bastard. Says it's all terribly confidential."

"It's not even a real museum — lost art, what does that have to do with anything important?"

"I understand starting it up was like a lifelong dream of the curator and his father. Maybe he deserves the gift," said the other man.

"Or was it the father? Someone down there was really into collecting Chicano Art."

"No one deserves money; they earn it," the first man replied sanctimoniously. "I, for instance, need to build another wing on the hospital. And this guy gets it all at once, finishes up the capital campaign and there you go, finished."

"So you're just jealous." The friend, I assume it was a friend; an acquaintance or prospective donor would have walked away well before the conversation turned.

"Yeah, maybe I am. I owe you a drink."

The two men drifted off. "I just wish I worked out of Marin. Stuart is lucky he found a job down there," was the final comment.

See? I discovered absolutely nothing, except that the cheap knock off Bruno Magli shoes I picked up at Nordstrom hurt my feet. And that tiny beads are very uncomfortable to sit on, and that Carrie makes a shark look like an ADD victim. Within the hour the woman was by the side of the scion of the Cooper Milk family and had wrangled an invitation to sit at the family table. See, she was the best in the room. I knew that.

"There was a last-minute cancellation. His sister is pregnant and couldn't make it, so I'm taking her place!" Carrie shrieked, but in a whisper. I didn't know a person could do that. Apparently they can.

"Are you okay on your own?" she had the grace to ask.

"Isn't that why you brought me?" I had the temerity to inquire.

"Oh, yes. Do you want to leave early? I probably can get a ride home with Patrick."

I looked at her in her short Norma Kamali dress ruched around her perky breasts, legs all the way up to her chin. Blonde hair. She was the whole package. This Beverly Weiss didn't stand a chance. Not that Ms. Wiess was after Mr. Sullivan. I did not know what Ms. Weiss wanted.

"I don't doubt for a minute you can get a ride home with Patrick Sullivan," I said sincerely.

That left me alone, story of my life, my own fault. Who knew I'd miss all this peace and quiet?

Chapter 3

"So he was the perfect gentleman." I turned off the freeway, easy to do at 12:50 p.m. on Sunday. The overcast that hung over my home this morning had already broken up down here; the sun was almost at full strength. I would have hung my head outside to feel the warm air but I was on the phone.

"Yes, damn it," Carrie was disgusted.

"But he took you home?" I pulled past the bright New Century/For Sale sign — bless the sign people, and the open gate and paused for a moment to put out my open house sign, even though I had a sign rider that announced "Open on Sunday" on top of the big sign that proclaimed FOR SALE. Sometimes you have to help the public along with extra information. No, I did not attach balloons; I hate balloons.

"In his Mercedes 550 SL," she informed me, as if sitting in a good car would help make the conversation inside that much more interesting. That is actually an urban myth. Yet she believes.

"Well, that's a start," I said cheerfully. I maneuvered back into my car and drove down the drive — ah, a replaced door. I couldn't tell if it was another Gilberto door or not, did not care. A door that locked was the door for me.

"I have to open the house. I'll call you back."

At some point I'll be able to stay on the phone, talk, and open my lockbox simultaneously. But so far technology has not caught up with my needs.

I called her back as I opened the two locks with the keys Hillary sent me via FedEx delivery (so I had to drive the damn keys down and place them into the lockbox just in case anyone wanted to view the house) and let myself into the house. The door had an odd smell. It was thickly carved with birds and trees or something like trees; maybe this was a genuine Gilberto door; if so, I was not overwhelmed. The varnish smelled terrible. I left the door open, hoping the smell would escape out rather than in.

"Yes," she conceded, her tone telling me she clearly was not convinced. "He gave me his business card with his cell number printed on the back. That's a start, right?"

"Absolutely," I agreed.   But I was distracted. I was worried the violent death in the kitchen would drive down the price. Sigh.

"Are you listening to me?" Carrie demanded.

"Oh sure." I walked out to the patio with its million-dollar view. The city burned white under the sun. The financial district looked like a cluster of points, like pencils stacked into a cup. From the financial district flowed neat blocks of low buildings and homes bisected with straight lines of streets, all neatly labeled in alphabetical order. And the tidy streets all roll toward the water and disappear around the curve of the Golden Gate.

The opening to the Bay is called the Golden Gate, which explains why the bridge itself is not gold; it is red. As a child I thought it should be golden color to match my expectations. It is not. That realization was the first of many childhood disappointments, like learning that M&M candies really can melt in your hand, if you try hard enough.

To the left of the city skyline, the Bay Bridge and the East Bay simmered in a low mist, not as clearly defined as San Francisco. At night the scene looks like scattered jewels. Cities often look better in the dark. San Francisco looks good in any condition. That's why it cost so much to look at it from your living room window.

"Why don't you marry a busboy or something easy?" I suggested, thinking that I should take the picture now, now, now. The fog could roll in at any moment. But, as you know, I couldn't take a picture, because my phone was also my camera, so I'd have to wait until I was off the phone to take the picture. Technology was not making my life less complicated.

"No way, my mother married a busboy and they struggled for years and years," she trailed off, and then came back strong. "I vowed to never let that happen to me, and it won't."

My, my, my, this was a side of her I hadn't seen before, or at least heard over the phone.

"What happened to you? Did your biological clock go off?" I squinted at the horizon — was that a wisp of fog? Where I stood, I couldn't see the bridge (that reduces the view price by about $30,000, give or take $500), which was the first to be covered by that band of fog so prevalent in the summer. Then again, maybe not. I didn't see anything suspicious.

I haven't heard many biological alarms recently. Had we all stopped listening? When did I stop listening to mine? Ah yes, if I remember correctly, the last time my biological alarm sounded, I threw the clock across the room and it broke.

"No, yes, I don't know. It's just time to stop messing around and start working toward something."

That something being marriage. Well at least she had her priorities straight — fall in love rich. I never managed to do that, being a sucker for the workingman. Or maybe I fall in love with the wrong man because the only opportunity I have to even meet single men is when I hire them to fix something — thus the blue-collar workingman thing. But they could be rich ...but then unable to converse. Oh hell.

"You don't have anything to worry about," Carrie continued. "You have it all together, a great house, a great career, and a great life. I just have my volunteer work and a less than impressive administrative assistant job. I want a family and a life, so why not upgrade?"

"Why not, indeed." I was beginning to feel sorry for the scion of the wealthiest family in River's Bend.

I murmured encouragement, told her to get call waiting instead of stressing over being on the phone in case he called — and took my fog-free photo. I took a number of pictures; you never know when you need a view of the City skyline for an MLS upload.

The new set of Gilberto doors had been installed, the kitchen tile cleaned. All was well.

I arranged the flyers for the house and my business cards on the long dining table — loaded up the refrigerator (cleaned out by a professional crew, Hillary would have nothing to do with that project — which also meant all those lovely cartons of Cooper ice cream were gone, oh well) with water bottles and wandered into the living room with my book.

I think open houses are boring and pointless, but sellers are under the impression that on any given Sunday a buyer will magically walk in and want the house so badly on sight that they will write up an offer for the list price by 4 p.m. It happens enough to other agents to make us all slightly superstitious — and continue to hang out in empty homes on Sunday from 1 to 4 p.m.

Usually my system for odious open house duty is to find the most comfortable spot in the house that has the best view of the front door or front walk, and read something uplifting. No mysteries. They look bad sitting on the table, you know, with those scary covers and suggestions of death in the title. So I brought along a copy of the newly revised *Think and Grow Rich*. Because if I think, I'm rich.

But the book held little charm. I was distracted by the house, the door, the afternoon.

Maybe it was the ghost of Mr. Smith. Maybe it was Carrie, bent on self-improvement through matrimony. Maybe it was the warm weather.

I sighed because I could, and no one was around to ask what the matter was, which was good since I didn't really know. I kicked off my shoes and wandered around the house.

Nothing had been moved. Ah, here was the problem. For all her snooping around, Hillary failed to take any of the art. So clearly, it was up to me to do a little impromptu staging.

You've probably read about staging and how setting a home with attractive furniture helps speed the sale along by a healthy percentage.

So it won't come as surprise to you that walking into an otherwise lovely home and being faced with three more or less authentic devil masks would be considered off-putting.

For the very Christian, these particular masks would make them run screaming from the room. So I started with those three. There was nothing behind them attached to the wall. I almost expected a tiny sign like "gotcha" or "Made you look," but no, the walls were blank and pristine white — heavenly white — now that the masks were gone.

I laid them carefully into one of the deep lower drawers in the kitchen among the pots and pans.

The canvass in the living room was lively, and the red and purple could grow on you, but it was definitely odd enough to distract a prospective buyer, so I took that down. The back wall was covered in cobwebs. I groaned and retrieved a dishcloth to swipe at the dirt. Yuck.

Then last but not least was the small, menacing figure in the foyer. It looked as if it could animate late at night, like in all those "Twilight Zone" episodes I wasn't supposed to watch because it would give me nightmares but did anyway because that's what my brothers were watching.

So the evil figure that comes to life at night would have to go.

Perhaps he came alive, stabbed poor Mr. Smith, and then turned into a statue.

Don't worry, I don't live in that kind of world. Besides, Mr. Smith hadn't been stabbed.

I picked up the little statue. It was quite heavy, made of ironwood or something like that, and hauled it into the guest bath, an odd little room. I had already used it once (the first time I was here — traffic south was clogged and slow and I had to pee so badly I hadn't even noticed there was no front door and a dead client on the floor, that's how bad it was. I really have to cut back on my coffee consumption, but I didn't want to be responsible for a dip in Starbucks stock). So I hadn't really evaluated the guest bath. The little guy fit neatly into the far corner next to the toilet. Its leer would prevent any visitors from actually performing any duties on the toilet, but that wasn't my problem. I closed the door on the devil.

Why didn't the thieves take that?

And Hillary hadn't responded to the art at all, which I thought was odd. If I reacted to the art, surely the daughter of an art expert would react, but she hadn't even noticed. I wonder if Mortimer Smith willed the collection to someone else rather than his children. If so, they didn't seem terribly upset. And why was Hillary looking under the rug?

I walked back into the living room and picked up the Asian patterned rug, pricey; the pattern on the back mirrored the pattern on the top —

hand knotted. But that hadn't interested Hillary. I lifted the carpet edge as high as I could, but all I could see was slightly dusty hardwood flooring.

Hardwood is very vogue. I already mentioned it in my flyers. But there was nothing else, not even a rough Picasso sketch carefully hidden under the rug. What did she expect?

According to Hillary the police found no signs of the gun. (The perpetrator took it with him, even I know to do that.) The police have no clue, because Smith must have let the murderer in, but how could we know that? The door was gone. Was it gone before or after poor Mortimer was shot? Had he been shot through the open doorway?

I walked back outside to the mailbox and wrestled out three days' mail.

Circulars, my listing postcard (a good photograph of me), and solicitations from no less than three fine arts museums. Two candidates advertising their immediate availability for public service including Mark Smith for DA — a little early for that, but if he wants to waste his money, that's fine with me. The PG&E bill (Hillary would have to pay that, it's difficult to display a dark house to best advantage), flyers, solicitations from other real estate agents, coupons, and a *Newsweek* and a *New Yorker*. Well, Mr. Smith had some taste.

Just before I came here to be bored out of my mind, I exacerbated the experience by having lunch with my mother.

At the club.

"I'm so glad you took this listing," Mother crooned over, yes, salad.

"You just did this so I'd visit." I twirled my fettuccini alfredo, made with real egg and bacon and balefully regarded my manipulative mother. If I had half her skills, I'd have twice as many dates, which at the current rate, would still add up to zero.

"What else do you know about Mr. Smith?" I quizzed.

"Well," my mother tapped her manicured nails against her lips. Were they newly plumped? Did I really want to know? I did not.

"He had a PhD in something. And when he tried Jazzercise it was quite a disaster. The man had no sense of rhythm at all, couldn't even do Zumba."

"A PhD in undeclared?" Usually a person announces that particular achievement and what their field of expertise is as often as they can fit it into the conversation. "Come on, what did he have a degree in?" The smooth sauce on the pasta was somewhat mitigating my circumstances. There must be a new cook at the club. *This* was divine.

"No, it wasn't general ed," Mom remained calm, swirled up another bite of greens and more greens garnished with funny lacy greens and popped it into her preposterously plump lips. I'd have to ask a sister-in-law. Since my brothers did indeed marry their mother; my sisters-in-law and my mother were very close.

"It was something to do with images and art and public influence. Hmmm, come to think of it, he was quite emphatic on the subject, even in retirement, he often became really agitated about the dangers of the wrong art, I think he called it."

"The dangers of the wrong art?"

She nodded. "According to Mortimer."

Since my mother has an AA degree in kinesiology, or as I call it, PE, her grasp of the complexities of representational art was limited at best. Then again, my degree isn't much better; I think I have a BA in something. Men? No, that can't be it; they didn't even count as an extracurricular activity at the Kappa house. No, I have my degree in business. Yes, business. How boring is that? Well, there you go.

But at least I knew what I didn't know about art. Which is substantial.

I did know, as I wandered around the house only an hour after lunch, that scary art is bad for business and frankly, I don't think I'd want to live with it either.

The downstairs art was disturbing; upstairs was not much better. Four-foot long canvasses covered in wild streaks of color overpowered the two guest rooms and den. The painting in the den showed suffering people falling into hell (any of my friends? I look closely at the distorted faces, but didn't recognize anyone), and a really offensive three-panel work featuring an angry Jesus and a mournful Mother Mary. But she always looks like she's suffering. How could Mortimer work with Jesus balefully staring at the back of his head? How could anyone? Maybe this was one of his techniques to keep the children from spending the night.

Since my art tastes lean more toward pretty illuminated village scenes by Thomas Kinkade, I am certainly not qualified to judge the merits of the works that currently dominated the house. I know what kind of art works as a natural complement to the living room sofa — landscapes and bowls of fruit are my first choice. Would Hillary want to sell the art? I'd e-mail and ask. I love e-mail.

I carefully closed the door on one of the guest baths that held a screaming man filled with arrows painted in thick Technicolor red. Okay, what does something like that really mean?

I couldn't stash all the art in the wine cellar, but I seriously considered it. The paintings were a little too big for me to take down the curved stairs by myself. I'd need help. And help I would have. There will be no paintings upstairs at the next open house.

See, I already doomed myself by mentally committing to the idea that there would be another open house.

I am often not my own best friend.

I walked back downstairs, and no, there was no crowd of people jostling for flyers in the foyer, panting to see the house and make an offer. There was no one at all. I knew this; I was not surprised.

People are even too busy to be nosey.

One of the solicitations in the mail pile was for a museum called "The Lost Works. A new experience in art." I pulled it out and tossed it in my bag. Same museum I heard mentioned last night? Maybe they would know something about this art? Did they perhaps specialize in losing art? Now that's a service I'd pay money to hire. I'd call tomorrow.

As odd as it sounded, was the million dollars he pulled out of his equity here on the walls?

I suppose it wasn't really my problem.

I glanced at my watch. Only 1:45 p.m. The afternoon drags so much when I'm alone in a strange house. There's nothing to do really. I can't work on the house; it's not mine. I can't nap. Someone may come in, and as much as I don't believe someone will come in, just the possibility is enough to keep me from relaxing. I can't do errands, hike, or get deeply involved in a book and stay there. Nothing. It's annoying.

I glanced outside and listened for approaching cars. No sound. I could use the facilities, which wastes a good three minutes out of my three hours of forced inactivity.

I sat down next to our scary figure. He leered at me, and I decided to take it as a compliment.

"You too," I said.

He was situated at the lowest slope where the stairs forced the wall down to only three feet before curving toward the front door. The highest point of the sloped ceiling was six feet right next to the toilet. I glanced up at that wall (no reading material in the bath) strangely, there was no picture hanging in here. The wall was blank and painted white. But up on the top, the dry wall was starting to sag. In fact, it was really sagging.

I finished, closed the toilet lid and stepped up. Now I was too tall and my head bent awkwardly to the right. But I was correct. The top of the dry wall was pulling away from the studs and there was a healthy 3-inch gap.

Well shit, that would never do. It was one thing to have this odd room, completely undecorated and unpainted, but sagging drywall is a very bad sign.

I'd have to point that out to prospective buyers or maybe get some one in here myself to pull it down and repatch it. Or replace it entirely. Damn.

I stepped down and walked into the kitchen. I had people in Sonoma County who were, well, my people, but I needed someone down here who knew the local vendors, permits, etc., etc. I retrieved the phone book from a lower drawer in the kitchen and flipped it open on the counter. I ran through the Yellow Pages and found an ad for Ben Stone, Rock Solid Service. Hey, consider my last mailing and ad campaign, A Little Will Get You More, I figured he must be at least a kindred soul.

I called this Ben Stone and left a message. It is Sunday, after all.

I wandered back to the bathroom, drawn to it like a roadside accident. Could I pull the sheetrock down myself? Was the homeowner's insurance paid up to the end of the year? I stepped out from the bathroom and listened for noise on the driveway. Nothing. It was as silent as Sunday afternoons get. No, I could not just rip the sheetrock off the wall with my bare hands. I thought about it though. For about five minutes. Then I gave up and wandered back out to the patio to breathe in the warm air and take in my million-dollar view. Well, I had to admit; I didn't have that terrible of a job.

My phone interrupted my moment of Zen. I didn't recognize the number.

"Hi, this is Ben Stone. You called?"

He had a nice enough voice, considering I was talking with him over the cell in a less than optimal phone space — only three bars.

"Hi, yes, wow, you called back. My name is Allison Little with New Century Realty and I have a sheet wall challenge. Is that something you do?"

"Do you want sheet wall installed?"

"No, taken down first, then I'll know more. Can you meet me on Monday?" I asked, hoping that if I have something to do on Monday I can miss the Monday meeting at the office. I will do almost anything to miss the Monday morning meeting at the office. It's an hour long — five minutes of useful information, and fifty-five minutes of people like Rosemary and Katherine alternately complaining about the market and competing with one another, either who has the worst listing, or who has the best. It's not an uplifting way to begin the working week.

"I can come this afternoon," he offered.

On a Sunday? So he was insane. Fabulous.

"I would love to have you come this afternoon. Can you get here by three o'clock?" I cooed. Oh, you don't think I don't court these contractors?

"Sure can." A manly response, a solid name. I imagined that this Ben Stone looked like most of my contractors, solid girth with a soft stomach from all the after-work beer. He'll be about fifty years old and will wear a baseball hat at all times because he's going bald. At least this contractor sounds more like a Giants fan than one for the Raiders.

Since it was only 2:05 p.m., I had plenty of time to worry about my decision. What if he pulls down the sheetrock while someone is looking at the house? What if someone comes and considers making an offer this afternoon and the bathroom quashes the deal? What if he, this contractor, attacks me? With that missing gun? What if I just sat down and took a breath?

Honestly, it's just sheetrock.

Yeah, but when it comes to a house that I've already committed to sell — it's never just sheetrock.

With visions of dry rot dancing in my head, I waited anxiously for this Ben Stone to deliver me simultaneously from my anxiety and my boredom. He had to meet very high expectations.

Twice I thought I heard the appropriate sound of a truck that would belong to a construction guy and not a neighbor, but twice the sound disappeared around the corner, only pausing at the for sale sign for a moment. Just looking. I hope they at least grabbed a flyer.

Promptly (and finally) at three o'clock, a truck pulled into the drive and Ben Stone walked into the house.

"Hi," he greeted me with an outstretched hand. "I'm Ben Stone."

Ben Stone stopped me cold.

Here's why.

Ben Stone was taller than me by a good five inches and sported those broad shoulders women always say they swoon over. Ben Stone had deep, blue eyes and a thick swatch of sandy brown hair, so I couldn't tell if he was going gray or not. He was imposing, self-possessed, and not 50 at all. Maybe 40, maybe.

I stood rooted to the floor, which is difficult to do since it's marble. Fortunately muscle memory took over and I quickly grasped his offered hand.

"Allison Little," I responded faintly. Good, remembered my name.

This was Radcliff Emerson. This was Ranger; this was Dietz. This was the man of my dreams and not just because he had the equipment to tear down walls. He towered over me, making me lift my head to look him in his blue eyes. (I had taken off my shoes and hadn't bothered to shove my feet back into them, not for a contractor, an omission I regretted.)

Oh, but this was a lovely man. However, I'm not a 19th century archeologist and he was not looking for buried treasure. He was looking to fix the drywall.

"Nice watch." He was the first to break the silence that had apparently fallen around us.

"Oh, this?" I was about to launch into the usual polite denial by dismissing the watch as *this old thing?* Because the truth is, I bought the damn watch because it was fancy and impressive. My clients like fancy and impressive and the commission on their house pays for things like this damn watch. Well almost. Well okay, I'm still paying for this particular watch. The faux alligator bags and shoes were purchased with cash and that was the same year my water heater exploded. Do you know how much a water heater cost? Well, okay, less than the damn watch.

"Thank you."

He waited expectantly as if the watch was terribly important and I had something interesting to say about the watch. It was actually a bit disconcerting, his blue eyes watching me; it took me a few seconds to realize he wasn't focused on the watch at all.

"It's a Timex," I blurted out.

"No it's not."

He leaned over and lightly held my wrist and flipped it over so he could look at the face — of the watch, not my face. That part of me was starting to blush, making me very happy he was focused on the watch.

"I see these for sale on the streets of New York. What'd you pay, $10? $20?"

He looked up and saw my warm cheeks. Damn!

"Oh, you paid $30 for this? You were ripped off."

I jerked my hand away. "Just look at the bathroom, will you?"

"Yes, ma'am," he grinned, making me doubt for just a second that he was a complete hick. Mind you, contractors are not stupid people. Or at least the ones I engage are not stupid people. But they aren't exactly opera buffs either.

He pushed his bulk into the narrow bathroom door, surveyed the situation, and came back out.

"Need a stepladder."

He retrieved the same from his truck parked outside and set it up.

"What do you think?" I called in.

"It's pulled away quite a bit. I think I may just have to replace it."

"Great, how much is that going to cost?"

"Just a minute."

I heard the ominous sounds of tearing and pulling, nails squealing in protest. Dust billowed out from under the door. Oh that's right, sheetrock dust gets into everything. Hillary would not be pleased, but then, I don't think anything pleases Hillary.

The sounds continued for another minute or two then there was silence. Silence is bad.

"Well," he said from behind the closed door.

"What? Termites, dry rot? Damn, the pest reports were clear!"

"No, I think you should take a look at this."

"There isn't enough room in there for the both of us," I declared.

"Give it the old college try anyway. By the way, where did you go to school? UC?"

"Chico State."

"Sorority?"

"Of course."

"I was a GDI."

God Damn Independent. That's what we labeled people who didn't join up with a sorority or fraternity. The category wasn't a great one when planning a theme party, but my sorority sisters claim that GDIs make far better husbands than frat men. Maybe better presidents as well. I wouldn't know.

"Of course you were," I replied. Maybe not the perfect man after all. But then again, I wasn't exactly running into perfect men at events like last night's dinner.

I waited another minute for more dust to settle, and then cautiously opened the door and entered the bath.

Half of the wall next to the toilet had been torn off. My little devil friend was covered in sheetrock dust so he was now a little white devil; nothing could turn him into an angel. Mr. Stone was covered in sheetrock, his hair was now gray, and it didn't look too bad on him. He moved aside, backing into the pedestal sink so I could see. The wall behind the sheetrock looked dark.

The wall behind the sheetrock? I squinted, trying to see through the thick dust.

"Is that a painting?"

"Yup."

"There's a painting behind the *sheetrock*."

"Apparently."

"Considering what's hanging in the guest room, I'm surprised he found something necessary to hide." I said.

It was so bizarre that I didn't even have a reaction. Someone hid a painting in the bathroom? Give me a break, and the devil masks in the living room come to life and sing every night, like in Disneyland's haunted mansion.

"It doesn't make all that much sense," he conceded. "But would you like me to pull it out?"

"You may as well," I backed out of the bathroom, brushing up against him and getting dust all over my jacket. Fine, another cleaning bill. I'd charge it to escrow.

While Mr. Stone wrestled out the painting, I took down the open house signs and stashed them in my car. When I returned, he had pulled the painting out into the kitchen and leaned it against the counter.

He gingerly wiped off the dust on the painting with a thick paintbrush.

"What is it?" I asked. My feet slid on the thick layer of dust on the tile. Damn, I'd have to call in a cleaning crew again. This listing was costing me every day. I shuddered to think of what Ben Stone, Rock Solid Service, charged for a Sunday afternoon visit, but that was the least of my concerns.

"It looks like it was part of a series. See how the edges of the canvass just stop with no definition? They were meant to continue onto another piece."

I thought about the angry Jesus upstairs. "Then where's the rest?"

He shook his head, scattering more dust into the air. "Not in the bathroom, there was just enough room for this. The place is pretty torn up."

"I'd like to hire you to fix it," I said, for once not looking at him. The figures of the painting emerged from his paintbrush in brilliant, almost psychedelic colors.

At the top of the painting were three large women dominated by an angry man who hovered over them like some kind of god, or dictator. Each woman held something, a bunch of flowers, a shaft of wheat, and a handful of strawberries. The angry man (what was it with Mortimer and angry men?) was twisting a river of water between his hands so there was no water flowing toward the women.

Oh yes, we have issues with water in California.

"It looks like the murals in Coit Tower. I mean, the style," I amended. There wouldn't be something like this in Coit Tower, not on public display. Maybe I understood more about Mortimer than I thought.

I gazed at the figures; the background was a riot of jumbled icons representing facets of California living.

Wouldn't put it on public display.

"I wonder who the angry man is."

Mr. Stone finished sweeping most of the dust from the painting and grunted as he rose. Aha, he's human!

He looked at the large male figure at the top of the painting. "I don't know. I don't know my Mexican/Californian history in the 40's. Lots going on though."

"Enough to need to hide this?" I asked out loud.

"Maybe. Look."

He gestured to another male face in the left-hand corner of the painting.

"Is that?"

"FDR, yes. The war was probably just heating up, even if this was in the late 30's, not a great time to denigrate the president."   "Or maybe an excellent time," I murmured.

Stone looked at me but I didn't notice. Art as insurrection, art as dangerous. I never thought much about it.

Maybe I should consider buying art with more meaning than my recent purchase; a picture of a bowl of apples. The red fruit matched the red in the couch. "Do you have someone to call to get an estimate on this?" He dusted the paintbrush clean on his jeans and placed it back into a huge toolbox.

"No, and I need to have the other work in the house appraised as well."

He nodded. "I can help, if you'd like."

"I'd like."

Oh, crap. How did that sound? Needy? Professional? Nope, I think needy wins. I needed to get away from his gravitational pull. It made me want to move closer to him, rub up against his messy jeans, as if I was one of Carrie's lost cats.

"I'll see about getting someone here tomorrow. Does that work for you?"

"Tomorrow?" That didn't give me much time to get ready — change my nail polish, touch up my roots, buy a new wardrobe, lose 79 pounds.

"Tomorrow would be great!"

Tomorrow was too soon, and not soon enough.

The bastard didn't even ask me to dinner.

Chapter 4

Ben Stone scheduled us to meet back at the house Monday morning at 9 a.m., which is a little too early. I usually don't schedule meetings until 10. You don't know me well enough to ask why.

I dragged myself out of bed, still pissed off about eating dinner alone, and dressed in the growing morning light, suffused with a heavy overcast of fog. I bound back my hair in a ponytail because between the weather and the time, there was no use in working on spectacular blow-dry effects; the effects will go limp within minutes of contact with the damp mist outside.

With all the energy I could summon, I pulled out of the garage at 7 a.m., swung by Starbucks, lost precious minutes while idling the car in line, silently cursing people who — at this hour — were not sure what they wanted to drink. I knew what they wanted to drink. They wanted a grande mocha with a shot of hazelnut. I finally picked up my order, gunned the engine and hit the traffic on Highway 101 that was — dead stopped.

Really, stopped. Actually, through the miracle of modern life, I wasn't completely stopped; my car magically inched forward without my even applying the gas, just the brake. And with that lockstep, I stopped and started all the way down to Marin.

Caltrans, California's Department of Transportation, does a pretty good job keeping the roadside clear of debris and weeds. I had a chance to admire their work up close, at five miles per hour.

My grande mocha with a shot of hazelnut didn't last long enough to entertain me. The radio morning shows are not only inane but the station signal faded in and out while I slowly crawled through high gold hills (gold from the dry grass, but we don't call it dead brown grass color, nope, we call the hills "golden") of Sonoma County, and I lost most stations entirely as I inched through Novato — a phenomenon I often attribute to some weird atmospheric problem, but sometimes I just blame my mother.

It was a very long two hours, but at least the drivers were fairly polite, except for the self-satisfied snobs swooping by in the commute lane — must they look so smug?

And why don't drivers of Jaguar convertibles look happy? I'd be happy if I could afford a Jag. I'd be ecstatic. I'd hop into that fabulous car and think — yes, I could have put a down payment on a house instead, but look at this car! And look at everyone looking at me in this car. And I am one hundred percent certain that a Jaguar makes a girl look 17 pounds thinner, and so yes, I'd be snotty about it as well. But here they were, the privileged Jag drivers zipping past me, and every driver looked stressed — as if the lease payments on the ultimate dream were actually more than they could afford.

Oh, and in case you are not lucky enough to travel in the center of congestion in this fair county, or anywhere in the state of California, yes, we are all on the phone.

To fit in, I also wanted to talk on my phone. I'm all about peer pressure. I wracked my brain trying to think of a client who was up at this hour. No one came to mind.

Of course, I didn't have anything interesting to say at this hour either. Besides, even Carrie would wonder what I was doing up so early.

Ben was already parked in the driveway when I arrived.

"Hi," I trilled cheerfully. I danced a bit while opening the lockbox, shoved the key into the new lock, and dashed upstairs to the master bathroom.

All that from one grande mocha with a shot of hazelnut. My life is not in balance. Maybe I should have skipped the extra flavor.

Ben followed at a more leisurely pace.

"I called the executive director of The Lost Works Museum in San Francisco," he announced as I walked down the curved stairway, newly dignified. I trailed my hand elegantly along the banister and got a handful of sheet rock dust for my trouble.

He was dressed casually in a faded polo shirt that looked like it was on the losing side of a Clorox bleach spill, and faded jeans that fit him rather perfectly.) He was gorgeous; his hair was still damp so I felt better about my own hurried hairstyle.

"The Lost Works. A new experience in art," I quoted. I carefully held my dirty hands away from my DKNY taupe suit and rinsed them off — again — in the kitchen sink. "I found information on that museum in Mr. Smith's mail the other day."

"He's meeting us here at ten," Mr. Ben Stone said.

"Ten o'clock today?" I was impressed. "How did you get him here on such short notice?"

Ben shuffled in the dust. "He had an opening and was excited about the painting. That's what they specialize in, recovering works that had been 'lost.'" He made quote marks with his long fingers.

"Lost?"

"Are you familiar with that mural in L.A. that was recently uncovered? The artist had made a statement slightly insulting toward the United States. The Los Angeles authorities thought it would be bad for city morale to see anything derogatory, so they white plastered over the work. Art historians just unearthed the mural after, what, fifty years or so? From what I remember from the article, it was like this one." He nodded toward the piece in the kitchen.

The piece in the kitchen didn't belong in the kitchen. Oh, in a pinch I could lean it against the far wall and arrange the spindly kitchen table and chairs in front of it, and I could get some kitchen towels and placemats in the same colors as the flower-covered dresses on the three women in the painting to pull the whole color scheme together, but it would take quite a bit of expertise to turn this particular work into an actual design element.

It would have to go.

"Maybe he could evaluate the other pieces here too," I said.

"What other pieces?"

I reached into the lower drawer in the kitchen and pulled out the masks and set them on the counter.

He let out a low whistle and gingerly touched the beard of one of them. "Thai."

I didn't pull out anything more. We needed to clean up some of the mess before our Lost Work expert arrived.

I cautiously swept away most of the grit and dust from the kitchen, working harder not to dirty my pumps — Gucci — than clean the floors. Ben, dressed for more vigorous work, easily broke up the sheetrock and stuffed the pieces into the tiny garbage can on the side of the house. What he couldn't get into the can, he stacked next to the recycling bin. We closed the door on the stripped half bath and I declared that was good for now.

By 10 the overcast was lighter, indicating that morning was somewhere around the corner.

Our man pulled up in a Toyota Corona painted a conservative blue. The executive director, a Mr. Fischer, Ben told me, was dressed in a blue blazer and khaki slacks, his version of Marin casual. As usual for the majority of the male population I encounter, Mr. Fischer was smaller than me by about 100 pounds. Any trouble and I could take him.

But there was no need. He was not the sort who would need "taking."

"Hello," I greeted him as if I were the lady of the house. "I'm Allison Little."

He nodded and offered me a limp hand to touch — eew. I dropped it as quickly as I could.

Mr. Fischer cautiously walked past me down the hallway. He evaluated each step as if avoiding landmines embedded under the rugs; he also held in his arms and legs as if there was a sheen of toxic containments on every surface.

The only reason for his behavior that I could think of was that he wanted to avoid getting white dust on his blue blazer. Or he was one of those odd people who are always worrying about germs and he didn't want to touch anything unnecessarily.

Or the place was really a mess. I squinted at the walls. Was there a layer of sheetrock dust covering the walls? Would I have to hire a cleaning crew for the walls as well as the kitchen? Damn.

I decided I felt better if I blamed his reaction on Mr. Fischer's own fastidiousness rather than blaming my listing.

"I'm Ben Stone," Ben's voice echoed in the kitchen, emphasizing the silence. Well, this will be a long, painful visit. I steeled myself and followed our director into the kitchen.

Mr. Fischer — did he have a first name? — nodded politely at Ben but didn't offer the dead fish that passed for his handshake. He crept toward the painting, as if inextricably pulled against his will.

"Ahhh." He let out a sigh, straightened, reached out, and almost touched the smooth paint.

"Where did you find this?" he demanded.

Ben was momentarily taken aback by the change in Mr. Fischer's tone.

"The basement," I quickly supplied. I don't know why I didn't want to say the bathroom, perhaps because it sounded so preposterous.

Ben glanced at me, and I shrugged in response.

"This is real," Mr. Fischer stated. He ran his hand lightly over the smooth paint. "My father is more an expert in 1930s Chicano art, of course, but he couldn't make it today. He'd like to see this."

"Your father?" I asked.

"How much is this worth?" Ben asked right on top of me so Mr. Fischer didn't hear my question. Or he ignored it.

"Oh," Mr. Fischer leaned back and squinted, not a pretentious squint; I see those all the time. This was a knowledgeable squint, born of dozens of years in the field. I recognize those, too.

"Rough? I'd say about $300,000, not much more than that. These are rising in value, of course, and Guerra is notable for his association with Rivera. See the lines in the water? The way the front face of FDR is turned, very Rivera like, not Rivera of course, that would be more valuable. Are you selling this?" he asked.

"We don't know yet," I said. "The children will have to consider the sale, but are you interested if they are?"

He shook his head, his expression changed from one of authority back to the timid man. "We don't have it in the budget."

Finished with his abrupt evaluation, he stepped away from the painting he couldn't have and glanced around the kitchen. At my encouragement he fingered the masks but wasn't particularly enthusiastic. I gave up engaging him in conversation and allowed him to be pulled, as I was, to the view out the back. He hesitated before entering the back patio, as if not sure of the steps or the sliding glass door. He hadn't been here before; he wasn't comfortable in the place.

Don't look at me like that; everyone's a suspect. He could have shot Mr. Smith so he could get the painting for the museum on the cheap. But even as I thought it through, it was ridiculous. This milk toast of a gentleman did not kill poor Mr. Smith. Mr. Fischer reminded me of those tiny men in cartoons who are constantly victimized by their large dominating wives. I wondered what Mr. Fischer's wife was like.

"Lovely view," I couldn't help calling out.

Mr. Fischer paused on the patio, his back to us. His shoulders were tense under the blue blazer. I could see that from where I stood, yards away.

"Mr. Fischer," Ben said. "Is there anything else you can tell us?"

"Since this is a piece of three," Mr. Fischer sighed and came in from the view. "I don't know how many private collectors would be interested. Many are donating these works to museums from their private collections already. Now I am authorized to accept this as a donation," he said. "But it's not in the budget to buy. We just completed a capital campaign to finish up our new museum building," he said with some satisfaction. A smile actually hovered over his mouth, but didn't quite land.

Well good for him and his museum.

"That's right," Ben murmured.

"I'll let them know," I replied.

I showed Mr. Fischer out and thanked him again and offered my card. He gingerly took it and after a breath, pulled out a card from his wallet and offered me his.

I paused at the door — the frame was still scarred but it wasn't too bad. I'll put it down in the disclosures, but compared to the violent death in the kitchen, the dings in the door frame will be inconsequential.

"Well, that didn't help much, sorry," I jumped, as he was right behind me.

"Uh, that's okay."

He nodded. "Well, I have an appointment. I'll see you later."

He edged past me since I apparently was incapable of moving from the doorway.

"See you," I echoed.

And that was the end of that. I may as well go to the office.

Inez called me on my cell while I was heading to the office. I had an appointment with her as soon as I arrived.

The New Century Realty office faces 101, and the front door faces 101, but the parking lot faces the frontage road, so you always end up walking into the back door. It's not terribly convenient, but the freeway exposure is priceless. Drivers who pass our office on 101 are often slowed by the increasingly congested traffic, so they often have plenty of time to view the office, recognize the office name, and if we made the posting big enough, they could read about new listings. Branding. I love good branding.

When I walked into the office, there was one new person at the desk mournfully staring at the silent phone. Patricia, our office manager, sits at the front desk as well. She was responsible for numerous important jobs but I think she thrives on annoying the sales team. I try to stay on her good side.

"You're late," Patricia remarked.

"For what?"

A snuffling sound from the bathroom distracted me.

"I don't know, but Inez wants to see you right now, or rather," Patricia glanced up at the clock and simultaneously gave her long hair a flip. "Ten minutes ago."

Patricia can be a lovely person when she's in the mood.

"I know. Inez called me already. I'll go right back."

Another mournful face appeared from around the corner. It was a new agent, Maria. I think she had children to support, a house payment, and an uncooperative ex-husband, at least that's what I gained from the New Century annual picnic last month.

"BOM," Patricia remarked as she saw Marie emerge. Back on Market, BOM, you can see why we call it that.

"911 Myrtle Place? I thought that was a done deal, who was she working with?"

"Christopher and Christopher," Maria supplied, dabbing at her eyes with a wad of toilet paper. Inez should really spring for a box of real tissues in the bathroom; it would look classier. I thought of my own bathroom trouble in Marin and decided to give Inez some slack on that after all.

"Ah," I said. "Didn't go through?"

"No, it's back on the market so I have to wait thirty days to resubmit the property onto MLS and my clients think it's my fault anyway, and they told me they need it on the market fast so they're going to use Christopher and Christopher so they can list as new tomorrow." Maria sniffed and blew her nose.

"What was the problem?"

"Christopher's clients didn't really have the funding, the pre-approval letter was bogus," Patricia summarized.

Happens a lot. Buyer comes in with a low offer, it's accepted anyway. The agent representing the buyer claims that it's all good, and the pre-approval letter is just fine and wonderful, and then three quarters of the way through escrow come to find out that the buyers actually need to sell their powerboat to come up with the closing costs and if the mother-in-law doesn't loan them that additional $100,000, they can't make the deal work. Oh wait, that was my last crushed deal.

"So Christopher and Christopher offered their services?" I asked.

Maria nodded, and dabbed at her dark eyes. Her lashes were spiky from tears and she looked beautiful. I envied her that gift; I would give up a three escrows if I could look that good when I'm miserable.

"Ask them," I encouraged. "Call your clients and ask them." Peter Christopher was known around town as queering the deal for other agents, then picking up the discarded clients on the rebound and acting as both selling agent and buying agent in the ensuring transaction.

There wasn't anything we, as a group, could do about it. And his reputation never caught up with him; there were always new clients in River's Bend who were ready to believe.

But I felt badly for Maria.

"Just call your clients and ask for another try. It's not your fault the buyer had no cash."

Maria nodded, but I could tell her heart wasn't in it. She was pretty, with long, shiny brown hair and big eyes. She was fluent in Spanish, perfect for this business. It was her bad luck that her first transaction was with one of the more notorious agents in town.

"Go on," I encouraged her. And headed to Inez's office.

The New Century–River's Bend office not only faces the freeway, it's a long narrow building, a series of rooms attached to a narrow, crooked hallway that seems to go on forever, especially if you have clients in the conference room and you need to use the copy machine located in the front office next to Patricia's eagle eye. Inez's office is located at the opposite end of the building. Sometimes I think she's the Minotaur and I have to snake through the warren of tiny offices to reach my nemesis. I am pretty sure this is unintentional. Sometimes I think I should bring string so I can find my way back outside, but I always forget. Inez wouldn't think it was funny anyway.

"The DRE called and they say you haven't sent in your renewal papers yet," she announced.

"Of course they did," I purred. I pulled out my phone/calendar/e-key/what-have-you and checked the dates.

"I sent in my renewal form by certified mail on March 3. I received that handy little card from the U.S. Post Office back on March 8. The post office, unlike the DRE Department, does not lie. So not to contradict you, but yes, the Department of Real Estate did indeed receive the paper work."

You may wonder why I would be so anal, but let me digress and rant about my least favorite institution, one that in comparison makes the DMV look like a paragon of customer service and efficiency. I am not even being sarcastic.

Like most bureaucracies, the DRE in our area is wedded to paper, hundreds of layers of middle management, and inefficiency. This department supposedly exists to help the public. Except they don't have e-mail and they don't answer their phones. Frankly as a consumer, if you have a problem with a real estate agent, don't call the Department of Real Estate; your better bet is to drive by the perpetrator's home and throw rocks.

Oh yeah, and if you think, hey, there must be another side to this, like maybe the DRE has some explanation, the odds are good we will never get their side of the story because there is no one there to answer the phone. And whose fault is that? See what I mean? So all you get is my side of the story. And since I'm all about customer service, it pains me to run up against institutions that are so clearly and fully devoted to not giving customer service. The only institution worse than the DRE is Country Wide. Just throw the rocks.

"I knew they'd lose the renewal," I said out loud. "I'll send them another copy, certified mail. Or should I drive up to Sacramento?"

Inez sighed. "What is it with you and the DRE?"

"Bad karma. I'll go there in person and renew."

It saddens me to know that when California does experience the "big one," Sacramento will not be affected. That means that while the residents of every coastal community from Crescent City to San Diego are wallowing in twisted rebar and accordion-pleated freeway on-ramps, members of the legislature, the governor, and the state senate can deny anything happened at all because, of course, there will be no sign of an earthquake immediately out their own windows.

I had time to return some calls on my drive up, or really over, to Sacramento. I left a message on Hillary's phone to see if I could meet with all the Smith children tomorrow. They needed to know about the art and I needed most of it out of the house. I had two calls back from agents. To summarize the feedback: the art was too scary and what was it with the torn-up bathroom?

I had two calls from other clients about the lackluster response to their homes. I'd have to address those. But I called back the agents first. I explained we had a small problem that was not pest related. They were satisfied and promised to take another look in a week. It was the best I could do.

After spending too much time searching for parking, I finally entered the hallowed halls of the DRE. There was a long line of people in front of the customer service sign, mostly agents. Everyone in line was frowning and texting into their phones as they waited. At the head of the line was a neatly hand-lettered sign requesting that phones be turned off.

I pulled out my phone and started up a lively game of Yahtzee.

It was my turn after only five games, a record. I was almost nice when I approached the elderly woman at the desk and handed in my extra copies of paperwork.

Always make extra copies.

"You real estate agents always wait until the last minute and then have to come down here. What a waste of time," she complained as she took my paperwork. She glanced through the papers.

"Where are the originals? We need originals for your renewal."

"With you," I said carefully.

She rolled her eyes, tossed my copies on her counter, and marched away in her sensible, low-heel shoes, leaving me standing at her desk with no additional explanation.

I toyed with the idea of playing one more game of Yahtzee. My high score was only 320 and I wanted to beat it. But I refrained. I shouldn't have; she took ten minutes.

"Well, we can't find your work, you'll have to fill it out again," she thrust the sheaf of papers at me, giving me no choice but to take them.

"You can go over there," she nodded to a row of hard plastic chairs; two agents were already uncomfortably seated, trying to fill out papers on their laps. There wasn't even a thick magazine on which to write. Kind of like that scene in *Men In Black*.

"You lost the paper work." I just made the statement.

"Did not," she retorted.

I opened my mouth and then closed it, like a wide-mouth bass. Hold it in; do not kill her; that will only slow down the process.

"Did," I said out loud. "Too."

I stood there, holding the paperwork and staring at the unlovely apparition before me. But what if killing someone sped up the process? What if something needed to be escalated? Oh hell, now I was back to the children. Or maybe it was an accident after all, that's what Mark suggested. But death by an accidental shooting? I wasn't ready for that explanation.

I smiled at the woman, frightening her a bit, I suppose. Bureaucrats never expect you to smile.

"I'll see if we can get the manager," she mumbled.

"I'll wait right here," I assured her. I was willing to wait because I always wondered if there was someone actually in charge at the DRE.

The manager, unearthed from the back of the offices, looked like the male twin of the front desk customer service clerk. I smiled again.

He grimaced. I said I would wait. He fumbled and scurried off.

After only one additional hour of waiting and a new personal best of a 400 score on my game, the manager found my paperwork and expressed great surprise that it was all in order.

"You know, you can phone us for matters such as these," he lectured even as he made certain all the information was correct.

I glanced around for something heavy to hit him. Nothing. I understood what could trigger a crime of passion. But that didn't help any of my situation. I received my renewal, asked for copies on the spot, and was finally released.

So to end my fabulous day that began too early with the immovable Ben Stone and me, the hard place, my happy drive to Sacramento in order to be abused by the DRE, Hillary returned my call and announced that they couldn't meet tomorrow; we'd have to meet tonight.

Did I make the evening worse by eating with my mother? I did not. I stopped at a Jack in the Box and ate my favorite meal, well one of my favorite meals, the grilled sourdough sandwich and a shake. I did not order the fries—too fattening.

Fortified, I was ready for another meeting with the Smith children.

The painting was where I had left it, just leaning against the kitchen counter. Mr. Fischer had mentioned that he could take the painting back to his museum to keep it safe. But as the youngest child with two older bullying brothers, I knew better than to let anyone take anything to keep it safe. "Keep it safe" is really code for "you'll never see it again." Kind of like letting someone move into a house before the loan funds and escrow closes. Don't do it. There are stories of people who never really get the funding but are already in the house and you suddenly have a very bad problem on your hands.

So the painting leaned against the kitchen counter, a 6-foot-tall reproach. Early evening light streamed into the living room and cast long rays of sun into the dining room where we all gathered.

Stephen leaned back in his chair because there was no one to tell him otherwise. Mark placed his hands on the table and focused on his long fingers, his wedding band sparkled bright gold in the kitchen light.

"So is that it?" Hillary sat across from her two brothers. I sat with my back to said painting because it wasn't my problem, and across from me sat the lawyer, or was he an attorney? He didn't state his preference. Attorney or lawyer, he did look the part. He was tall and skinny with a shock of gray hair. He took my offered hand and stared into my eyes for about a minute — a long minute. He had no laugh lines; I had that much time to notice. I suppose this was his way of being sincere — I'm so sorry for your loss kind of sincerity, but I was having none of it. I pulled my hand away, and when he turned to Hillary, I carefully wiped my hand on my skirt.

Okay, yes. Every time an attorney gets his wings, another three-part form appears in my "IN" box. Every time a lawyer wins a frivolous lawsuit, I have another set of disclaimer and warning contracts to present to my buyers to sign. The disclosure statements for any home sale currently weigh in at 9 pounds. The paperwork includes important information like: remember, you may possibly live in an earthquake zone. Really. California is one big earthquake zone, but apparently there was enough legal discussion and lawsuits that we've created an abundance of paperwork explaining degrees of earthquake possibilities. I think that if you move to California and are surprised by tremors, you should not have left your home state. Just sign here.

So I'm not a fan of attorneys. Sorry. If you are an attorney, you can redeem yourself by purchasing twenty copies of this book. Tuck them into your holiday gift baskets. Share the love. Thank you.

But I seemed to be even less a fan of this particular attorney, which just shows that I am capable of seeing beyond my own stereotypes and can dislike a person on his own merits.

"Is that what he spent a million dollars on?" Hillary's voice warbled with distaste and distress.

"Of course he would. The art was all, remember?" Mark drummed his fingers for emphasis.

"So what do we do? Sell the damn thing?"

A million dollars disappearing out of your inheritance wasn't something to calmly acknowledge and then shrug with an "oh well, it's only money" attitude.

Because the term "its only money" is never true.

Here's what I know to be true. Dear old dad drew a million dollars of equity out of the house so the sale of the house would only net another million, which split three ways isn't something to be ignored — a person could buy a decent car, invest in more real estate or travel the world (if you leave out Antarctica), but I'm guessing that the amount wasn't even close to the windfall these perpetually disappointed and angry children expected to make up for years of being ignored. Nope, not enough at all.

I had many interesting thoughts about murder while at the DRE, but nothing really panned out or made sense. And the police had no clue at all. At least none when I called again to ask about progress. (I had a lot of time on that highway as I was driving home).

"We will contact you, Ms. Little," the detective answered as patiently as she could. "But if I am always talking to you, how can I do my job?"

She had a point. But then again, I hadn't called in twenty-four hours, just to give her a break. I made a note to check in on Friday.

"I think," Mark, the man running early and often for Marin County DA, spoke directly to the attorney — I think the attorney's name was Mr. Peterson, or it was Peter? A P-word. There is a class available on remembering names, but I keep forgetting to sign up.

"The weird stuff." Mark dismissed the art he could see and apparently the art he couldn't see. "We can give away or sell. Whatever, that's just dad. But this," he gestured with his head. "Could be a problem. Can we donate anonymously?"

Peter Peterson, Attorney at Law, nodded his head, but Hillary would have none of that.

"Anonymously? Are you crazy? Why wouldn't you want your name and picture on everything you do? Hello, running for office, you need the exposure."

Mark shook his head. "Maybe not this kind of exposure. Dad's right. This stuff is pretty weird."

"Mom always thought it was weird, his lifelong thing about art," Stephen put in.

"At least Mom didn't have to live through this," Hillary snapped.

"Neither did Samantha," Stephen pointed out back.

"Did her family get anything?" Mark suddenly asked.

Did this Samantha have a family? History? Maybe her family had information about who may want to kill the lovely, if a tad uncoordinated at Jazzercise, Mr. Smith?

The attorney shook his head. "Nothing. Everything was left just to you. What's left."

Mark groaned, Stephen groaned.

"Did she have any children?" I asked, you know, for fun.

Peter Something shook his head. "She was childless."

"Child-free," I put in.

"What? Oh." But before he could even ask about my knee-jerk correction, Hillary turned the focus of the meeting back to her.

"Do we have a buyer?" Hillary turned to the lawyer who, I thought, was actually earning his money today. I'd charge these kids, what, $400 an hour just to sit in the same room with them.

Oh sure, as if it would be any prettier with my own brothers and me. Worse, my lovely accomplished sisters-in-law would insist on being included, and that would make any tense situation twice as painful.

But Hillary had a fine handle on her siblings. Whatever they said, both men automatically looked to their sister to give the final blessing to their thoughts and words, and she managed to keep the spouses out of this entirely. I admired that.

"I don't like it," Hillary insisted. "It represents everything I hated about Dad."

"Oh, he wasn't that bad," Stephen protested mildly.

"Bad? You didn't have any paintings in your room," Hillary cried.

"I had Cheryl Tiegs plastered over that weird bloody one," Mark serenely replied.

"Dad must have killed you."

"Never went into my room," Stephen grinned. Ah, he was the baby. Sometimes the baby does well in the lineup.

"Lucky you," Mark said with a little rancor. "Oh, and speaking of twerps, where is the Polynesian figure?" Mark looked around, and then craned his neck to look down the hall.

"The little devil of a guy?" Stephen asked.

"I put him in the bathroom," I said.

"See if you can have an accident and make it go away," Stephen said quietly. I smiled at him thinking, 'Ah, here is some spunk, someone with a spine.'"

"Maybe we can sell the whole collection," Mark suggested.

Hillary glared at both brothers and they backed down. I was impressed; maybe she'd share her secret for dominance. But I realized that her authority came from years of absolute terrorism. If you began life taller and could reach the cookies first, if you could sit on your sibling's head, or smash your sister's Stonehenge made of red and green wood blocks, it established you as the dictator for life. And I didn't have the right background. As the baby in the family, I was the designated victim; I was the one who fit into the dryer. Not on purpose. Mom still doesn't believe me.

Now, since I don't even fit into commercial size dryers, I've been upgraded from perpetual punching bag to "Poor Allison," usually when my sisters-in-law alluded to my unmarried state.

"So is that what he took the million for?" Hillary demanded.

Peter Petersen, attorney-at-law-JD-esquire-something, sighed and looked at me as if I had the answer and more, an interest in helping him out. I just looked at him with the same bright expectation as his clients.

"He donated the million dollars directly to a museum," Peter, the lawyer, reluctantly announced. "Anonymously."

The boys rolled their eyes in frustration while Hillary remained silent.

"Apparently, according to the museum executive director, the painting has been here for years," the lawyer finished, his voice trailing off as he saw the furious expression on Hillary's face.

"The museum?" I asked.

"Where was it hidden?" demanded Hillary.

"In the guest bath," I offered, "behind the sheetrock."

"So what do we do?" Mark asked. His hands had not moved from their position on the table surface. He appeared relaxed, immovable. I looked more closely at his hands; the fingertips were white around the edges, but his demeanor was calm. Maybe that's what you need to be a DA, I didn't know. My attempts at complete calm usually fail. Although I did not kill anyone in Sacramento today, that should count for something in the self-restraint department.

The $400/hour man cleared his throat. "You can donate it and defray the profit of selling the house for tax purposes."

"Is that what you would do?" Stephen looked like the youngest and had a baby face, but he was, in my opinion, the better behaved of the three siblings. Only three; sometimes it seemed like there were thousands of them, and they didn't even move fast.

"It's up to you," Mr. Peter Peterson said sanctimoniously.

People don't pay other people $400 an hour to finally conclude, "It's up to you." They pay you to be the expert and to TELL them what to do. For instance, I do not have a problem telling my clients what to do. They are enormously grateful for the advice and I'm often right.

"Can we get the million dollars back?" Stephen asked.

The lawyer shook his head.

"Which museum?" I whispered.

"Lost Art," Peterson whispered back.

Hillary dropped her head into her manicured hands. "Oh God," she groaned, leading me to conclude that it was worse than she thought. First her dad wants to sell the house to disguise the fact that it was mortgaged to the hilt, and then she discovers that the big secret hiding in the house was art she couldn't use and apparently didn't like.

"And you," she shot daggers at Mark. "You should be the most upset."

"I am," Mark said. He slowly dragged his hands across the table, as if those white-edged fingertips were suction cups. He finally managed to move his reluctant hands onto his lap.

"I am very upset," he said more quietly.

What next? There was no what next. Well, her father had been murdered. But we weren't even discussing that. The children had apparently distanced themselves from that fact; perhaps that was the best way to cope for now.

"When is the funeral?" I asked, apropos of nothing. Well, to them it was apropos of nothing; to me it was a logical course of my mind. Have you ever seen a wonderful cartoon, "Pinky and the Brain"? Brain is a lab mouse with an enormous head that plots nightly to take over the world. Pinky is Brain's sidekick whose own head is filled with little more than non-sequesters of which he only utters the very last part so there is no way you, the audience, can follow his odd train of thought. I love the show because everyone is so focused on his or her goals. If you haven't seen the cartoon, then never mind.

I love cartoons; it's almost all I watch. Why would I waste time with depressing reality shows and the news??

So that was my thought pattern.

"The funeral is tomorrow afternoon. Come," Mark said, suddenly the generous politician. As if a funeral was an opportunity. I gave him a look and he met my eyes frankly. Yes, it was an opportunity; he knew it and so did I.

"I may," I replied. Fine, I had no offers on this house, I had no offers on my three other listings, and one listing needed a price reduction — always a tricky conversation with clients. So it was not a good week for me work-wise. Do murderers attend funerals, or was that something I read? Okay, maybe I watch more than just cartoons.

Don't judge me.

Chapter 5

The day of the funeral was sunny and warm, just like summer. Marin and Sonoma counties are on the coast, so we don't get long, hot weeks of summer. We get summer days randomly. A beautiful 77-degree day in January. A heat wave in March. And freezing fog-filled mornings in June. I like to think it's our way of living on the edge.

Today it was August. The temperature clocked in at 90 degrees according to the temperature gauge on my dashboard. I parked and greeted the clear blue sky and ubiquitous golden hills with more enthusiasm than the event warranted. Unlike the natural state of the landscape at this time of year, the hills at the cemetery rolled up from the parking lot in artificially green mounds and valleys. The grass was the same cheerfully improbable shade as the grass covering the eighteen-hole course at the Marin Country Club. I suppose it made sense that the greens should match — same people, same demographics; just some underground, some still upright in a golf cart.

I stepped out of the car and took a breath of the hot air. I was on time, so I had a few minutes before I needed to appear. So I took the quiet moment (Katherine, a top agent in my office, is always harping on me to take deep breaths and center myself. She frequently travels to India). I lowered my eyes and expectations and I pretended I was outside on a hot, breezy green hill in the country and had nothing to do but nap in the warm air. The fantasy did not last very long. If I lifted my head just slightly I could catch more than a glimpse of the slow-moving freeway traffic just beyond the last hill. You can see the graveyard from 101.

I wondered if die-hard commuters actually requested the sites overlooking the freeway, just to remind them that they didn't have to be on the road everyday anymore. Their children could visit the gravesite; look out over the traffic and say, "Mom always tried to leave exactly at 6:45 because that was best time to miss the worst of it." And now she overlooks the freeway, secure in the knowledge that she never has to enter the 101 corridor again.

Our event began in the farthest of the narrow rooms that make up the funeral home. We were competing against a beloved mother resting in room five. Smith's funeral guests were gathering in room seven. I found the room, signed the guest book propped up next to a studio portrait of Smith as a much, much younger man, and strolled in.

"Oh Allison, you came," Hillary bustled up. She was dressed impeccably in a Chanel suit of navy with white piping; she even wore the de rigueur gold chains to match her gold chain belt. Her bare feet were smashed uncomfortably into navy pumps. I can say uncomfortably because really, you need to wear pantyhose with pumps, it just feels better.

But I didn't feel that sorry for Hillary.

"You must meet the girls," Hillary said.

I glanced around for my mother, who assured me she would attend dear Mortimer's funeral. She was talking to a couple that I recognized as regulars at the club and golf course (they were still in the upright in their golf cart category and probably thanking their gods for that at this very minute). Mom didn't see me yet. So I couldn't use my mother as an excuse to not meet Hillary's offspring. I dutifully followed Hillary to the front of the room. A spray of white lilies covered the lower half of the coffin and three arrangements marched behind the coffin, roses, carnations, and a mixed collection; every one was embellished with the banner: Dearest Father. I assumed there were not a great many pre-printed banner choices.

"These are my children," Hillary announced.

At one point Hillary's triptych of girls must have looked like a perfect set. It was easy to visualize the three little girls dressed in their annual red velvet outfits for the Christmas card photo and they probably all dressed as fairy princesses for Halloween and of course, they wore Easter dresses in yellow, purple, and pink. I wondered if Hillary also made the girls wear hats and carry tiny purses. I know my mother gave it a try.

But the years of the matched set of perfect girls was officially over. Hillary may have complete control and authority over her brothers, but it was clear, even to me, that the dictatorship at home was slipping.

"Girls," Hillary pointed out three disparate females. They glanced at their mother and reluctantly stepped forward. I could see that despite their mother's best efforts, clearly the sisters' own personalities were beginning to show through. The oldest girl was stuffed into a miniature Chanel suit that probably looked just like Hillary's on the hanger. The child had pulled the skirt down over her bony hips, pushed up the jacket sleeves and embellished the outfit with an ancient black Whitesnake tee cut off right below her small breasts. Her stomach was fantastically smooth and firm as only a 15-year-old can have.

I didn't want to tell her that the window of opportunity to enjoy that flat stomach was a narrow one. Yes, I did want to tell her. I'd kill for that stomach and I was jealous.

Hillary merely glared at her eldest.

"This is Allison Little. She is the realtor for Grandpa's house."

"Nice to meet you," the girls mumbled as a unit, ducked their heads, and glanced over at the coffin.

The youngest wore a purple and green striped Rugby shirt under her short navy jacket and had hiked her skirt up to reveal enviable narrow toothpick legs. She didn't shake my hand, but instead sniffed conspicuously, as if a sudden surge of grief would excuse her from performing social duties.

"Jackie?" Hillary raised an eyebrow.

Jackie, the oldest, handed over her limp hand and I shook it.

The middle child shifted her weight, tugged at her skirt, and glared at me. I smiled back. The girls gave me hope for my own tightly organized nieces; they do grow up. And bite you back.

I glanced around for Hillary's better half, but he wasn't immediately apparent. No husband? No, her left hand was weighed down by a couple of carats so no, there was a spouse somewhere. But she didn't volunteer to introduce me. Why I even thought of it, I don't know.

I pulled away to survey the group, perhaps a contrite or gleeful murderer was lurking in the back of the room, and I would see him (or her) and know immediately that he (or she) was the culprit. Because wouldn't that just move everything along nicely? But I was interrupted as soon as I broke free of Hillary's grasp.

Not to be outdone by his sister, Mark sidled up to me and insisted I meet his brood too. I sighed and wished for some distraction to prevent further juvenile introductions, but there were none to be had. The minister or preacher or whomever, was nowhere in sight. I didn't particularly want to stand next to mom; she was busily speculating on Mortimer's untimely (turned out he was 85) death and I didn't want to stand too close and feign innocence about said untimely demise. I looked around the bare hall, noticing the gray folding chairs and single podium adjacent to the coffin; a spray of white gladiolas masked the podium base for that festive touch. It all seemed so plain and anticlimactical.

I wondered if it was too late to join up with the Catholics or even the Episcopalians. I think there should be some more ceremony, more pomp and circumstance for the last goodbye. Perhaps a choir and some incense. I don't know how Mom would react to that wish. But if I wanted, I could probably make a last-minute switch, just to satisfy my own needs. She'd be dead; she probably wouldn't care.

Mark steered me to his own group of upstanding young citizens. He had produced three sons; all were broad shouldered and sported "Smith for DA" buttons on the lapels of their ill-fitting jackets. As children of a politician, they were much better at the meet-and-greet than Hillary's. Score one for Mark.

"And your wife?"

"Wife?" Mark glanced around much the same way Hillary had. "She's probably in the ladies' room."

"A campaign is a lot of work," I commented. "I suppose she helps you quite a bit."

Mark was still scanning the room but I sensed it wasn't to find his lovely spouse to introduce us. "She is critical to my work," he said absently. "Excuse me." He headed off for some new arrivals, all men.

"Have you met my kids?" Stephen waylaid me before I too could sneak off to the ladies' room. If all the wives were huddled in there, that's where I wanted to be. You hear a great deal in the ladies' room, almost as much as you hear in the grocery store checkout line. But I digress.

"No," I said brightly. "Do you have three children?"

"How did you know?"

"Lucky guess."

He led me across the room to meet his brood of little darlings.

"A political campaign is a lot of work," I repeated to Stephen.

He patted his hair and looked at me a big strangely. "Yes it is. You mean Mark and Hillary?"

"Mark and Hillary?"

"They were always as team. Mark is three years older than me but only a year younger than Hillary so they were in high school together. They always ran for student body officer or prom queen or some damn thing. I remember they would hole up in Hillary's room to strategize. I played outside. Here they are," Stephen gestured to his children, as if they were prizes won at the school raffle.

His were a mixed group of three boys and a girl all jumbled together. Each child sported peeling red swatches of skin across the bridge of their nose. Each exuded the glow of excessive sports activities. Each child announced the results of their last soccer game as I was introduced.

"We beat the Zip Drives 82—9," said one small sturdy child. A few feet away, I could see Hillary's oldest roll her eyes. Well, this probably wasn't the most cheerful group at holiday time. With little in common, they were probably reduced to spending their hour at the children's table tossing peas into each other's milk and tormenting the youngest or smallest.

"Lovely," I murmured.

"Well, I need to greet some people, I suppose. But they have that pretty well in hand as well." Stephen glanced at his siblings.

"What about Mark's wife? Doesn't she help with the campaign?"

"Karen? She's around here. She usually keeps to herself. She and Hillary never got along."

"Jealousy?"

Stephen gave me a look of surprise. "That was pretty astute of you. Yes, Hillary was always jealous of anyone Mark dated. Poor Karen." He shook his head and wandered off, finished with me. Fair enough; during a funeral I think it's wise to cut the immediate family members some slack.

I would have liked to talk to Stephen more, but I had to remember that I do not get involved in the family dynamics. I am just a realtor, and in fact, I didn't really need to be here at all. But I was. And now I felt somewhat at a loss.

I backed into the entrance, and for a time took over the job of greeting people.

"Yes, it was sudden," I commiserated. "Won't you please sign the guest book?"

I may have recognized a few people, either from the club — Mortimer Smith's friends and acquaintances — or reporters from the local paper — those guests were greeted with hearty enthusiasm by Mark who then dropped his eyes after the initial loud greeting and looked chagrined and saddened by the necessity of them meeting this way.

I directed at least three couples to the guest book and accepted condolences from five couples that were certain they recognized me. I want you to know I resisted slipping my business card to any and all participants. Maybe once but only because they asked.

Half an hour later, I was ready to retreat. My black suit didn't fit me as well as I wished, as if wishing magically expands the fabric of a skirt or better, magically reduces the circumference of one's hips.

It doesn't. I sometimes wish anyway.

I did entertain myself by discovering the answer to the question: what does one wear to a funeral in the summer? The men had it easy; they wore the same jacket and shirt they would have pulled on in the dim morning light to get to work in the City. The women chose linen, the real deal that wrinkles with the slightest movement. So the majority of women were elegantly wrinkled; that's the only way I have of explaining it.

My mother was dressed up in tailored linen slacks (wrinkled) and a black silk blouse with a huge, floppy bow that I hoped to god wasn't a sign that they were coming back in style. Huge floppy bows, not mothers.

Everyone carried their designer sunglasses in their hands, as if they were on the verge of dashing back outside.

I joined my mother and her big bow. We sat toward the back of the room with the country club and exercise class friends. Five rows of empty chairs divided us from the family sitting in the front row. We sat in a room with a two hundred-mourner capacity; an optimistic number ordered by Hillary. There were maybe fifty people attending if you count all the little grandchildren. But since Hillary and her spouse sat in the front row, they could just visualize the crowd piled in behind them and no one would ever point out that the number of mourners were low.

I settled my purse under the chair in front of me and glanced at the line of people waiting patiently to pay their respects to the dead.

Well, look at that. Mr. Fischer had slipped in right after I had left my post; see what happens when I'm not vigilant? Mr. Fischer firmly held the arm of a smaller frailer version of himself, the father who was the expert in Chicano art, I presumed.

"Who's the old man?" I leaned over and whispered to Mom.

"Shhh, we don't say old."

"Excessively mature then. Do you know him?"

Mom squinted, "An old war buddy, isn't that what they call them?"

"Only if he went to war."

Mom thought for a minute, and then shook her head. "Almost. Mortimer had money or influence in the family or something. Maybe he had influential friends. He mentioned that he even worked for Rockefeller, can you imagine? Anyway, he went to college and avoided the draft. I don't know how that worked out really. No one avoided the draft then, not like they do now."

"As if you remember," I taunted her. Mom wasn't that old, a good seventeen years younger than the gentleman who staggered slightly as he approached the coffin. The viewing was open coffin, which I think is tacky. But it was not, as you noticed, my funeral.

And seventeen years is a colossal amount of time in American history. So what my mother remembers and what someone as elderly as Mr. Fischer senior remembers could very well sound like two different histories. And of course, anything that happened before 1976 in my book didn't happen at all. I'm looking forward to what the next two hundred years will bring to the United States. Our whole history amounts to a bad phase in Egyptian or Chinese history. We are nothing, historically speaking. I think of things like that at funerals. It seems appropriate.

Mr. Fischer helped the elderly man, his father, walk away from the coffin. Fischer had a pretty strong grip on the old man's arm. Maybe Mr. Fischer the elder was unsteady because he was thinking it was his turn next.

That's what I'd be thinking if I were his age. But I'm not. I'm young and healthy and have enough chutzpah to think that death will not happen to me.

Keep that in mind.

The ceremony was simple. Recalling what the art in Mortimer's house looked like, I guessed he wasn't exactly a pious man, and I was right. The ceremony part of the program was spare. I let my mind drift to thinking about what I'd wear to my mother's funeral.

Smith's children had little to say during the funeral. Hillary read Mr. Smith's biography that included a list of all his published articles and his PhD thesis in representational art and its influence in the community. His work was even sited by McCarthy in the 50's. Not something I'd ever mention, but this group seemed impressed. Hillary touched on Smith's work with the Rockefellers in New York before the war, his move to California for his BA and his graduate work.

Hillary read carefully, without much emotion. She mentioned her own mother and added a few scattered adjectives to that beloved person. But she only listed her stepmother by name. Samantha was relegated to a short addendum in Mortimer's life. Those who survive write the history.

"What about this Samantha?" I whispered to mom.

"She died two years ago. She was much younger, no children."

"Cause of death?"

"He never said."

Well that wasn't helpful at all.

Hillary and company sat upright and quiet in the front row. The Smith children, either unconsciously or not, arranged themselves in the second row by size. Hierarchy — size, weight, and influence, we all line ourselves up. The soccer siblings kept kicking each other.

Hillary finished the list of accomplishments with the tag line "and he was a devoted father." Both boys squirmed at this line but didn't object. I kept my expression grave. Because that's how you should look at a funeral, grave. Practice this look in front of the mirror before trying the expression in public because sometimes you just end up looking silly.

The funeral director said a few words of comfort, general things that applies to anyone already dead and not likely to contradict. Then we were allowed to break up, talk to the dead, talk amongst ourselves.

Peter Peterson, attorney-at-law-esquire, spotted me before I spotted him. My first instinct was to thrust Mom in his path and deflect his interest, but she was distracted by Hillary and wasn't available. I had to face the lawyer alone.

"Have you met Mr. Fischer?" Peterson, or some name like that (remember I am just making this name up, I didn't bother to take his card the other night plus we were not issued name tags, but again, at my mother's funeral...) Anyway, he fetched Mr. Fischer and dragged him back to where I stood.

Fischer ducked his head and nodded to me as if we never met.

I, in turn, had to touch his limp hand again. So I squeezed it too hard. He didn't react at all.

"The children would like to donate the painting to the museum after all," Mr. Peterson said.

"After all he's done," Mr. Fischer murmured, glancing instinctively back at the coffin.

"Well, a person can never do too much," I replied.

The lawyer snorted. I felt a little more kindly toward him.

We stood together like a tiny island of silence, nothing else to say to each other after that first revelation.

"Peter Reilly Klausen the Third," I heard a voice behind me bellow. "How the hell are you?"

"Ben Stone," Peter let out a sigh along with the name. He straightened his shoulders and his tie at the sound of Ben's approach.

So that was his real name. But I still liked the alliteration of Peter Peterson. Maybe Peter Peterson could become an imaginary friend. I had to give up that fantasy and concentrate on the drama at hand.

Peter Reilly Klausen the Third looked a trifle pale as Ben approached. Ben strode confidently towards our group. He was dressed in a black suit that fitted as perfectly as good tailoring can. His shirt was white. His tie was dark purple. He cleaned up nicely.

Peter stepped to one side to allow Ben into our cozy island, which was no longer silent. Ben must have been Reilly Klausen the Third's schoolyard nemesis. Had Ben Stone been a bully on the playground? Did he beat up skinny, annoying boys who would grow up and become attorneys for the county and tangle Ben up in lawsuits involving EPA reports and endangered Red Back Frogs until he choked? Ben didn't look that concerned.

But P. Reilly Klausen the Third did.

"I'm fine," he squeaked as Ben grabbed his hand in a firm handshake.

"Do you know Mr. Fischer from the Lost Art Museum? And Ms. Allison Little?" Klausen amended at the last minute, as if I'm hard to miss. I was certain the introductions were a way for Reilly Klausen the Third to deflect Ben's attention, but it didn't work. Unless Peter crawled over half a dozen folding chairs, which would look like an obvious attempt to escape, he was stuck making nice to Mr. Stone.

"How the hell are you?" I leaned past the stiff figure of Klausen and gave Ben as hard a handshake as I could. He just grinned in response.

He crushed my hand to counter my crush. I smiled in spite of myself. Great grip on that man, he must be good with his hands. Oh my. I sucked in a breath and forgot all Katherine's admonishments to breathe deeply. His hands. Don't even go there with me because this is a solemn occasion and we'll both go to hell.

"Great watch. Did you get that on the streets of Beijing?" I greeted him.

"No, on sale at Mervyn's," he countered. "It could very well be a Timex." He held my hand, easing up a bit on the full crush part, but he didn't let go. I released first.

Really, we should not be having this much fun at a funeral. I didn't even bother to glance around to see if anyone was watching. Mom was deep in conversation with the exercise club members, so I was free for a moment or two longer.

"So Klausen, representing the family or Mr. Fischer?" Ben bellowed.

"Just the family," Peter responded faintly.

"By the way, where did that million dollars go?" Ben asked.

Now that was interesting. How did Ben Stone, contractor and general handyman, know about a million-dollar gift to a museum in the City? And, of course, how did I know? Because Klausen slipped up and told. Not great with a secret, is he? I was looking forward to the answer.

Klausen cleared his throat, but Mr. Fischer pursed his lips and shook his head at Ben. "Our donor insisted on keeping the gift anonymous; he didn't want his name attached, but he did help finish up the capital campaign. We are thrilled, as you can imagine."

Fischer looked almost thrilled.

"Well, thank you," Ben drawled. "That clears that up."

I don't think Mr. Fischer realized what he said.

Klausen cleared his throat again. Ben glared at the smaller man, who cringed in response.

"Okay, well, lovely to meet all of you. I need to make sure my mother is okay," I said and pulled away from the scene. I did not get far. Hillary pounced on me as soon as she saw me move away from her lawyer.

"We want a second opinion on the painting," she announced.

"I thought you were donating it to the museum?"

"We are. I think we are, unless it's valuable."

See how skewed my world is? As if $300,000 wasn't very much at all. Sometimes it seems that nothing is valuable unless it comes in at a half million. Homes listed for under $500,000 are considered bargains and affordable. I have actually heard people say things like, "If only I could get my hands on a half a million dollars, I could turn it into a fortune." I know, the greed of people can be astonishing and when there are so many deserving cats to be rescued.

"A second opinion? That's great," I encouraged her. One must sometimes indulge one's clients. Okay, one must encourage and indulge one's clients all the time, nature of the business.

"I don't have time to take it to the City myself, I haven't been home much this week and the girls need me. And we have Mark's campaign. You do it," she commanded.

I bristled up as only a youngest child can, then tried to control that initial reaction.

"I'm not an art curator," I pointed out as calmly as I could. "And the last one," I nodded to Mr. Fischer, "made a house call."

Mr. Fischer who made house calls, had managed to extract himself from between the lawyer and the hard place (that would be Mr. Stone) and was now was alone and hovering around the back of the room glancing through the door that I believed led to the restrooms.

"Well this one is more important." Hillary dismissed the current curator for the powers of a new, unknown curator. Opinions from the new and unknown always carries more weight with people than the opinions of the known.

"He's from the de Young so you have to bring the painting to him. I made an appointment for tomorrow. Ask for copies of the estimate or whatever so I can review it over the weekend. Here's my fax number. You can just drop the painting back off to the house on your way home."

I just stared at her, willing her to understand how preposterous her request was, but she did not budge. She blinked at me and smiled. "Uh, please?"

Please.

Oh, damn. "What time did you make the appointment?" I managed to squeak out. I braced for the answer. If she said 8 a.m., I'll slit my wrists, which ought to produce an interesting performance art project.

"Eleven. He doesn't come in much earlier than that."

"Why the rush?" I finally asked. "The house won't sell tomorrow, and you have at least thirty days after the sale to clear out the art and furniture. Why do we need to take the painting in now?"

"We need the money," Hillary said simply. She would have said more but Mark swept up behind his sister and gave her arm an affectionate squeeze that looked like it may leave a bruise.

"So are you joining us at the gravesite?" Mark bared his teeth in my direction — it was supposed to be a happy smile. I just took the smile at face value and did not ask more questions.

"Sure," I replied, a newly dug grave being easier to deal with than Hillary.

"Then that's settled," Hillary nodded, extracted her arm from her brother's hand and left to herd her section of the family outside to the gravesite.

I returned to the mean-spirited group who obviously knew each other and had history, because the vibes among the three men were strong and not terribly friendly. I bared my teeth in a smile and invited everyone to join me at the gravesite, perhaps to throw fastballs of dirt into the open hole, or at each other, something.

Fischer the younger bustled up and excused himself, regretfully, from a gravesite appearance. He looked a little damp around the edges, as he had been hiking in and out of the building from cool air to the hot summer afternoon.

"Have you seen my father?" He asked us all in a general plea.

Ben shook his head and gave the director a look of sympathy. "Where did you see him last?"

As if a parent was a set of car keys.

"I thought he went off to the restroom, but he wasn't in there," Fischer admitted.

"Did you check the ladies' room?" Ben asked.

"Ladies' room?" Fischer squeaked. "Oh, Lord. Excuse me, I have to go."

All three of us did the exact same thing. We nodded gravely, and no one smiled. No one. Because as funny as it is, not a single person wished to tempt the gods who dictate what kind of elderly parent you are likely to end up with. We were sympathetic to Fischer but we were also thinking, *better you than me*, and surreptitiously making the sign of the cross. Hey, whatever god works well at the time.

The gravesite service was not particularly special, the situation wasn't mournful, and the sun was actually hot.

We all squeezed under the temporary canopy where the site and the coffin lined up perpendicular to one another. The children, Hillary, Stephen, and Mark, winced at getting their hands dirty when they threw the symbolic handful of dirt into the grave. But it was a great photo op for Mark; he looked serious and sad as camera flashes filled in the shadows. It was a nice — albeit bizarre distraction. But even the presence of the press couldn't mitigate the terribly final sound of dirt hitting the top of the coffin. It made me feel squeamish but I resisted looking for my mother in the crowd.

Hillary surreptitiously wiped her hands on a clean handkerchief.

It wasn't until the group broke up that I remember that I couldn't fit the painting into my car.

"What do you think?" My mother spun in the foyer of the family home and looked at me with great expectation.

I came back to the house after the funeral because frankly, I had nothing better to do. I was disappointed that I didn't meet with anyone suspicious, unless you count Hillary's and Mark's rather unhealthy regard for each other, but there was historical precedence for a brother and sister to marry; I think it happened in both ancient Egypt and ancient Rome, so that wasn't far out of the question. But their relationship had nothing to do with hidden art and stolen doors.

So I was mildly depressed and I told myself that if I got a call on the house, I was closer to showing it. In my dreams.

"What do I think of what?" I asked as I walked into the two-story foyer. The foyer opens to the living room that is backed by a series of French doors that in turn open to the patio and pool that in turn backs into that bright green of the thirteenth hole. This is an ideal location because my dad, like his neighbors, can sneak out the back gate and get in a few rounds before the sun sets. Whatever keeps them off the streets is all I have to say.

Dad? Yes, you may wonder, is my mother so powerful that she can keep Dad out of the loop and out of meddling in her life forever or at least on a consistent day-to-day basis? No, she is not. Dad is a consultant over at Lawrence Livermore. He is a nuclear physicist and still likes to play with atoms. Just try to top that as a kid. I had the thin, perfect mother, and my brothers had the brilliant, talented father who once flew to Washington, DC, to testify on behalf of the beleaguered atom (that was many administrations ago, when decisions were influenced by facts). We, my brothers and I, are, by comparison, underachievers.

Anyway, Dad was in the East Bay this afternoon.

Absence does seem to make my parent's hearts grow fonder. I personally would want my spouse around. You know, to open jars and stuff.

Back to mom. She was indulging in that quintessentially female activity where the girl stands in the middle of the room and challenges her mate with the words, "notice anything different?" And the poor man has to guess what the hell it is and if he gets it wrong, she will crucify him even though it was something hard to spot, like a new color eye shadow, or that she trimmed her bangs. I know this not because I indulge, but because I see it often, and I despise the practice. My friends like Carrie do it all the time.

"What?" I checked to see if Mom had trimmed her bangs, was wearing a different shade of taupe eye shadow, or was employing a different moisturizer, anything at all. Her blouse was new, the latest thing, she assured me at the funeral, but we've already been over that. So I honestly couldn't see anything.

"The door," she said in disgust.

"The door?" I rotated back around to look at front door. Did I notice it when I entered? Nope, I did not notice the front door because I came into the house through the garage. Hah, I win on that one.

"The door," Mom repeated stubbornly and adjusted the bow on her blouse a fraction to the right.

I focused on the damn door. It was new. The old door had a vaguely arts and crafts feel that didn't necessarily go with the 1960s track home, (lest you get all worked up, a 1960s track home in the country club of Marin, remodeled twice over, runs a respectable $1.2 million; in some areas of California it's still all about location, location, location). And now this new door — was no improvement at all.

The door was big; although it couldn't have been much bigger than the original door; otherwise it wouldn't fit into the frame. It looked larger than the previous door. It was heavy and thick. The carvings of exotic plants, birds, and a tiger were completely unsuited to the cool mid-century interior of the rest of my mother's house — my old home, I supposed. The scent wafted toward me. I remembered that scent, but at first I couldn't place it; maybe it was the shock of the door.

It was one of those awkward situations that inspire responses like, "That is a very large door you have." Because that response is better than shrieking, "What the hell were you thinking?"

I swallowed back the shriek and said, "That's a very large door."

"Isn't it just magnificent?" She crowed. "It's a Gilberto, arrived yesterday. What do you think?"

"It's very unique," I assured her.

"I would hope so," she retorted. "Especially since everyone has one."

I was foolish enough to hang around Mom's just a half hour too long. I passed a truck on the way out, a little late in the day for mow and blow, but maybe the landscapers forgot something. The County Club CC&Rs, the most specific home owner rules I have ever encountered in my career, clearly state that no one is allowed to indulge in cleanup landscaping after three o'clock.

I hit traffic, stop-and-go, but mostly stop, through the Novato Narrows, and had little else to do but return Carrie's three messages waiting for me on my phone.

"Where have you been that you can't answer my calls?" she demanded as soon as we connected.

"At a funeral, where have you been?"

"Work," she said morosely.

"Well there you are, we were both busy."

"I'm going out tonight," she announced, but she didn't sound terribly pleased at the prospect.

"What? Enthusiasm waned so soon? Not the man you met? He's changed?"

"Oh, it's not that, but this will be our second date and it's another big public function."

"Well, I imagine that's what it's all about for the boy. You want to buy into this lifestyle, remember?"

"I know, but his sisters will be there."

Ah ha.

"So?" I prompted.

"So they don't like me. They think I'm dating him for his money."

"How astute," I said dryly.

"Well," she continued, intent on her own agenda and purpose. "Well, maybe he's busy and this is the only way we can see each other. He told me he was really busy, all these events, the foundation, all that stuff. You know, he practically runs the dairy now that his dad retired."

"Milking the cows?"

"He's not milking the cows," she cut me off.

"Maybe he can donate some milk to your Forgotten Felines cause," I suggested.

"Oh my God!" she perked right up at the thought. "That could be like, a test or something. Like will he do something for me? Will he contribute to something I believe in?" Carrie enthused. Her mood and tone picked up considerably at the prospect of entrapping an innocent male.

"There you go," I finally was able to accelerate to a blazing 30 miles per hour and I enjoyed the speed. I gradually pulled up and past a makeshift sign for Mark Smith, DA. No picture on this one.

"You can bring it up at the dinner tonight. It will give you both something to talk about."

"He doesn't talk much," she admitted.

"You'll be fine," I reassured her.

I clicked off and considered my options for getting that monstrosity called art into my car and down to the City in time for my appointment with, I glanced at the card Hillary claimed she had found in her father's Rolodex files, Dr. Samuel Jones, Curator at the de Young.

Okay. You know my only option and I did too. But I didn't want to ask him for another favor. So far I haven't been able to return any of his favors. This was not a good thing. I like balance in the relationship, and so far the expected give and take with a new business acquaintance was all take on my side and all give on his. Not good at all.

But he had a truck. And I don't have many friends who own trucks. My clients own things like Jaguars and Porches because those are the clients I like best — big incomes with equally elaborate and expensive housing needs.

I dialed as I snaked up to River's Bend. Pink trumpet-shaped Naked Ladies flowers hovered in random clumps around the base of trees; sometimes a long line of them filled the edges of wire fencing. Just to give you some late August atmosphere. "Oh good, I was going to call you."

My heart constricted, just a bit, at that sentiment.

"I had to leave the funeral for a job, but I wanted to know if the house would be open tomorrow so I can finish up the guest bath."

"Oh." He was calling for business. I was disappointed. I admit it. "Um, well, yes, the house can be open, but," I paused. "can you help me with something else before that?"

"Depends on what it is."

He waited. I waited, just for a second. But he was going to make me speak first.

"Hillary has engaged another curator, this one is at the de Young, and I have to take the art down to get it appraised. Tomorrow." Silence at the other end of the phone.

"It doesn't fit in my car," I pointed out helpfully.

More silence. Oh shit, he thinks I'm a moron.

"Why you?" he finally said.

"What, you don't think I can be trusted?" I shot back.

"No, it just seems that this should be a job for Peter Reilly Klausen the Third at $350 an hour."

"I think he's charging $400 for Hillary and company."

"He should."

"How did you know him?"

"High school. He's a prick."

"Really?" I let it linger. Ben didn't fill in the silence, which only means he's as good at negotiation as I am. I let the moment linger for about another mile. He wasn't giving it up. Another mile. I broke first. I deserve two pints of Ben & Jerry's after this.

"If you can help tomorrow, I'll pay your standard hourly wage," I finally said.

"You don't have to pay me," he growled.

No gentle Ben here.

"Fine, no money for you. But can you help?"

To my unreasonable relief, he agreed.

Instead of focusing on what to wear to an odious errand in which none of the participants wish to participate, I called back clients. Guaranteed to put me into an even worse mood.

Oh, yes, here's what you're thinking right now. You're thinking, oh, Allison, I would never be an uncooperative client. I know all about real estate sales so I'd be the ideal client for you, Allison.

That's what you say in the beginning, but then you morph into a typical client trying to sell a typical home. As soon as we sign the listing agreement you'll be regaling me with stories about how the red dining room will enhance the selling price by at least $20,000 because your brother-in-law is a professional painter even though he painted this dining room for free, it looks professional. Or you'll explain to me how the rock wall in the front yard should really increase the value of your house over your slovenly neighbor's who rarely mows his lawn at all. Sellers are all alike. And speaking of garish interior colors, I had to call Norton, currently my least favorite client.

Let me tell you a little bit about Norton. His wife left him and made it his job to sell the house so they can split the proceeds. Okay, all that is fine and good; it happens a lot in my business.

But when I showed up to list Norton's deceptively normal three and two, a big home on the east side of town in the hills, which looked great on paper, I thought I could list it for somewhere in the high 700's. But when I walked into the house, I actually had a moment. One of those sit-down-and-drink-a-cold-glass-of-water moments. And I don't have those.

It was the paint. Not the off-gassing from a new paint job. No, it was the interior colors, assault quality colors.

Norton's house is painted like the inside of a sherbet factory, after an explosion.

The unadorned kitchen walls were painted bright lemon yellow, the adjacent living room glowed lime, and was furnished with one purple couch and a flat panel television. The guest bath was filled with sprays of dried lavender that exactly matched the purple walls, and the master bedroom was painted — and I do not exaggerate — a Pepto-Bismol pink. Norton's ex took the bedroom set, so the only thing in the bedroom was a single mattress placed in the center of the bare wood floor. His wife took custody of most of the furniture and the cat, leaving nothing in the house to even mitigate the pink.

I almost didn't want to know why, but I heard anyway.

Norton claimed he and his wife had hired a feng shui expert to help them harmonize the home and enhance their relationship.

But after all the paint and mirrors and moving items to the most auspicious areas of the house, it turned out that Norton can't sleep in a pink room, and lime green gives him gas. So for the last three years he slept in the study (painted beige) and ate out (Taco Bell).

But has Norton learned his lesson? He has not. He refuses to paint his house white; he is still convinced that the "expert" he hired was right.

"No," he told me flat out when I suggested a fresh coat of paint. Not even my description of how humiliating it would be to show the house at the brokers' tour moved him. I had to host the house during the Broker's Open and suffer through countless pitying looks and worse, those thumbs-up gestures that are supposed to be encouraging, but are really a bit on the condescending side, if you want to know the truth of it. And every realtor in town scribbled on the back of their cards — PAINT! Even after showing the suggestions given by disinterested third parties who don't even necessarily have my client's best interest at heart, Norton did not budge.

It's been three weeks; no one has come by to view the house. And the house is priced right because I always list a house right. Priced right means what a buyer is willing to pay, not what a seller thinks the house is worth — those are always two different amounts.

I had left a message for Norton while I was driving down to the funeral. So now, bolstered by an extremely bad day, I called again.

"So Norton? How's the painting coming along?"

"Do you know how much painting costs?" he shrieked over the phone.

"Yes I do. I also know how much it will cost you if we lower the price again."

"Miranda won't be happy with that."

"She's not happy with anything." Except the cabana boy at the Costa Sol in Mexico, but I didn't say that out loud.

He sighed. "You're right. I know you're right."

I could hear it in his voice; he wasn't going to paint. He was going to save $3,000 and lose $15,000 on a price reduction. Really, and he is not the exception, people employ logic like this all the time.

"Look," I was feeling a little desperate. I started to argue again, but then a happy thought came to me. I had a friend who often comes to mind when I'm faced with a desperate situation.

"How about I send you a new feng shui expert?" I suggested, making up the scenario as I went along. "She specializes in..." I paused, thinking fast, and trying not to slam into the car ahead. The driver was apparently trying to move forward with one foot on the gas and one foot on the brake, not a very effective way to get ahead.

"She specializes in feng shui that enhances the chi for selling a house. How about that?"

I held my breath and braked again.

"Well," he hesitated.

"I'll pay for her services myself," I offered.

"Well, she's an expert?"

"She has helped me sell many homes," I assured him. Which is actually true; she has.

He paused and I braked and started, waiting. But he did not hold out like our Mr. Stone.

"Okay," Norton capitulated. "Can she come tomorrow?"

"I'll check her schedule and get back to you," I promised.

Now don't get me wrong. Norton is not a loser. Norton is gorgeous. He's about 50 years old and his hair is still dark with only a few streaks of silver. He is a slender man with long, gangly legs and he is just clean enough to make me suspect he may be gay. But I like the way he towers over me and he has a great ass, particularly when he wears jeans and a tight T-shirt with Queen for a Day written on it, a gift from his brother.

Actually, the only way I'm certain that Norton is not gay is that if he were, he would have never allowed those paint colors in his home in the first place.

So I called the feng shui expert who specializes in selling houses.

"Hi, Joan. I need your help."

"Of course you do," she replied with equanimity.

"I'll owe you one if you can pull this off."

"You always owe me, Allison, but since I find you vastly entertaining, I'm at your disposal."

I told Joan about Norton and she listened with more than a little interest.

"Wounded?"

"No, the divorce was a long time in coming, but they need to split the proceeds from the house and Norton will buy a condo with his half."

"And she?"

"Is licking her wounds in Mexico. I don't care what she does with her money."

"Should I even ask what she's doing in Mexico?"

"Something about the whale migration and mating habits."

"An environmentalist," Joan purred. Joan is not surprised by anything, probably because Joan knows too much. She's currently working on her third master's at the local university, this one in art history, which is why I called her for this particular job.

Joan is necessary because a real feng shui expert would never do what I asked. Because what I ask for is often the antithesis of feng shui. I'm a fan of white. Everywhere. Here's what I know for certain about feng shui: the charlatan who did Norton's house should be tossed out of her office along with her credentials and be made to live in a split-level ranch at the base of a road with a dead tree in front and northern exposure across the back of the house, and a heavy, swampy place in the northwest corner.

Yes, I know what should be, and I know what sells a house.

Not pink.

Write that down.

I gave Joan Norton's phone number and address. Joan was sure she had never met him, which will help.

What would a real feng shui expert say about those new heavy doors of mom's? Mortimer's doors had been stolen and he had been shot. Was there a connection? Should I warn mom? But no one mentioned doors at the funeral. We talked about art and missing parents. There was probably no connection at all. And since Mom has been on her own and raising a family since she was 17, she probably can cope.

Chapter 6

According to something Carrie read about couple compatibility, spending the day on errands is a more intimate activity than say, going to the movies. Intimate. She read that somewhere. I've never heard such a thing. I need to subscribe to better magazines.

I tried to remember that as I helped Ben (I held open that awful door) load the painting into his truck, secure it with ropes and a tarp (kind of kinky, but I kept my weird opinion to myself) and take off down the freeway to the infamous de Young Museum.

You should be familiar with the de Young. The image of the new museum appeared in all the papers and magazines because it had to be rebuilt after the earthquake. (The Loma Prieta earthquake, 1989 — during the World Series, it was in all the papers — don't worry, we didn't feel much of it in River's Bend. Much of the town was built on bedrock, but thanks for your concern). In the case of the de Young, a building on city-owned land and funded by private money, the collision of public and private interests, created all sorts of interesting reports. For instance, at one point there was an excellent rumor that the City of San Francisco wasn't really building a museum, that they were using $50 million to build a parking garage.

And as much as a parking garage could function as a massive homage to what is really important in California; clearer heads prevailed and we have a magnificent structure that has been described as either:

A. An artistic abstraction that resonates with the de Young's tree-filled park setting.

Or B. An internationalist building in a beaux arts concourse that is about as relevant as a screen door on a submarine. (That pithy remark was from the *SF Weekly*, Oct. 6, 1999)

Then the museum attendance broke all records and everyone stopped complaining and decided the new building was wonderful.

Money is the great leveler.

We couldn't very well wrestle the painting into the front doors. But that was the only entrance we were familiar with.

"Come on, we'll leave the engine on — a gesture of impermanence," Ben parked against the red painted curb and leapt from the truck.

"Okay." I didn't really leap; I sort of slid down the side of the seat until my feet were firmly on the ground.

Yes, I wore high heels, but with a chunky heel, Gucci. They were the latest thing a couple years back, now they're just comfortable and practical to wear with slacks.

I slammed the door on the humming truck and we both hustled through the main entrance. The main entrance to the museum is decorated with large, immovable rocks and a deep split in the cement. Not an accident, but done on purpose. I think it represents something about earthquakes, which makes sense, that's why the building is here in the first place.

The guard waved us to some area "around back."

We headed back to the truck — still there.

"I'll go find out where 'around back' is, you wait here, keep the engine running."

Business must be pretty good, to waste all this gas.

Ben disappeared in the direction of "around back" and I slouched down in the seat and smiled at the disapproving matrons walking slowly by the no parking area and pushing umbrella strollers burdened with small children and large diaper bags. The diaper bags were large enough to double as carry-on for a week-and-a-half trip to Europe.

The mothers, in turn, frowned at me, and then scooted their little Einsteins off to enjoy another dose of fine art. I admire their sincerity, but I did not envy their lifestyle, or their scowling faces.

Shouldn't little babies be more fun? Oh, maybe it's like that Jaguar metaphor earlier. Sometimes the dream costs more than you expected.

Across from the new de Young was the new California Academy of Sciences. I'm sure it's fabulous. I could take a niece or nephew to check it out. Or not.

Mom loved the city, so my brothers and I spent a number of afternoons running in and around the trees. I was often running away from my brothers. My brothers saved their allowances and bought rubber snakes at the Academy of Sciences gift store. The snakes were quite realistic, enough to startle me. Which delighted them. I'm not fond of snakes.

"We're seeing a Dr. Charles Wang." Ben slid easily into the driver's seat and backed out of his temporary parking spot. "It is, quite literally, around this way."

Dr. Charles Wang did not greet us at the back door, but two nice men who apparently do this kind of thing for a living helped Ben wrestle the painting out of the truck and through the back corridors filled with the busy internal workings of the museum and up the service elevator to Dr. Wang's office.

I am far more conversant with the façade of the famous building than the art inside. In fact, I've only been as far as the front lobby of this particular museum. My two restless brothers dictated the family activities. We visited the aquarium. Not the museum.

And even when I did enter the museum, it was to attend one of the opening parties. I was in the lobby the whole evening. I didn't even bother taking the complimentary tour; it would have taken me too far from the buffet table.

I told you art was not my thing; Hillary picked exactly the wrong person for this.

To my relief, Dr. Wong was as charming as Fischer was nervous. He smiled, greeted us cordially, had a firm handshake, and immediately examined the painting.

"It's like that one they found in L.A.," I said helpfully, mostly because it was the only fact I knew.

Ben glanced over at me, and raised his eyebrows.

I smiled, having delivered my one fact and waited for the verdict.

Dr. Wong smiled as well, and stroked his bare chin. "Well, this is the real deal, and it's political, which always adds to the interest. You know, we had 10,700 people in the building for the Chicano art exhibit; huge interest, and growing, so this will become more valuable over time."

"But how valuable is it right now?" I asked. Since NOW is what is important to my clients.

"Now?" he shook his head. "We would pay about $250,000 for it. It's probably worth a bit more, and I can write that up if you want to take it to Sotheby's or Christie's. That's what I'd recommend."

"No, that's fine. Hillary just wanted a second opinion."

"Hillary?"

"Yes, Hillary Smith, the woman who hired and I assume paid for your services."

"Hillary? No, Mark Smith called and asked me to look at the painting."

"Did he write the check for your fee?" I asked.

"Most assuredly. Now if you'll excuse me, I have a lunch meeting."

We nodded and he nodded, and he called the staff to take the painting back down to the truck.

"The oldest always makes it sound like his idea," I said. "Or in this case, her idea."

Ben merely grunted.

We followed the staff members outside and waited while they loaded the painting back into the truck bed and deftly tied it down. The painting, not the truck. Who is that artist who ties up islands and bridges? Christo. Maybe I know a little.

"Can I leave the truck here for a minute?" Ben asked them.

"Sure." Our two helpers hopped off the truck and disappeared.

Ben turned to me.

"Have you been to the top of the tower?"

"No, it wasn't open when I was here last." How does that sound? As if I travel down to the de Young every month or so to catch the latest exhibit. See my earlier statement about a party in the lobby.

"Come on. Let's go up. It turned into a great day."

To reach the top of the de Young tower, you have to stand in line and take the elevator. Taking the stairs is not an option. While we waited in line, Ben entertained me with fundraising stories. Dee Dee Wilsey emerged as one of his heroines in his tale.

"Everyone wants a rainmaker on their board," he concluded as the guard, or at least the uniformed staff member, directed us to the elevator on the right.

We rode up in silence because in an elevator one does not speak too loudly or God help you, too intimately. Why? Because you just don't.

"So are you on any boards?" I twisted to look at him; he made sure I left the elevator first, quite the gentleman.

He was still focused on the recent history of the museum; it had only been a year since it opened — more or less. "She probably raised $100 million of the $180 million it took to get this together."

"What do you give to museums?"

He shrugged, "I'm a member of this board and a couple others. And I often give in-kind, you know, the use of materials, or I donate my labor to fix things. I do what I can. The reason I know about the Lost Art gallery is because I helped with the restrooms during their restoration and expansion — made them compliant."

"The restrooms or the museum?" I had to ask.

"The museum needed to be compliant too. Ever try to negotiate a wheelchair through a noncompliant art gallery, let alone a noncompliant restroom?"

I shook my head. The very thought of my mother or father confined to a wheelchair made me cringe, so I changed the subject.

"This is beautiful." I gestured to the floor to ceiling windows that surrounded the top of the museum tower. Below us spread the park, the City, and beyond, the sparkling ocean. Nope, it was the ocean not the bay; we looked out past the avenues to the beach and the Pacific. Behind us was the bay but you can't see it from here.

He stood next to me, very close, which could be a good thing, or he was just crowded against me. Different languages in different intonations flowed around us.

"You have an odd mind."

"You don't even know. Do you watch cartoons?"

"Read the funnies every morning; more cheerful than the front page."

"Do you miss Calvin and Hobbes?"

He drew in a breath, a movement that showed more emotion than anything I saw yesterday at the funeral.

"Every day."

I cautiously inched to the left to take in another part of the city view.

"This must be gorgeous at night."

"It is."

"How did you get up here at night?"

"Party, during the opening ceremonies. And no, I don't recall why I was invited. Oh yes I do. It was my grandmother; I came as the attendant."

I nodded, now that made sense.

"Would you live in the City?"

"I did as a kid, we lived," he glanced around at the panorama spread out below us, "can't see it from here."

"The only thing you can't see is Pacific Heights." And the bay, we covered that. "Where the fabulous Danielle Steel lives."

"Yeah."

He must have lived in the gardener's shed. And I'm going with that explanation.

"Grandma liked the Wine Country better than the City. Mom stayed in the family house. I moved to be with my grandmother."

"I've thought of doing that," I mused.

"Where does your grandma live?"

I smiled at his affectionate use of grandma, instead of grandmother. "Claim Jump," I said.

"Gold Country," He responded immediately. I was impressed he knew the town at all. Claim Jump is not on the Highway 80/50 trips to Tahoe; everyone knows those highways. Claim Jump is just east, off on Highway 49, not a popular route since, well, 1855. Plus Claim Jump never grew past 5,000 residents. Long story, another book. Anyway, I was impressed with his grasp of California geography.

"So you're native?"

"Born and raised."

"I bet your parents made you tour every mission down the coast," I said.

He smiled at me. Not a formal smile, but a drop-dead-killer-melt-me smile.

"Every damn one of them, including a couple that were just foundations in weeds."

I smiled back. "Me too."

And that's it. Really, that was the whole exchange. We smiled like idiots at each other for about a minute, sharing in that peculiarity of a California childhood that includes eating crushed acorns in the first grade (to learn about the native Indians) and building a mission — any mission — out of sugar cubes. My nephews informed me recently that the fourth grade mission assignment is far easier now because there are whole kits one can buy in the craft store. Good for them. But I think it takes the sport out of it. Maybe the sugar cubes were deemed bad for the children. Certainly the missions were bad for the natives.

Our mutual reminiscence was interrupted when his phone vibrated, and mine made that chirping sound to tell me that I had a message but failed to hear it ring in the first place, and we both needed to make our way back outside the museum to take the calls.

"How about lunch before we leave?" He finished with his call just as I was leaving a message.

"Where?"

"The overpriced museum café would be the closest thing."

"Okay, but I'm buying to thank you."

"Okay then," he agreed.

Sometimes summer can be as simple as eating lunch outside in the warm sunshine, watching children play on the green grass — in and around the huge outdoor sculptures. I observed the tourists, the families, and those mothers still finding every moment an educable moment.

"It's a Claes Oldenburg honey," a mother lectured her toddler. "The clothespin is supposed to be that big."

"Regret not having children?" He had followed my gaze.

"No," I said honestly. "You?"

"No, not really. My nieces and nephews are enough."

"Mine too."

We left right after lunch and he courteously dropped me off at Ocean View and even carried the painting back inside, and carefully placed it — wrapped — down in the half cellar. After all, it had just lost $50,000 in the journey; it could stay under the house since I hadn't figured out where the hell to display it. So the cellar area was a good choice.

"Well, goodbye. I'll be back to fix the bathroom if you're still interested."

"Yes, I'm very interested. When can you get to it?"

"Don't know, give me a call this weekend."

"Okay, I'll do that."

He shook my hand; no big squeeze like the game we played at the funeral, but a polite exchange: colleague-to-colleague.

Yes, I know. It sucks.

I had floor Saturday.

The definition of "Floor Time" in real estate is that you, the Realtor, have assigned times every month during which you must hang around the office and direct calls to other agent's voice mails. In a buyer's market, floor time is not a great boon. My turn was this Saturday morning. Floor time is right up there with open houses, excitement-wise. But here is the reason we keep doing it. It's the myth of floor time.

Here's the myth: a potential buyer or seller will call your office randomly and be convinced, by your brilliant selling skills, to list or buy, that afternoon. Or better, one Saturday afternoon a shabbily dressed man pulls up to the otherwise empty real estate office on his motorcycle and asks the agent on floor if there is any land around for his mother's mobile home. The floor agent says yes, and takes the nice, if shabbily dressed client, around. The client turns out to need acres and acres of prime Marin real estate because the client is George Lucas.

True story.

That's why we all still show up and take our time on "floor."

I busted my considerable ass to get to the office at 8:30 knowing full well that even if there was another George Lucas driving around, he was still in bed. But that's what Inez wants, so here I am.

Rosemary followed me into the office. Rosemary stomped in for her open house signs. She flung a bright pink scarf edged in silver over her conservative navy jacket.

"Like it?" She flipped the ends of the scarf in my direction. "I picked up quite a few in Thailand. They have beautiful things there! You should go, Allison."

Rosemary is older than me by about ten years although because she's lost and gained about a thousand pounds since I've known her, she looks 50. Do I point that out? Never.

"How did your new herb regime work on the trip?" I asked.

"Oh, just a few hassles at customs but they worked fine. The box was difficult to carry in some areas, you know, but it was mostly excellent." Rosemary was currently in a health phase (please, we do not call it a diet, everyone knows that diets don't work. Well, at least I know that.) involving Chinese herbs. These herbs must be stored in a special compartmentalized wooden box and every morning Rosemary is supposed to finger each herb selection and ingests the herbs that smell best to her at that time. The herb box is very big and heavy.

"So it worked out in Thailand," I encouraged her.

"Well," she rolled her eyes and adjusted her sari/scarf. "Some of the herbs did stick together a bit in the humidly. Sometimes I couldn't really smell them, you know? So I had to guess a bit. But they loosened up with a chopstick I found at the bazaar. Oh Allison, you must see the shopping there! Just fabulous!"

"So where are they now?" Since for three months Rosemary dragged that box to work, plus took it with her on her recent trip, I automatically glanced around, she usually slaps the box on the front counter and startles Patricia every morning. Patricia has been crankier than usual these last three months — must be the Chinese herbs.

"Oh, you didn't hear?" Rosemary pulled up the sleeve of her jacket and displayed three gun metal colored bracelets digging into her soft fleshy wrist.

"I met this wonderful man in the Frankfurt airport, you know they herd you into these waiting areas where there is nothing to do for hours and it's barbaric — no restrooms, no concessions, just terrible, the

Germans, honestly. Anyway, I told him all about my herbs and he told me all about his magnets. Have you read about these?"

I shook my head, but I knew I'd learn. The phones were silent, not even a wrong number to interrupt Rosemary.

"No I have not," I admitted.

"Oh, magnets are fabulous. They cure arthritis, back pain, headaches, and all sorts of emotional problems. I haven't had trouble with my feet since I started wearing them. You should try them. There's a website to visit."

"I'm sure there is," I echoed politely. When someone gives me one more thing to look up on the everlasting Internet I always listen politely and pretend I'm memorizing the URL when I'm really ignoring it. I only have so much time.

Rosemary's phone chirped a disco tune that I couldn't place, and she disappeared into her office.

Much to my surprise, the office phone rang and I snatched it up. Rosemary poked her head from her office, just out of morbid curiosity.

"New Century Realty," I chirped in my best phone voice.
"Is this Allison?" My mother's suspicious tone wafted over the phone line. I shook my head at Rosemary, who of course was hoping it was a call on her property and as soon as she realized it was not, she ducked back into her office.

"Yes, Mom, this is Allison."

"Mary Jane!" Mom's voice kicked up another three octaves. She may have been a member of the high school chorus, I couldn't recall, but she was working well into the soprano range.

"Her doors!" Mom repeated.

"Mom, you need to calm down. What about Mary Jane?" Mary Jane was the mother of a grammar school friend of mine. I don't see the friend, but I still see Mary Jane at the country club. I liked her, and mom's sudden outburst worried me.

"She was attacked last night — I cannot believe the police didn't catch them. She was hit on the head, right in her home. In her home!" Mom's voice ran up to the top of the soprano range.

Mom has a couple of triggers.

"Mom, is she okay?" I interrupted.

"Well, I wouldn't have called you this morning if something had really serious happened to her." Her voice dropped a bit. Now we were at semi-serious. Fine.

"And?" I prodded.

She took a noisy breath over the phone.

"Mary Jane was home alone, Fred was out. Why Fred was out on a weekend night I don't know."

"Mom," I urged.

"And she said someone knocked, she opened the door, and that was all she remembered," Mom concluded.

"How is she?"

"They're keeping her overnight for observation. Fred is beside himself and the police don't have any answers, and you want to hear the worst of it?"

I waited because you and I know exactly the worst of it.

"The doors are gone!" Mom wailed.

"Her front doors are gone," I repeated.

"Completely gone! The Gilberto doors! And she had the ones with the carved giraffes. I can't believe they are gone!"

I could.

A door a night, that's all we ask.

"How are your doors?" I asked tentatively.

"Right here, I'm looking at them. I called the police but they said they don't guard doors and I was being silly."

I admit that wasn't fair, especially since I think that Mom has a real point and no other reference. I didn't think she knew about Mortimer Smith's doors or how he came to his end. Mary Jane got off easy.

"What are you doing today?" I asked carefully.

"Golf at 3 and my club this evening."

"Dad?"

"He's in Washington again."

"Good, when is he coming back?"

"Tomorrow afternoon." Her voice and tone were back in the familiar range.

"Okay, I have an open house tomorrow. I'll check on you before I go and when I come back. But you should be fine."

Mom drew a ragged breath. This really had rattled her. I thought she was impervious to any event that wasn't directly affecting her. But perhaps I was wrong.

"I'll call you when I hear more about Mary Jane," she promised.

I hung up, dropped my head in my hands, and considered my options.

Even though Mark and Stephen didn't seem to really care what I was doing with the house, Hillary cared, and she was convinced that open houses were the way to sales and riches. She mentioned reading that in an article somewhere. I'm sure it was in a doctor's office while waiting for a touch-up. But now I'm just being bitchy.

So, Hillary was all about open houses. And since whatever Hillary wanted, Hillary got, I had little choice but to follow with her regime. Even though Hillary was safely in Danville for the weekend, and I could have just pointed to the ad in the paper as proof that we held an open house. Even though I could do all those things, I still knew I'd show up and actually hold the house open. I had no choice, because if I say I'll do it, I'll do it.

Except I would be doing it alone. And the Mortimer Smith house had just acquired new Gilberto doors.

"You can look up the magnets on the Internet," Rosemary emerged. "Was that a lead?"

I shook my head. "Hey," I remembered. "Can you sit with me on an open house tomorrow?"

Rosemary narrowed her eyes, the only part of her body it was possible to narrow.

"Where?" she asked suspiciously.

"Marin," I admitted.

"That's not my territory."

"Mine either," I replied.

I picked up a book off Patricia's desk: *100 words to Make You Sound Smart*, it looked like Patricia left off at word eighteen.

I spent most of the morning trying to find help for Sunday. But no one could help me. It's high season for the exuberance of open homes, so no one could be spared and Katherine asked if I could sit on one of her homes, forgetting what I had just asked her.

I even called Carrie.

"I can't, I volunteer at Forgotten Felines on Sunday afternoon. You know that."

"Oh, of course." I was tempted to tell her more about why I needed her help, but I didn't want to scare her.

"What are you doing for Forgotten Felines?" I asked, just to keep the conversation going. The company phone, after delivering my mother's hysterical call, was now silent.

"We're rounding up the cats," Carrie said.

"You actually round up cats?"

"It's harder than it looks."

I called Mom in the evening and again first thing in the morning, ostensibly to get an update on Mary Jane, but really to make sure Mom was all right. The scare ended at midnight, when Mary Jane's condition was downgraded from critical to just a bump on the head. But the police weren't really saying one thing or another about the doors, or the attack. No one was talking about my parents being in danger. I thought the best thing was to keep calling and pretend it was about something else. I didn't want to panic my mother. Could Dad stay home for a while? Would they be willing to play a round of golf together? They never play golf together. I thought that was strange. Actually it was strange that I never noticed it before. See? We all take our parents for granted.

For this open house, I did all the tedious stuff we discussed earlier and for fun brought champagne to reward anyone brave enough to drive into deepest darkest Tiburon and submit to viewing yet another beautiful home. I had new reading material and was prepared for three hours of boredom. I already took apart the bathroom. I suppose I could check out the laundry room, pull back the sheetrock in there and see if Mortimer Smith had stashed a Picasso or a racy Gauguin behind the wall. But I didn't have the heart for it.

I squinted at the front doors. Mark had just ordered more Gilberto doors to replace the Gilberto doors. Hillary has protested the cost and there had been a lively discussion that I had not been part of. I wouldn't have spent the money either, but Mark, according to Hillary, had been adamant about it and she had backed down.

Now I would have paid money to see that. But alas, I missed my opportunity to see Hillary back down.

And we had the doors. Doors and More must be doing land-office business out here. These doors looked like Mom's. The carving was a bit different, but each door was unique. Mom had explained that at length.

"See," I could hear Mom and her friends as they compared their recent purchases, "on my doors the hibiscus carving is slightly to the left and a bit lower than the bananas on your doors." Really, they discuss things like that. My life should be that simple.

Actually, not that simple. Mary Jane's doors were gone and Mary Jane was — I checked my phone — still fine. Mom promised to call immediately when Mary Jane was released from the hospital. Apparently, according to Mom, Mary Jane did not remember what her attackers looked like.

Which is a shame, the police love information they can actually use.

The varnish on the doors was slightly sticky even after twenty-four hours. And it still smelled odd; I still couldn't identify the scent, but it wasn't pleasant. So I stayed away from the doors.

I turned on the lights, moved the furniture a bit to "stage" it, which amounts to angling large pieces like sofas and pianos on a diagonal to the room because it makes it — the room — look larger. The rooms in this house do not need help to look large; they are large. But I moved furniture around anyway. I took the classes, I had the certification, and I would Stage The Room, just as I promise in my brochures. See? I'm a woman of my word.

I also checked my key program on my PDA, only four showings all week. All Marin numbers.

The downstairs guest bath was still ripped up. Damn, I was hoping Ben would get to that yesterday, but I had to admit that taking the painting down to San Francisco took up most of the day. I glanced down at my phone; I had programmed his number into it. I listed him under my category of "Useful Person." I gazed at his phone number and name on my tiny screen. Did I want to call him? What kind of impression would that make? Needy? Business-like? I didn't know. How odd to be this indecisive about a worker.

Maybe the bathroom wasn't an issue. Before I called Ben, I'd call the four agents who had viewed the house. Only two picked up. Both commented on the ravaged bathroom. Am I offering credit for the bathroom, say about $40,000?

No, we were not giving credit back to the tune of $40,000. I'd rather give it to this Ben person who looked like he could use the cash.

So I'd have to call Ben after all.

I took a deep breath and hit send. Fortunately he was out and I could leave a message that I hoped sounded business-like.

"Hi, this is Allison again. I don't know if I remembered to ask you: can you come in like, today, to finish the bathroom at 2389 Ocean View Court? Call me as soon as you can with your schedule. Thanks."

See? Business-like. No problem. He's a contractor. A professional. As am I.

I opened up a bottle of the champagne, took a sip to make sure it was okay. Then I settled down in the living room armed with three fashion magazines and a trade magazine to put on top of the fashion magazines if anyone really did walk in. I could see most of the driveway from my seat, and what I couldn't see, I could infer. I just want to be ready for visitors. It was already 2 p.m., which meant I only had two hours to go.

The latest styles hot off the runway did not hold my attention. I flipped through a whole magazine, then dropped it on the floor and got up again. I prowled around the living room. Would the thieves come back here? Had Mark purchased the doors for this house before Mom purchased her doors? Were they coming back to the homes in order of installation orders?

Was this an inside job? It would have to be, wouldn't it? I just had that thought when a truck pulled into the driveway.

Okay. I straightened my shoulders because I can take on anything. This is it.

I looked out the window and watched my potential clients (because I prefer to be optimistic) disembark from a pockmarked Toyota truck. The driver leaned into the back and pulled something out, but I couldn't quite see, and I didn't want to stand at the window and stare; it puts people off. So I walked toward the foyer to greet them.

Warm bodies looking at the house! How great was that! And better — and this is the point of the open house exercise — I could report to Hillary that yes, there was some activity but not enough to need to hold another open house for at least a month.

However, on the down side, these two men didn't look like likely buyers, really. In retrospect, I wish I could say something like, they seemed a little shifty around the eyes, or they were skinny and nervous. But they looked healthy enough, like regular dudes from Marin or even Sonoma. Think of your best California stereotype, *Bill and Ted's Excellent Adventure*, cute in their own way, but their appearance and demeanor automatically excluded them from being potential buyers. Why? Because, George Lucas aside, there is grungy and there is grungy. The only way I will believe a grungy person has the wherewithal to buy a $3 million home is if he is followed around by an equally and artfully grungy entourage. (**C**: I added a word here because it seemed to need one. Does this change what you were intending? MM)

I know, don't pre-judge, but I've been in the business long enough that actually, I can. But I'm not supposed to. At least not legally. So I put my best face forward, good hostess that I am.

I left the doors slightly ajar so it looked more welcoming. One young man pushed open the door and stepped across the threshold.

"Hello," I said warmly.

He was startled and stopped, leaving his friend standing outside.

"Welcome, would you like to sign in?"

"No." He let his friend in, a similarly dressed young man who looked exactly like his friend. I smiled to greet the second friend, but just then something hard hit me, and the newly staged living room disappeared.

I know I'm stubborn, sometimes hardheaded. But I was out cold. Out cold, where does that come from — out cold?

Well then, let me tell you, cold or warm, everything went black.

I must have swum around in that blackness for quite a while because the next thing I knew someone was cradling my head and whispering something. It sounded like, "Allison, wake up."

But I wasn't late for school. I was pretty sure I was finished with school.

My eyes fluttered. Oh please, really? I hoped they didn't flutter like some hopeless, helpless, romantic heroine.

"Tell me I didn't faint," I said out loud.

"You didn't faint," said the voice.

"Tell me I'm finished with high school and I do not have to get up for that eight o'clock chemistry class."

There was a pause. "No, you do not have to go to chemistry class. Can you move?"

The tone wasn't one of general joviality, which made me suspect that maybe I couldn't move, so just to prove it — the voice — and myself that I was in fine, fighting shape, I struggled to sit up and feel my feet or whatever it is you do when you've fallen. I think my brothers say something to their children after a fall. "Can you feel your feet?" But I think the question has more to do with making sure the child is not paralyzed for life and thus becoming a burden to the family than anything else.

I could move my feet. They looked good in the shoes, thank you.

And I looked around. There wasn't any sign of a struggle, and nothing looked out of place. I could see down past the foyer from where I sat, but I really didn't need to strain much to see what had happened.

"The doors are gone, aren't they?"

"Yup," Ben said.

Ben. I stifled a groan because heroines in novels are constantly stifling something.

"What are you doing here?"

He grinned. "I'm rescuing you. How am I doing so far?"

I rubbed my head. "Pretty good, especially if you have some Aleve or Advil pills on you. And why are you here?"

"You didn't pick up. I know from experience that when a real estate agent wants work done, they pick up. Morning, noon, and night."

For you, I bet they do pick up. But I wasn't so far gone that I said that out loud.

"So I figured something was wrong and I was in the area, so I popped by."

"You popped by Tiburon? No one pops by Tiburon. This is a destination, it's not on the way to anything."

He gave me a level look. "It was on my way."

"Oh," I backed down.

"How's your head?"

Hurt like a son of a bitch, but that wasn't the most ladylike sentiment and since I was already into the damsel-in-distress identity what with the stifling and all, I thought I might as well run with it and for once, try not to swear.

"Very painful," I said. "Do you have anything?"

He shook his head.

"Can you get my purse? It's under the kitchen counter."

He retrieved it, winced at the weight and brought it to me.

I spent as little time as I could rummaging through the contents and pulled out my tiny bottle of Aleve caplets. I popped two pills and swallowed without any water.

His eyes bugged out a bit — it's my best parlor trick. I smiled beatifically and relaxed, even though I was sitting on the floor and couldn't remember if the living room had been vacuumed after the drywall extraction. That drywall dust attaches to everything.

I was afraid to stand. I was wearing a burgundy colored silk suit. Even a little dust would show. Damn.

"Do you want to go the hospital?" he asked.

"No. My mother would find out and freak out."

"Okay then, I'll take you to my doctor just to make sure you don't have a concussion."

"I don't have a concussion," I retorted.

"Look into my eyes."

Looking deep into his eyes would be a very bad idea considering the state I was in, but I was compelled to do it, as if he was his own force of nature. His eyes were deep blue, dark, not girly, and intelligent. More intelligent than your average contractor to be perfectly frank, (since I had, on occasion, gazed into the eyes of semi-professional and sometimes semi-successful contractors) his look hit me simply like a semi.

"No, your pupils are the same size. You're probably all right."

Thanks.

He waited a beat. I held my breath.

"And they are a beautiful color green."

I let out the breath and thanked him more sincerely.

He just grinned. "So, what do you want to do?"

I glanced at my watch — the one he mocked me about the day we met, but I'm not bitter - it was 4 p.m., straight up. I am so out of here. But what about the doors?

"The doors," he said out loud. "Well, we can't leave the house unattended; there are still things in here."

"The painting?"

"It's still downstairs in the wine cellar and I locked the cellar door for good measure. So our thieves are really stealing doors, not paintings," he mused.

"They didn't seem all that bright," I commented.

"You saw them?"

"Well, they walked inside in order to hit me," I responded.

"What did they look like?"

"They looked like they couldn't afford the asking price," I said shortly. The Aleve caplets hadn't kicked in; I was not ready for interrogation.

"Okay, kind of short, kind of tall?"

I smiled. "He look-a like a man," I said, quoting the nail salon character on *Mad TV*.

"I'll quiz you later," he promised. "Right now, we need some doors."

"Don't you have some laying around?"

"What? Oh, no, I buy them new from the store. My clients like their doors fresh."

"So what store?"

"Where did these," he gestured to the open gap in the foyer, "come from?"

"Doors and More in San Rafael." I looked out through the empty gap. Hillary was going to shit bricks. And I'm not even sure that's a metaphor. After all the cash Mark put up to replace the damn doors and now they're gone again? Not good.

I wondered if I could get Mr. Rock Solid Service to make the call. No, now I was just being a chicken.

But hey, my head hurt. Cut me some slack.

He nodded. "I know it. They specialize in imports, very high-end. Very," he waved his hand to encompass the house, the view, and the hidden narrow driveways that made up the hamlet of Tiburon, "from around here."

"Then let's go."

We ended up calling my mother anyway. I did not explain that I had a growing bump on my head and was seeing double (only a few times, not worth mentioning). I did not explain that I suffered the same fate as Mary Jane because I wanted Mom to focus on our problem at hand and not go off on a tangent about how her friend was doing.

And I wanted Mom out of her own house. Right now.

"I have a problem here, can you come down and help me out?" I asked her as politely and calmly as I could.

"Well sure, honey, I don't have bridge until 5 this evening. It's our monthly potluck. I'm bringing that casserole that your brothers always liked."

Macaroni and cheese, the one casserole mom doesn't burn.

"That's great. Can you come down and watch an open house for me?" I repeated. I got silence back on the phone.

"Only for a half hour or so," I amended.

"Well, okay, but you know, Allison, you should be doing your own work."

"I am doing my own work, I have to," I searched for a reason why Ben could not get doors by himself. He was shifting in front of me from one foot to the other. His movements were making me dizzy.

"Just until your club meets," I cajoled her. I made a rude gesture at Stone, and he stopped moving. Thank god.

"Think of it as a favor for Mortimer," I finally said.

"Well, all right, if it's for Mortimer's house."

"Yes it is." I hung up.

She made it down in record time. And I didn't ask how. Dad always drives when they're together in the same car, but when Mom's alone, well, I know her car does 160 miles/per hour, my brothers know her car does 160 miles per hour, and I suspect Mom has tried it out a couple times herself.

Ben was already in the truck when mom pulled up, squealing the tires dramatically.

She climbed out, dressed in her casual bridge ensemble — suit, pantyhose, and closed toed shoes. I admired her very much, but I was still a bit out of it, and just wanted her in a safe, or at the very least, an already burgled spot.

"Thank you Mom. See, I couldn't just leave the house open," I explained.

"Well what do I say when people come by?" She wrinkled her nose in the direction of the open door.

"Just make something up," I told her. "And don't quote any prices, just hand them a flyer; it's over there," I gestured to the hall table.

"Okay, but hurry up, I'm going to bridge from here." She paused in the empty doorway. "Who is in the truck?"

"The contractor. He wanted to nail plywood over the entrance," I explained.

"You can't do that," Mom said gravely. "Get more Gilberto doors. They go with the house."

Considering the house was faux Tudor with a turret on the south side to defend against possible Goth invasions, or perhaps affordable housing proponents, I didn't think there was much a person could do to enhance the façade, but then there wasn't much you could do to ruin it either.

I waved to Mom reassuringly and climbed into Ben's truck.

I don't know; his truck is blue. It's just high enough for a girl to climb into the cab. Not a good idea if you're wearing a skirt, but fortunately I was wearing slacks. It was the perfect wardrobe choice for the recently assaulted.

Doors and More is located in a small warehouse in south San Rafael, an architecturally abandoned district of mostly warehouses and, increasingly, big-box retail stores that anchor strip centers filled with smaller-box retail stores. I knew from experience that during the course of this recent buildup, many locals, some with jobs, most without, stormed every single city council meeting and spent hours decrying the intrusion of big-box stores into whatever neighborhood they have decided is filled with charm and uniqueness. Yet, as soon as something like Lowe's opens, the first people to belly up to the patio furniture display are those very same unique community bleeding hearts. Why? Big-box stores stock the necessities in life rather than the cute things in life. A person can only own so many candles, shells, and yarn before a person is forced to shop at the Container Store for matching plastic boxes in which to store the yarn. And the shells. And the scented candles, and tiny pieces of fair trade imports.

I am not making this up. Go to your local city council meeting and bring up the word Starbucks and watch what happens. I do it every chance I get. Especially if those sitting on the council were those I specifically voted against.

"On our way back can we stop at a Starbucks?" I asked.

"Sure," he glanced at me.

"Medicinal." A venti mocha with a shot of vanilla would really hit the spot right now.

He turned into Doors and More, a freestanding warehouse-like establishment with contractor hours to match. Not open. Closed on Sundays.

Who is closed on Sunday? Me? Never. Ben wasn't closed on Sunday either. I respected that.

"Now what do we do?" I asked.

"Home Depot," he said, although he didn't sound happy about it.

That store anchored similarly minded establishments including my Starbucks. So in the end we all got what we wanted.

The doors weren't something to write up in the MLS but they would serve the function. Ben also purchased a deadbolt and, of course, a door handle. I almost forgot about that little detail. But I did need something on which to hang my lockbox. My new lockbox. I'd have to supply another, and those things are expensive. Damn and double damn. I used my credit card to pay for the door ensemble thinking the money would be better spent on a direct mail campaign, or a scarf, but what the hell, right? It's the cost of doing business.

I almost forgot about my mother.

We found her almost exactly where we left her, except she had pulled up a dining room chair and was sitting in the empty door frame. Give her a shotgun and she could have been Granny from the Beverly Hillbillies. Don't tell her the thought even crossed my mind. It was just the way she was sitting, not the way she was dressed, or did her hair, or that she wore granny glasses, just the way she was sitting. She looked kind of belligerent. Good thing she didn't have a shotgun. Oh never mind, my mother is complicated.

As soon as Ben climbed out of the truck, my mother was on the alert. She stood and greeted Ben with a wide smile and cheerful greeting.

"And you are?" she trailed off fetchingly as he approached. Mom is good at flirting, did I mention that? And I am not, but you saw for yourself previously.

"Ben Stone," he reached out and shook my mother's hand.

Allison Little Stone. Allison a little stoned. Stone Allison. Little Stone.

It will never work between us.

"You are so wonderful to do this work on a Sunday," Mom continued, finally releasing Ben's hand. "Can we thank you with dinner tonight?" Mom fluttered her eyelashes completely forgetting she had macaroni and cheese cooling in the trunk of her car.

"I'm sorry, I always have dinner with my grandmother on Sunday, but thank you," he said politely.

"Your grandmother?" Mom beamed. "And who is your grandmother?"

"She's from the City, but she lives up north. She's pretty elderly. That's why I have dinner at her place; she doesn't get out much."

My mother nodded knowingly. I knew she lived for the day when her own mother would be too disabled to get out of the house and too frail to care. But that wasn't the case yet. I could see a flash of envy in Mom's eyes. My grandmother, her mother, was her Achilles' heel, and I was the only person who knew. It was one of the few situations I could leverage particularly since the same woman who drives my mother to distraction is my own personal fan — Grandma is always on my side.

And from Ben's easy refusal of mom's invitation I could tell that he too was loved by his grandmother and wasn't sorry to miss out on dinner with me in favor of dinner with her.

That's the other problem with dating, or god help us, falling in love; we all have full lives. And trying to combine those lives at a later age (Okay, it's not that late for me, but I don't know how old Ben is, I should find that out) is difficult, to say the least. Maybe Carrie was right in working on marriage and a relationship while she was still in her 20s. I suspect it's too late for me.

I helped Ben install the door, with my mother hovering and offering suggestions, which highlighted why my father played golf and still drove into the lab every other day. Mom was very, very helpful.

"Shouldn't it swing the other way?" she asked. "You know in, instead of out?"

Ben grunted and gestured to me to hold the door steady as he mounted the hinges.

"We're just installing this temporarily," I said. "We'll get the better doors later on." My head hurt again, I didn't know getting hit on the head carried such long-term repercussions, so to speak. I braced myself against the door and closed my eyes for a minute while Ben worked.

"You okay?" he whispered.

I nodded, not trying to do anything more than help him. Mom was the flirt, and she was working hard at her craft. I was just the assistant, the muscle. Ah well.

When Mom deemed the project satisfactory she headed out to her bridge night out. Ben followed quickly after.

"I'll go to the store tomorrow morning," he said to me as he left.

"I'm coming with you," I declared, not bothering to flutter my eyelashes or any other part of my body.

"It will be early."

"I know."

"It will be boring and we won't really learn anything."

"I think the door seller is key, and I'm going with you." I did not relinquish.

"Is there any way to stop you?" He rubbed his eyes.

"No."

"7 then."

I struggled with the time. "Sure," I said as calmly as I could. "I'll be there."

Chapter 7

Inez called as I was driving home; unfortunately, the cell phone worked all the way up the freeway. There were no drop-off points that I could use for an excuse to cut her off. At least not legitimately.

"You were attacked this afternoon," Inez accused.

Had Ben called in to report the theft? Maybe. Should I ask how Inez knows these things? It wasn't relevant to the current conversation.

"It wasn't personal," I assured her.

"Any attack is personal," Inez declared. "We need to report this."

I had my opinions about reporting. Not to belittle my own experience or that of anyone else, but real estate agents get attacked, molested, and killed on a disturbingly regular basis. How could we not? We advertise in the paper that we will be alone in an empty house on Sunday from 1–4 p.m. We walk into deserted homes with people we don't know and we are constantly getting into cars with strangers; we are statistical nightmares. And since this was the first time for me and since it had nothing to do with me per se, or me as a realtor per se, I was not interested in adding to already depressing figures piling up and increasing our insurance rates.

"No," I said. "It really wasn't personal, it wasn't about my job. It was about something else."

"What something else?"

"Just something else," I hedged. "I'm starting to lose you."

"I can hear you just fine."

"No, really, I'm going over the hill. Oh, before I lose you, I can't make the meeting tomorrow morning. I have a client."

I clicked the phone to vibrate. I can't turn it off completely, but I can turn off the ringer. When I turn up the volume of the radio; I can't hear the phone vibrate. If someone wants a million-dollar home, they will leave a message.

And if Inez wants to labor over this further, she too can leave a message and I'll pick it up, oh, sometime tomorrow. I wasn't in the mood today.

I passed by the huge Christopher and Christopher billboard. The billboard featured an enormous photo of Jill and Peter Christopher. The two of them were posing so close together that tendrils of her hair stuck to his head. They portrayed the perfect couple: blond and beautiful. *God is our business Partner* was scrawled across the bottom of the billboard — their tag line. It's on every ad, every sign, including applied over their generic open house signs, and of course, the saying appears on each and every one of their business cards.

I'd have to check and see how Maria was doing with her back-on-the-market client.

But that would all wait until tomorrow. I needed to get my sore head under a hot shower and into bed.

It's dark at 5 in the morning. No one should be up before the sun; it's not right. But many people were. Note to self: no commute. Ever.

We have already reviewed the whole commute thing in the early morning hours. Getting into San Rafael as the sky lightened wasn't too bad, and I was smart enough to start my trip at Starbucks and end my trip at Starbucks. I did not want to damage my dignity by dancing around full of coffee while trying to interrogate the owner of Doors and

More. So I used the restroom at the San Rafael Starbucks and picked up more coffee for both Ben and myself.

I felt very smooth as I presented his coffee order to him. Of course, I just assumed a flavor and gave him tall frappuccino in case he didn't like it.

"I must say you are always on time," Ben took my offering with a smile.

"Always," I replied easily because it's true. He too is always on time. You may think that is a small thing, but in our businesses, showing up on time is huge. It's enormous; it can make or break a relationship. Which is why I got out of bed in the dark. Being late is not allowed.

I don't know what I expected from Doors and More. It wasn't really a retail outlet, so I expected to find a seedy place — dusty shelves covered by rusted deadbolts and bent door handles. I expected an equally dusty, perhaps even shifty-eyed proprietor hovering behind a high counter, not eager to see customers at all because they interrupt his day. Or at the very least, we'd see the dudes themselves lurking around the back, swapping stories and nodding in that most excellent way.

"They looked like surfer dudes," I said out loud as we walked toward the building. The air was cool in the early morning, the sky was clear; another hot day was on the way.

Ben glanced at me and raised an eyebrow. He can pack so much into that single expression. I wish I could do that. But then I wouldn't be able to speak. Won't work; must talk.

"Dudes?"

"I know, it's like saying a house is really clean and the seller is really motivated. Tells you nothing."

"No, it tells us something," he held the door open for me. "Surfer dudes don't fit the current criminal profile, so maybe they haven't been doing it long enough to pick up the uniform and the mien of hardened criminals."

"Well," I rubbed my head. "They were good at hitting."

He nodded at me and then addressed the proprietor who was waiting patiently for us to approach. Even at 7 a.m., the hour contractors rise to walk the earth, we were the only customers.

Our salesman at this fine establishment was not a dude; he was older than me, which moved him completely out of the *Bill & Ted's Excellent Adventure* category and into the perpetually old person category. Okay, maybe just the middle-aged category. But he was old enough to know better.

Ben took the lead and started to ask questions. I thought he would use complex contractor-like language, but I understood every word.

Ben described the doors and asked intelligent questions like where did he, the proprietor — he did not wear a name tag — find the doors?

Imported, like his entire inventory, was the answer.

"I heard they were the thing to have," the man continued. "There was a lot of word-of-mouth hype about them. I order these things six months in advance, especially handmade items like the Gilbertos. But I only got a small number. They misplaced the shipment at first so none of us got what we ordered. It took weeks to get the doors to the store, then it was piecemeal," he shrugged. "That's the beauty of COD, sometimes it works out."

"Anything unusual about the doors that you noticed?" Ben asked. He sipped his coffee as if he had all the time in the world. At this hour, who didn't?

"A couple of my contractors noticed they were pretty heavy," the other man admitted. "I had to order thicker hinges to handle the extra weight, but other than that, nothing, they're just doors."

"And can we get some of these famous Gilberto doors?" Ben asked.

"No, all sold out. Just yesterday a couple of guys came out here and bought up my whole inventory."

"Guys or dudes?" I asked dreamily.

He thought about it seriously. "Dudes. They looked like they were from Bolinas or from out on the coast somewhere."

I glanced over at Ben; I hadn't said dudes loud enough for the man to hear me. At least I didn't think I had. I was whispering. And we were still in the parking lot, but I don't have an indoor voice; he could have heard me.

"And there are no more doors to be had?" Ben asked.
The man sighed and pulled out a thick binder. He leafed through the pages for a minute or two, and then stared at a page covered with tiny numbers and faint lines. "Says here they're discontinued."

"I thought you just got the first shipment."

"Well, sometimes they can't keep up with demand. This started big this spring, the doors everyone wanted, so we all ordered, we had to jump through so many hoops just to get the doors delivered, and then just this trickle of orders came in. Maybe it was too much for the supplier."

"Is the supplier someone you recognize?" Ben asked.

The man frowned as he studied the pages in his binder. "No, it was a new company, never heard of them." He slammed the binder closed. "Probably won't use them again either — too much trouble."

Ben and I both nodded in agreement.

Great. Now they are rare; my mother is going to love this.

"Anyone else carry them?" Ben asked.

"Not around here. There's an outlet in the East Bay and one down in San Jose, but that's it. The manufacturer didn't make too many of them. I know, Steve told me he heard there was only one container from Columbia and that had been lost. I thought I wouldn't get my doors at all, but I was able to get a few. Must have found the inventory."

"How do you lose a container?" Ben asked before I could.

The man wrinkled his forehead. "I was told it happens all the time. They all look alike, people pick up the wrong ones, and cart them away."

"Doesn't seem likely," Ben said.

The man shrugged. "That's all I know. Is there something else you need?"

"No, no. Thank you." He put his hand on my elbow and ushered me out.

"Do you think he's legitimate?" I asked as we walked to the parking lot. The sun had cleared the hills; the sound of the freeway was more muffled as the air thickened with the sounds of movement and activity. I don't do things this early, but I didn't point that out. I wanted to look tough and competent.

I needed to go to Starbucks, just one more time.

"Can I buy you another cup of coffee?" I offered.

He stopped walking, and glanced at the small cup still in his hand. "Sure."

We drove separately to the same Starbucks I had just left, oh, minutes ago, and met inside. I automatically took my place in the ubiquitous line to make my order. Ben glanced around as if he had never been into one of the franchises. Three women standing in line ahead of me glanced back at Ben.

"Let me get something from the car," he said. "Can you order a grande non-fat latte, no foam, for me?"

Aha, then he wasn't thrilled with the calorie-ladened frappuccino family of coffee drinks. Then again I'll be honest, he and I probably weighed about the same. In a wrestling match we'd be evenly matched and compete in the same category. On him, it looked good. I didn't offer to wrestle him even though the image was more than a little intriguing …But to the point of the coffee, if I didn't indulge in my favorite frothy drink (or two, or three) on a daily basis, I may look as trim as him. Or I may not. Never mind, not worth it.

He returned and headed to a small table and set up a laptop. By the time our order was called up, he was typing away like a computer nerd. I was impressed, only because it seemed incongruous for a man in jeans, faded blue T-shirt and heavy work boots to be hovering over the latest, sleekest laptop computer.

I sat down next him and glanced at the screen.

"Thefts of doors in the East Bay," he said out loud. "Three reported. San Jose, two reported."

"We have a problem," I said.

"Yes." He took a sip of his non-fat latte, no foam, and frowned at the computer screen.

"No one was hurt at the scene of the crime but many thefts seemed to have happened in broad daylight when the victims were at work."

"What about the distributors?"

He ran another Google search, but all we came up with was a small newspaper report about a theft at Lowe's in San Jose. The stolen items were not named.

"That fits," I pointed out. I paused, waiting for my mind to continue to work. It would work, I was confident on that; there was something.

"Oh my god, my parents." The foam went down the wrong pipe and I choked a bit. "I need to see my parents."

To his credit, Ben did not blow me off. He did not say, "I have work to do." In fact, he did have work to do, that bathroom. "Do you want me to come with you?"

"Yes," I said simply.

Southbound traffic was still backed up, but our northbound passage was relatively clear.

My phone rang as I turned off the Novato (one of them) exit.

It was Melissa, she of the impossible loan.

"Okay," she said immediately, before I had a chance to say hello. "I can do this on her credit rating rather than his, which just went into the toilet with that boat deal. Are they still in?"

"They are still in — let me know." I clicked off the call and took a deep breath as I rounded the corner to my parents' house. There they were, those awful doors, thankfully still intact.

I could only wave at Dad; he was already in the golf cart waiting to drive out to his first hole. He waved at Ben and me and briskly moved forward to catch his tee time executing a neat hairpin turn with the golf cart. Mom rushed to the door and greeted me with exaggerated parental joy, showing off for the guest. Even this early in the morning, she was dressed in a skirt and jacket, tan open toed Marc Jacobs shoes highlighted her professionally painted toenails. My mother is always perfection on two legs.

For a moment, I wanted to just throw her to the dogs, or dudes right there, but I resisted. What would my brothers say if they knew I killed their mother? Naw, I don't really want to kill her. I probably drank too much caffeine. Is there such thing as too many Starbucks coffee drinks? I didn't think so.

"We're here to admire your doors again," I said instead.

"Yes, they are lovely aren't they?" Mom said.

"How many in this area?" I tried to sound conversational rather than completely panicked.

"About three. Then the store ran out, which is a shame, don't you think?"

But I know my mother; she didn't think it was a shame at all. She loved having something that no one else had. My father is a case in point.

"Any?" How do you say this delicately? Any more thefts? Anyone killed in the last forty-eight hours? Any additional matrons whacked over the head, which seems to be the MO of these thieves, not violent in their way, just needed to get those doors and they needed to get the witness temporarily out of the way. They must either have a huge home with many front entrances, or they are creating an art sculpture and are up against a grant deadline. Oh wait, or they are building a multi-doors-to-the-world sculpture for Burning Man. If so, they are under deadline; Burning Man was at the end of the month.

"Any unusual activity last night?" Ben finally asked.

"Oh, no, unless you count Linda's shower for her daughter. I had no idea they hadn't married yet. The girl wants to have the baby first so she'll look nice in her dress for the wedding, as if that was the only important thing." Mom harrumphed in disgust.

She shook her head and glanced at Ben. "What do you think about a trend like that?"

He shrugged. "I always thought getting married first was the better way to go."

"Aren't you a lovely man?" Mom relaxed and beamed at him. "So can I get you some breakfast?"

My mother has the same culinary skills that I do, which is to say, none at all. She wrapped herself in a bright yellow and blue Provence patterned apron that looked to be brand new, and created her best meal: English muffins and scrambled eggs. She even had some cheese laying around to melt into the eggs. I was impressed; this kind of meal was usually reserved for high holidays. I hoped Ben appreciated the effort.

He seemed to be eating at least.

Mom was doing an excellent job quizzing Ben who, naturally, would put up with that kind of thing from a mother, never from a peer.

Where did his grandmother live? Aha, Mom remembered that detail.

Up north in the Dry Creek Valley.

"Oh that's lovely up there," my mother crowed. She served him more eggs.

That's expensive up there, I thought, more so than in Tiburon because there are fewer opportunities to buy land or a home. If he's a good grandchild, maybe he could inherit.

I glanced at Ben complacently eating his second round of eggs. I tried to subtly get Mom's attention to get the rest of the eggs. But she glanced at my plate and whisked the pan away and dumped the rest of the eggs into a plastic container destined for the refrigerator.

"How old is your grandmother anyway?" I asked.

"90. She still lives at home."

"Oh that's wonderful," Mom poured him more orange juice. "That's what I want to do, live at home, be comfortable for the rest of my days, have my loving children beside me."

"May I have more juice?" I interrupted her.

"Sorry, honey, that was the last of it. And your parents?" She kept her full attention on Ben.

"They are still alive," he said shortly.

And that was the end of the conversation because that was the end of breakfast. I was still hungry, but I refused to beg.

Mom fortunately had another bridge meeting this morning — hence the formal little suit — so Ben and I were left with each other and the doors.

Ben regarded the doors on the frame; he then walked to his truck and returned with an impressively large toolbox. In no time he had knocked out the pins on the hinges and released the doors.

"Here, let's take this outside."

I helped him move the doors outside and held them up while he searched for sawhorses in my father's immaculate garage. He found two folding chairs instead, extra for the holiday dinners, and managed to balance the doors on a total of six chairs.

Now, I bet you think I've forgotten about Carrie and her romantic challenges, but passing out on the floor distracted me somewhat. To be honest, I didn't think that much had happened since I last spoke with her. She was back at work; I was pretending this was work. But I called anyway.

"Hey, how are you?" I greeted her.

"How am I? You were assaulted yesterday and you didn't even call me!"

"How did you... ? Never mind. Sorry, it was complicated."

"Still seeing that contractor guy?" She could refocus instantly, that girl.

"I'm not seeing him." I watched him as he walked around the doors and squinted at the ends, or rather the bottom and top. I don't know the technical term for it. I haven't spent that much time around doors; they open, you walk in, that's all I know.

Oh, sometimes you need to plane them down so they don't catch on the carpet. A door has to open all the way, that's good feng shui, okay, so I know a little about doors and enough about feng shui to be dangerous. I wondered how Joan was doing.

I know A Little About Everything. No, that doesn't work as a slogan.

"We went to dinner again Saturday night, but he didn't talk to me at all! We just sat there and listened to his sisters complain about how restricted their lives were, what with the charity functions and dressing up and everything."

"River's Bend is not San Francisco," I pointed out.

"Tell me about it. I don't know. It was so awkward. Oh, sorry, got to go."

"There's about an inch unaccounted for," Ben said at the same time.

I clicked the phone call off and focused again on our spontaneous project.

"What do you mean?"

For me personally, I have many inches that are mysterious and unaccounted for, like I can't remember what I did or did not do to create those extra inches around my torso. But he wasn't looking at my body. Damn.

"The carving is thick, but not really thick enough to account for the weight and heft. . ." He took a screwdriver and poked at the top of the door.

"Hmmm," he made a soft noise.

"What made you go into contracting work?" I asked as he rooted around in his deep toolbox.

I'd like to root around in his toolbox.

"When I graduated from Stanford, there were no vice president jobs open, so I started working with a friend in the trades. Liked it."

"You graduated from Stanford?"

"Philosophy."

"Your parents must have been so proud," I said sarcastically.

He retrieved a cordless drill. "They recovered, as long as I was working and subsequently out of the house, they were happy."

"Well yes, that was a goal back then. When did you graduate?"

"June."

He took the drill and pressed it against the center of the door top. I looked over his shoulder; the door was made in three layers. It looked like there was a center to the door about an inch thick, and the carving layers were pressed on either side of the layer, like an Oreo; the cookie was the carvings and the creamy center was, well wood. I didn't see the big deal, but I'm not an expert. I know you figured that out early on.

My phone rang and I took it while he drilled. I kept one eye on the process, which took less time than it takes to explain, and one-half my mind on the conversation, which took less time than it did to record it.

"Your feng shui expert is very interesting," Norton reported.

I could imagine. Joan would interpret her assignment as feng shui expert as an opportunity to dress up like an Oriental table decoration. She probably swept into Norton's candy-colored house draped head to toe in black and red. I know she took the opportunity to wear a red hat. She owns nine red hats already because she's turning 55 next year, and she's stocking up — and she probably carried a handful of small charms, crystals, and candles to light up various corners of the house. I can always depend on Joan to dress the part.

I do not care about the means, just the end.

"What did she say?" I asked as casually as I could.

"She's very interesting. We're having coffee later this week."

Oh great, everyone is getting some except me. Am I cursed? Yes, I suppose so. I glanced at Ben, who was carefully drilling into the top of the door; he seemed to be going at it rather gingerly.

"And what did she say?" I repeated to Norton.

"I never knew that Navajo white was an auspicious color for selling," Norton mused.

"I've heard it's ideal for selling, very auspicious," I confirmed.

"And I need to get the rugs cleaned and she told me how to move around the furniture, but she'll help me with that once the painting is done."

"And when will the painting be done?" I prodded.

"The painters are coming tomorrow."

"Marvelous," I said. What a relief. I loved Joan more than anyone on the planet just then.

"Damn." The drill pressed through the wood then suddenly pressed all the way through the wood to the hilt, as if nothing was there to stop it.

"Gotta go. I'll call you about an open house date and a good time to take new pictures." I signed off quickly.

"Hollow door?" I asked Ben.

"Not for the weight of the thing. I thought it would be completely solid." He reversed the drill to pull it out. It slid out quite easily, along with a stream of white powder.

The two of us looked at the stream of powder for a full minute, the crystals glinted in the morning sunshine.

Very pretty.

"Call the police," he said.

Chapter 8

Unfortunately, Mom returned from bridge a minute after her precious doors were confiscated by the police but far too many minutes before Ben returned back from another trip to Home Depot loaded with replacements. This unfortunate configuration of events found me as the guardian of the yawing empty space in the front of her house as well as the woman who had to explain to Mom that her doors were more than just ugly — they were a felony.

I was grateful that when the police did show up. Fortunately, it was not the Tiburon police; it was the Novato police. I was more than grateful. I did not want to be seen with stolen doors twice.

Oh, and yes, Ben and I did look in the garage for the old doors in case they were miraculously propped up somewhere in the back. But my mother does not save anything — a reaction, I'm sure, to my grandmother's propensity to save everything, something I understand completely and in fact, do myself. In my business, it pays to save. Clients not only regularly forget what they said; they often forget what they said they wanted. So I found it best to save all notes, comments, and conversations on either paper or on computer. I save notes; my grandmother saves everything else.

My notes look like this:

November 21, 5:05 p.m. Informed client that if they don't drop the price of their house they will lose the option on the new house they have in escrow.

November 21, 5:09 p.m. Client refuses to drop price. Quote, "hell no."

November 23, 12 p.m. Client loses house, escrow falls though.

November 24, 11:05 a.m. Client withdraws his listed house from the market

November 24, 11:09 a.m. Allison is out about $1,500. December 20 Client and family blame Allison because no one could make up their mind in time to either sell or buy.

That's when I submit the phone logs. It slows down the buyers and sellers somewhat, and protects me. And why do I need protecting? Well, the average person is completely stupid and the average lawyer is completely devious, and as much as it's a profitable combination for both of those parties, it's potentially disastrous for me. So I keep the logs.

I wonder if the door thieves have a lawyer on retainer. I would if I were stuffing doors with kilos of coke.

I do not keep a running log of conversations with my mother. Too long.

"What happened to my doors? Allison." Mom slammed the door of her Mercedes and gave me that look; the one that immediately blames me for whatever situation has surrounded me, by accident or not. Like the time my brothers hid in the garage, leaving me standing next to the arrow implanted in the wall, and holding the bow. I remember I immediately pointed out that at least it missed Mom's favorite painting. But that hadn't helped my cause. Nothing ever did. But it was great sales training.

"There was a problem with the doors and the police had to take them away — material evidence," I explained.

"Material evidence? They're *doors*," Mom emphasized the noun.

"But very special and unique doors," I reminded her.

"Allison, tell me now, why did you let them take my doors!" Mom placed her hands on her slender hips and stared at me.

"The police took them," I explained again. "I can't obstruct an investigation."

"What kind of crime can be committed by doors?"

One of taste?

"Mom," I took a deep breath. And fought down years of resentment and history so I could respond to just the single question between us. It doesn't do to bring up half a dozen slights or perceived slights (I admit that) when there was really only a single question to be answered.

"We found cocaine hidden in your doors. The police had to take them away," I said as simply as I could.

She paused, waiting for the punch line.

"If it's any consolation," I continued, "your friends are getting their doors taken as well."

Mom let that sink in for a moment.

"How was bridge?" I asked.

"But they were so unique!" Mom wailed. "Where am I going to find doors like that?"

I hope the answer was: nowhere. But I kept my mouth shut. Rare for me.

"And where is your lovely friend? Did you scare him off?" Mom quickly recovered and returned to her favorite activity, attacking me.

"No, I did not scare him off," I retorted. I swatted at a wasp hovering under the porch roof. Maybe it will come into the house. Maybe it will sting my mother. Nature has a way of getting even on our behalf.

The wasp drifted across the street. Stupid wasp.

Just then Ben drove in, a set of new doors rattling around the back of his truck. I noticed he took the trouble to match the look of the house façade. These new doors were embellished with glass inserts and brass trim — not bad, actually.

"Oh, aren't you the sweetest thing?" Mom recovered and clasped her hands like a child and smiled winningly at Ben.

"It was the least I could do," Ben gestured to me to help him unload the doors.

I helped him heft the doors over the tailgate and carefully unwrapped them.

By now I knew what to do to install a set of doors. It was like having an applicable skill. Maybe I could get a real job.

Ben worked quickly and deftly, all the while giving my mother no more than generous grunts to her barrage of questions.

As soon as Ben washed and accepted a glass of water, he turned toward the now secured doorway.

"Well, you've been just wonderful." Mom was reluctant to let him go. Honestly, I have never seen her drool over a man like this before. And he was a common worker to boot. "Let me at least pay for the doors," she said.

Ben waved away her offer. "No, I wouldn't dream of taking your money. I consider it my fault you lost your lovely doors in the first place."

"Oh nonsense, you were just doing your citizen's duty. Wasn't he Allison?"

"Uh, sure."

"Well then, join us for dinner tonight, I insist. We'll meet you at the country club at 7. Allison knows where it is."

I glanced at Ben wondering how he was going to slip out of this one. But he inclined his head and nodded. "Seven, thank you. I'd be delighted to join you."

I hid my surprise. But he passed me and headed out the door before I could gather my wits. I followed him to the driveway.

"So what's next on your agenda?" I was now stuck down here for the rest of the day, mostly because I didn't particularly want to drive north, and then come back down again. I'd probably just return to the Smith house.

The sun was warm on my shoulders, promising another perfect summer day. The thought of just hanging around the pool for the afternoon was more than tempting. But I'd have to hang around with my mother as well — not so tempting.

"I have time. Want me to fix the bathroom at the Ocean View property?" He placed a hand on the door handle and turned to me.

"Yes, that would be very nice of you," I responded politely.

He nodded and jumped in. I slid into my car — oh, it's a Lexus, I know you were wondering about that — and we convoyed out of the driveway and headed south. I didn't see her, but I could feel my mother looking out the kitchen window. Allison with a man. Mom was probably executing a neat victory dance in the kitchen.

She'll be tremendously disappointed when this fictitious romance doesn't work out. Mom doesn't understand that I have working relationships with men. Doesn't get that at all.

I was getting a little tired of the house, of Tiburon, of bathrooms, of everything. The tile floor was chilly, the bathroom was trashed, and no one had shown the house in the last twenty-four hours. Not even my alleged (according to the papers) attack drew people in. So what did a woman have to do to get attention in this county? At least in Sonoma

I'd be able to draw on some prurient interest. The violent murder alone would at least bring in other agents. But in Marin, no.

I aimlessly wandered around the Smith house while Ben grunted and swore and generally acted like a contractor should.

What he needed was an assistant. A young assistant. A young assistant who is about 23 years old with a washboard stomach and a $150/ month text message bill. A young man perpetually hooked into his iPod, one who is easily led by promises of the simple life and easy love. A young assistant who was smart enough to be attracted to me, Allison Little. That's what Ben needed.

Has it been a while? Yes it has. Don't tell anyone.

"Do you want to paint this as well?" he called out from the bathroom.

"Oh sure," I looked around the kitchen again. I still couldn't get the image of Hillary moving determinedly around opening cupboards slamming them closed. The million was gone; the art wasn't worth as much as everyone thought it should be worth — old story.

Then what was she looking for?

I called Carrie on my way to the club. Ben had to stop off and change, which I thought was sweet, but he didn't offer to show me his place, wherever it is.

"Probably because you are so difficult," Carrie offered.

"Probably, but shouldn't he pursue me a little? You know, gallantly try to break down my barriers?"

"Your barriers are like the Great Wall of China," Carrie chided me.

"And what do you know about the Great Wall?"

She paused; I turned into the parking lot of the club and turned off the engine.

"We attended a lecture on the trade issues of China last night," she admitted.

"That was your date?"

"Yeah."

"Are you perhaps rethinking your goals?"

"He took me to John Ash afterward." She named one of the better restaurants in town. I only eat there if I've just closed escrow.

"And?" I prompted.

"He kissed me good night."

"Good kisser?"

"Great kisser."

"Well, you're ahead of me."

"I didn't know this was a race."

"It's not a race," I said, suddenly impatient. The closed car was too warm. I opened up the door, the car beeped because I left the keys in the ignition. I pulled them out and struggled to get out of the car. "It's not a goddamn race," I repeated at Carrie.

"Have a nice dinner." My agitation must have put her in a better mood; she was quite cheerful when she said goodbye.

Oh fuck everyone.

I stomped into the entrance, air kissed my mother, hugged my father and of course, awkwardly shook Ben's hand. They were all waiting for me. You know what I was thinking.

We toyed with menus and bread as Ben started up the conversation.

"I heard a story about smuggling coke in ready-made cupboards," Ben said. "But no doors, this is a pretty unique approach."

"Did the smell of the wood deflect the dogs or whatever they use for drugs?" I asked.

"Probably," Ben agreed.

Dad beamed, when he heard Ben attended Stanford, Dad's alma mater, Dad lit up like a Christmas tree. I attended a state school, and my brothers attend UC. That was all we could get into. This lack on our parts was pointed out every blessed Thanksgiving dinner. For the most part, my holidays are not pretty.

Dad and Ben enthusiastically compared notes on their school while I toyed with the idea that I should order a salad like Mom so I could look ladylike in Ben's eyes. Then I saw the special, homemade ravioli stuffed with chicken, asparagus, and feta smothered in pesto sauce. Forget the damn salad.

So I redeemed myself somewhat by bringing in a Stanford alum for Dad. Mom was beside herself because Ben was male and sitting next to me. I think my mother is worried that I, like many of her friend's daughters, am really a lesbian. She shouldn't, I own 130 pairs of shoes. No lesbian owns more than three pairs of shoes. Everyone knows that. That's how you can tell.

"Now," my mother jumped into the conversation. "The one thing we were disappointed about the college experience for Allison was she started smoking pot there. Do you know what that does to your reproductive system? And it makes you fat, well we can see that." I took a slug of the cabernet and glared at my mother, who, as you probably figured out by now, was oblivious to my feelings.

"Mom," I tried to sound severe and warn her away. This is not good for my professional life, nor is it particularly good for my soul.

"Well, you know if you hadn't smoked so much pot you wouldn't have gained so much weight." Mom beamed at Ben as if she made a salient point about drugs.

The waiter served the food — I don't even have to tell you what Mom ordered. Dad always orders the steak because mom won't barbeque it at home. But Ben ordered the ravioli as well and I was grateful. I took a bite of the pasta — delicious — to deflect my own arguments; there is nothing I can say that will move my mother off the discovery that I smoked pot when I was 16. I gave it up in college, made me too mellow and I had things to do. But no, it's the only thing Mom can remember about my childhood. She brings it up every chance she has. For my mother, if you make one mistake, it's over; there is no way to ever redeem yourself. So whenever I call her with some good news, like a prestigious award, a fantastic sale, or when I bought my own house with my own money, she brings up the pot. I think she does it because she was always the perfect child in her family, just ask her.

I took a deep breath and practiced my smile, a sunny I-don't-care-anymore-what-you-think smile.

"Thank you, Mother, for that background, but I'm sure Ben is more interested in other issues besides my sordid past."

"Well, I think he should know about you," Mom protested.

"Didn't everyone try pot at least once?" Ben asked mildly.

I should have stayed in the car.

I shot him a grateful look and changed the subject.

"Don't people get killed for possessing drugs?" I asked innocently.

Ben gave me a strange look. We hadn't come across anyone during the day, but we did not know about the night. Nothing had been released about finding the coke in the doors; the thieves would not know that the doors had been confiscated. They had gathered up the new doors, they would want the rest of them. And my guess was they would want the doors tonight.

"Do you have a place to stay?" Ben asked immediately.

Mom and Dad looked at each other.

"Oh, I don't think it's serious, what could happen?" Mom said.

"They'd shoot you in your sleep," I offered helpfully.

"Don't upset your mother," Dad chided me.

"Sorry, just pointing out the obvious," I said. "It's not that safe," I amended, as if I were the concerned daughter. Well, for the most part I am. But not tonight.

And Mom wonders why I didn't live in Novato; she actually said that when I bought my house in River's Bend. "You could buy a house in the country club and we could have dinner with you every night," she had offered, in total sincerity.

Well, there were two reasons why I will not buy in Novato; one, it was too expensive in Novato; and two, I'd shoot myself before I'd have dinner with my mother every night. Really. I would like to point out that both brothers live in northern River's Bend. They are close enough to the City to commute for their jobs, far enough away to discourage mom from spontaneous visits. They don't even mind that she's too far away for convenient babysitting. I find that interesting.

"You shouldn't stay in the house," I said. "At least not tonight."

"You can take me to the City," Mom suggested to Dad, always generous. Dad nodded. "We'll be at the St. Francis. The house is locked. You still have the key, honey?"

I nodded.

"Good. Well," Dad gestured for the check. Ben and I split the last of the wine. The idea of leaving for San Francisco propelled my parents into action and we ended up leaving before dessert and coffee. Just as well.

We said formal goodbyes in the parking lot. It was already dark.

"It was very nice to meet you again, Mr. Stone," my mother offered her hand and Ben obediently took it.

"You too, and again, I'm very sorry for the trouble," Ben said politely.

"Well, it wasn't your fault," Mother reassured him.

So it was probably mine. I waved silently and my parents headed off to the house to pack overnight bags. To their credit, they were treating the situation as if it was just another adventure.

To Ben's credit, he played it cool. If we could get them out of the house, even if the thieves accidentally stole the wrong doors, not much harm would be done.

Except I think I need a frequent purchase card at Home Depot for the doors. After ten door purchases, I get a free window.

Now, if I was a drug runner and I wanted my drugs, and I knew the drugs were in the doors but I wasn't sure whose doors, wouldn't it be easy enough to drive around and just look for the doors? It would be very easy indeed. And since our new doors looked like the Home Depot special that they were, there shouldn't be too much trouble.

"Do you think they'll come by?" I asked Ben as soon as my parent's car turned the corner.

He shrugged, "I don't know, they're stupid enough to come by in broad daylight and attack you."

"Not that stupid, they got away with it."

"True," he conceded. "And your parents are away. So it should be okay."

"Yes, it should be okay."

"I better use the restroom before I drive home," I said. "Goodnight."

He looked at me a little strangely. What, he never uses the restroom? Maybe he just repairs them.

"Goodnight."

I headed back toward the club and waited for his truck to start up, and for it to turn out of the parking lot. Once he was around the corner, I stopped, turned back to my car and drove back to my parent's house.

I passed them as they were driving out, and I was driving in, but they didn't notice me. Mom was talking a mile a minute and Dad was nodding. Perhaps that was the secret of their marriage; she talks, he listens.

I let myself into the back door because even though I owned a key to the old, old door, I did not have a key to either the Gilberto doors or the new doors. So many doors, so little time. But I always could get into the house by opening the side gate, sliding along the patio and jimmying the lock to the bathroom that doubled as the pool changing room. No, I'm not going to tell you how; you could be after Mom's collection of Provençal linens.

The house was quiet and dark, illuminated solely by the under-cabinet lights in the kitchen.

Remember, I grew up here. I grew up during the remodel phase and was here for the pool renovation phase. (They did it during the summer, how stupid was that? And it had been a very hot summer. I can't even begin to tell you.)

So this was my home, but it still felt strange to be here. I tiptoed across the living room to the master bedroom. My parent's king-size, four-poster bed dominated the medium-sized room. It was perfectly arranged with eighteen tiny embroidered pillows arranged neatly in three rows. The master bath, another remodel, was as big as most apartments in this area, complete with a Jacuzzi tub that I don't think Mom ever uses and a walk-in shower. All was quiet. Streetlight filtered through the skylight over the tub.

So far, we were in control and the house was secure. I walked back across the living room; light from the patio — a few up-lights to illuminate the olive trees — cast the heavy antique furniture inside from my great grandmother into shadow. I hesitated in the living room. I could read a magazine; I could watch TV (hidden in an antique armoire, and you are correct, that means the TV is pretty small). But if the point of this exercise was to pretend that no one is home, then no one would be inside with the lights on and watching television, yes? That meant I had to sit in the dark and keep very quiet.

Well, that wasn't fun at all.

Maybe I could practice meditation and become one with the universe? Katherine insists that sitting, meditating, and becoming one with the universe is like a fast-track ticket to better sales. Really, she says things like that. So, since meditation is something I could practice in the dark, I gave it a try.

I sat still on the Oriental carpet and took in deep breaths. One, two. I hate my mother. Three, four, I hate Ben Stone. Fortunately, before I got much further my phone vibrated. Vibrating phones aren't necessarily silent; they make this vibrating sound and sometimes jiggle across the table, which is kind of interesting during a formal dinner. And the sound was very loud in the silent meditative space.

"Yes?"

"He's coming to the Forgotten Felines fundraiser."

Better him that me.

"He's coming to one of your events?"

"I think he thinks he owes me for the China lecture," Carrie admitted.

"And that's good," I said.

"Yesss," she drew the word out with caution.

"What's the matter? You are dating the most eligible bachelor in the county. You made this your quest and now you are getting everything you want."

I struggled up from my meditative position and began wandering around the house again. I like to pace when I talk, which, I know, wasn't a silent activity, but I couldn't help myself.

"I don't know, Allison. Am I up for this? He's so handsome and smart and his family is so, so."

"Good old boy?" It's one of the big downsides of working in River's Bend, the good old boys. We live in a ranching and farming community. We grow our own wine and cheese. That's good. The attitude of third and fourth generation farmers is not so good. They've all been here since the Bear Flag rebellion; they know everything and like to say, "We've never done it that way before." Just try getting these guys to sign the piles of disclosers it takes to sell property. I get lectures with every form I make them sign. As if it's my fault.

"Yes, good old boys, and everyone asks me where I'm from," she admitted.

I wandered into my old bedroom as I listened to her. I could meditate in here, on my old bed, but that was too weird. I wondered why Mom hadn't redecorated this room? My brothers' rooms, the two past the pool bathroom, had long been altered to accommodate whatever hobby mom was currently pursuing. It made no sense, but I stopped trying to follow my mother's train of thought years ago. I take the freeway.

"You're from River's Bend," I reminded her.

"But not from the right side of the river," she pointed out.

"That just means you're exotic. Buck up, this is your chance and you should not blow it over one tiny little lecture about the trade deficit in China." My window was closed and locked. Half of me was happy about the security and the other half wondered what my parents were so worried about.

"How did you know?"

"I read about the lecture, and I'm sorry I missed it," I replied. I ducked back into the bathroom and tested the lock on the door leading to the patio. It was secure.

"Okay, okay, we're going this Friday," she meant the Forgotten Felines event, not another lecture on China. "Want to come along?"

"No, I do not, and bless Patrick for taking my place." Because last year I had to attend the Forgotten Felines Fantasy Dinner and Litter Box Competition, or something like that. It was deadly. Not as dead, however, as poor Mr. Smith. Which reminded me why I was stalking around my parents' house in the dark testing to make sure all the windows were locked. Even though I knew the bad guys would come through the front door. And take it.

"Okay," Carrie signed off. "I thinks that's him on the other line. I'll call you back."

"Don't worry about calling back, go to your prince."

She didn't even deny it.

Now the house was feeling really stuffy. I opened the two back windows in my brother's old rooms, one for Dad's home office and one for Mom's projects. I didn't recognize any of the heaps of things on various card tables and didn't stop to look closely. I punched up Joan. No one would hear me at the back of the house.

"So this Norton," Joan start immediately, she has caller ID. "What else do you know about him?"

"Why? Did you trade a painted interior for sex?"

"The hint certainly moved him along. That's one lonely man."

"Careful of the lonely ones." I paused and squinted at one of the tables, scrapbook paraphernalia.

"Honey, I spend enough time in academia to know the signs. What does your Norton do, anyway?"

"Music teacher." The second table was covered with old family photo albums and loose pictures. I once suggested she should go digital, if only to keep track of the granddaughters, but she prefers the old fashioned versions.

"Music teachers do not live in houses that size."

"He worked for Cerent when Cisco bought it out. That's why he can teach music," I explained briefly. I checked to make sure the windows weren't open too far and moved back down the narrow hallway.

"Any money left?" She asked.

"You were just in it." I paused at my bedroom door and decided I did not want to wait in there, it was still haunted by old Barbie dolls and probably the remnants of my first joint. Perhaps Mom could make a whole scrapbook page devoted to my wicked encounter with the bad weed.

"Ah, I see," Joan said.

"Change your mind?'' The dining/family room seemed more neutral territory; from here I could see the living room and, I was sure, hear the sound of a front door being opened, or stolen.

"Maybe, maybe not, but I did get you what you wanted. The house will be ready for the open house this Sunday."

"You're pretty optimistic." I flopped down on the leather sectional couch, the only piece of furniture not from my great-grandmother's estate, and the only piece my father had any say in. The couch was ugly, but very comfortable. Maybe I could meditate here in comfort instead of twisted up on the hard floor.

"Not really, but I do still look pretty in a low-cut tee."

I love my friends.

"Let's have dinner and talk after you sell his soon-to-be irresistible home."

"Let's..."

Headlights swept across the front of the house. SHIT.

"Let's do it next week. E-mail me." I stood up, realized I could be seen that way and quickly crouched down lower than the back of the couch.

"Are you all right?" Joan asked.

"I'm excellent," I whispered. The headlights shut off. A car door slammed.

Shit and fuck.

I had parked in the garage so it didn't look like anyone was home just to catch them.

It never occurred to me that I may need another plan to "catch" the crooks should they show up. On TV, the heroine has a gun, or a black belt in karate, or superpowers. And she thinks on her feet. I should have made some notes ahead of time.

"I'll call you back," I whispered into the phone. I stashed the phone in my pocket and crept back toward the kitchen. Mom keeps her knives in a big wood block on the counter. I pulled out the lowest one, because crouched as I was, it was the only one I could reach.

It was the big cleaver. Menacing and shiny, maybe it would scare the dudes, if they were on this particular assignment.

So I had no super powers, no retroactive karate skills, and one of Mom's good knives, which would do me no good if these other guys had guns.

Mr. Smith had been shot.

I didn't know if everyone knew that.

The front door rattled and opened. A key? The bad guys had a key? I crouched down in the kitchen as if I could hide my bulk behind the granite-covered island.

Footsteps approached.

Chapter 9

I snuck around the kitchen island toward the living room. The thief was still at the doors, fumbling with something. I waited from him (or her, I'll be fair and politically correct, I was going to hurt them either way) to open or jimmy the lock. It clicked and he/she entered through the front door. The step on the floor was heavy; it was a he. He took one step, paused. Another step.

I could follow the steps on the hardwood (new) and waited, waited. He was heading right toward the kitchen.

I bunched up my courage and held my breath. Okay, okay. He took another step.

Ha! I jumped up and almost managed to bring down my cleaver onto the head that finally appeared against the back glass doors.

My perfectly aimed blow was neatly deflected. The cleaver clattered to the floor.

My heart stopped. Now what? I had just taken a class on what to do when your goals fail, but I've never taken a class on what to do you're your meat cleaver attack fails.

"Allison?" said the thief.

"Ben?" I squinted, as if that helps in dim light. It was Ben. He was dressed all in black, black jeans and a tight black T-shirt decorated with a faded prism shot through with a rainbow. He looked much better than me, more appropriate for the occasion, since I hadn't had time to change after dinner.

"What are you doing here?" he demanded.

"Stakeout." I retrieved the cleaver. Fortunately it landed on the kitchen tile instead of the living room hardwood floor. I didn't want to have to explain a gouge on Mom's pristine cherry hardwood.

"And," I pointed out, "this is my house. So the question really is, what are YOU doing here?"

"Guessing that you would do something silly like staking out your parents' house."

"They won't come in anyway," I pointed out. My voice was a little shaky. "We replaced the doors."

I moved back to the kitchen and returned the cleaver to its place in the block on the counter. He followed me. In the half-light cast by the under-cabinet illumination, I could clearly see how well his chest muscles filled out the top of the shirt, how nicely his biceps strained the sleeves. The shirt was so old he had been much smaller and thinner when he bought it. Why is that a good thing for men and a bad thing for women? Just asking, but let's go back to Ben.

"But that doesn't mean we can't wait for them to come, then follow them," he pointed out.

"Is that what you plan to do? Follow them?" I asked.

"And then call the police," he assured me. I had a vision of him as the hero. I'd love to see him crash through a flimsy door (not the Gilberto doors, those are too big and solid) and catch the smugglers red-handed.

I could just see him standing tall and holding a scruffy dude in each hand saying, "Boys, we need to talk."

That's my fantasy. You have yours; I have mine.

"For audacity, I can't help being impressed with the idea of smuggling coke in a door, and I can't help being impressed with the sheer stupidity of losing track of the shipment and having to retrieve the doors piecemeal. These are not the sharpest tools in the shed."

"Nice construction metaphor. But if you plan to follow them, why come inside?"

"Just checking. I found you, didn't I?"

I had to admit he did.

"So are you planning to spend the evening in your truck?"

"Probably."

"I'll come with you." I didn't want to let that T-shirt out of my sight. Hey, I was going to enjoy what I could.

We locked the front door (he had the extra set of keys, clever, I have to admit), and climbed into his truck. I've already spent time in it, so I'm not going to dwell on it here, but he did keep his interior pretty clean. I liked that.

We sat in silence, watching the road. As you can imagine, I lasted about a minute in that state. There was no room to meditate, okay? Plus there was no way I could relax sitting so close to the man.

"I don't smoke pot anymore, you know," I started in, artlessly I admit, but there was no graceful to bring this particularly sore point up and no other way to deflect it.

"You don't strike me as someone who does," he replied.

"I hate my mother."

"Everyone hates their mother," he kept his eyes straight ahead, which makes sense because we were watching for the bad guys. But I wouldn't mind if he turned and gazed at me with something resembling adoration or attention, or even tolerance. Not happening.

The night breeze wafted through the open windows. It's warmer in Marin at night, warmer than fog-shrouded River's Bend. You pay more for your property, you get better air; that's a rule.

The silence folded around us; in its own way the atmosphere was sensual, evocative, but I was having none of it.

"Why is Peter Reilly Klausen the Third so afraid of you?" I asked into the night. I thought I'd begin with an obvious question and move into more subtle questions, ending with the ultimate feminine question: and how do you feel about that?

He sighed and shifted in his seat. He checked his keys to make sure they were in the ignition. They were. He adjusted his rear view mirror.

Now I understood some of Carrie's frustration with Patrick. It's difficult to come up with conversation when you have no starting place. The only thing Ben and I had in common was fixing a bathroom in Tiburon. Once that was finished (he still needed to paint), he was out of my life.

So I may as well learn a little, since I obviously have nothing to lose here.

"Ben?" I prompted.

"Shhh, they could come at any time," he replied.

"Answer the question or I'm going to think the worst, and perhaps repeat it out loud,"

I threatened.

He stopped fiddling with the keys. He arched back in a stretch and ran his hands through his hair. "Okay. A number of years ago, and it doesn't matter how many, because I've forgotten; Klausen had an affair with a friend of mine. She was his client."

"Ouch."

"Yeah, plus she left her husband and family for him, but in the end he did not marry her and left her high and dry. I couldn't just stand by helplessly, so I took her in and donated my lawyer to the cause."

"Is he a jerk too?"

"Oh probably. She tried to sue, but of course there was nothing she could do. So then I hired a private detective to follow Reilly around."

"What did you discover?"

"Hmmm? Oh many, many things, none of which was useful in this case," he grinned. "But I can use it for other purposes. I think Klausen knows that; that's why he's so jumpy around me and that's why, well."

"You goad him all the time," I finished.

"Come on, you saw him at the funeral. He thinks I'm a walking emotional time bomb, liable to blow up at any moment, for any reason and blurt out inconvenient truths."

"And are you?" I eyed him; he was impressive, much bigger than me in muscle and stature, which was part of the appeal of course. But would he blow? Was he a volatile guy? Klausen seemed to think so.

"No, I'm pretty calm, pretty easygoing." He checked the rear view mirror again, but there was no movement on the street. It's a pretty quiet neighborhood, part of the charm.

"Are you sure you just sued him? Are you certain, deep in your black little heart that you did not hurt him or threaten him?"

"Well, she was a good friend."

"Good friend or like a really good friend?" Now who was goading whom?

He shook his head with a smile at me. "We won't go there, but just a good friend. I don't like to see people taken advantage of and that's what Klausen did. He did it to women back in high school and he did it again in this situation, so I finally had had it."

"So you're saying she really thought he loved her?"

"Yeah, she really thought he loved her. The idiot."

"What happened to her?"

"I stopped the lawsuit and just gave her money to start over. She left the state."

"Why did she leave her family and husband for someone like Klausen?"

He regarded me, but I couldn't make out his expression in the dim light. "Love makes people do stupid things?"

"That's your answer?"

"It's the only one,..." he began, but we were interrupted by the sound of a truck. It was loud and from the sounds of the muffler, pretty beat-up. It slowly turned the corner towards my parents' house. One headlight was cockeyed and caught us head on. Before I knew it, Ben dived on top of me and pushed me down on the seat.

"Shit, they may have seen us." I could feel his breathing against my chest and my breasts reacted to the pressure in a rather embarrassing manner, but fortunately I wear nipple-proof bras.

"I can't breathe," I whispered.

"Oh, sorry." He pulled up just a bit, but didn't lift off completely. We spent what felt like hours chest to chest. My arms were pinned to my sides so I couldn't even push him away. Perish the thought, he could stay here all night if he'd like.

"Wait until they pass," he whispered.

"Oh, of course we'll wait," I whispered back. I wiggled a bit just for the fun of it, and in response, he dropped his full weight back on top of me. I know what you're thinking, but I could not tell if he was interested in me or not. Maybe it was the glaring headlights that reduced his enthusiasm.

I could hear the rattle of the truck as it slowly turned around our circular driveway. Ben and I knew what they were looking for. The car did not pause; the engine gunned as the truck pulled out of the driveway with a roar that sounded like it — the truck — was disappointed.

"Here we go," Ben popped off me like a prairie dog, a little too fast, and without enough regret, and started the engine of the truck. We were off, following, I might add, with no headlights.

"Shouldn't you have the headlights on?"

"And risk being seen?"

"Well, won't we be pulled over?" I asked. Ben followed the truck south onto the freeway, which, at 11 at night, could accommodate traffic traveling the speed limit.

"I certainly hope so, then the cops can help."

He had far more confidence than me. But he did turn on the headlights as we merged onto the freeway. The truck stayed ahead in the slow lane traveling at exactly 55. They didn't have to, but the speed limit between Novato and San Rafael changes seemingly randomly from 55 mph to 65 mph with little or no warning. Our truck driver obviously did not want to be pulled over for a mere infraction of the speed limit.

We crept behind our quarry, completely silent, as if drivers ahead of us could hear if we spoke.

They led us to south San Rafael, but not to the Doors and More store. That rhymes; it could be a haiku or something. We passed the Doors and More and continued down the frontage road toward San

Quentin. I wondered if our dudes felt any irony about the location of their lair. Probably not. Not many people understand irony.

"Great location," Ben mumbled under his breath.

We traveled down the narrow streets, keeping what we hoped was a safe distance. The truck pulled into a small parking lot and the loud muffler was blessedly silenced. Two men jumped out of the cab. They were empty-handed, sans doors, sans handy packages of incriminating coke. Not even a baseball bat or a tire iron. I never did figure out what they had hit me with. I hoped a tire iron; it was edgier and less wholesome than a baseball bat. Getting smacked with a baseball bat seems like such a cliché.

One of them said the F-word out loud several times. His friend was equally aggravated.

"The cops must have the stuff then," said one. "Otherwise why are all the doors gone?"

"Fuck!"

"Is that all you have to say?"

"Fuck, this is all your fault!"

"My fault? Blame him, it's his fault. He gave us the wrong shipping number."

"Yeah, he forgot to mention that cargo boxes all look the same. Fuck, now what do we do?"

"I don't know, you got us into this."

"Did not."

"Did too."

We didn't stay for the rest of the scintillating conversation because we didn't need to. I had their address and Ben had a GPS in his truck. We pulled away during the debate, leaving them reduced to chanting, "did not", "did too" back and forth like a mantra.

"I think the house is safe now," Ben commented.

"I probably should just go home," I said. I saved the address in my contacts list.

"Can I take you home?" he offered. At last, a gallant gesture.

"Oh, thanks. No, I need my car," I said with some regret. It would have been nice to spend a few more minutes in the car with him.

He pulled into the driveway and I got out.

"Thanks for your help," I said, circling around to the driver's side of the truck.

He leaned his arm on the open window and peered into the dim light at me. I could still feel the imprint of his hard body on mine — muscle memory.

"You're welcome," he said.

I paused. How much did I have to lose? Nothing, except the bathroom still needed a coat of paint. But I could even do that myself. But before I could launch into something clever, he beat me to it.

"You know, my parents have never let me forget I like to work with my hands for a living. My father makes comments about my rough calluses and wasted potential."

My chest felt a little less tense.

"Thanks for understanding."

"Anytime."

He even waited while I walked to the side door of the garage (it's always open because my parents don't think anything bad can happen once you've passed the gated entrance of the country club) and climbed into my car. Satisfied that I was on my way, Ben pulled out, I was close behind.

There are some mornings when I work and some days when I actually stop by the office. I needed some door hangers for the open house for the newly painted Navaho white Norton place and to print up some contracts using the office printer and more importantly, office ink cartridges.

"Did you hear about Rosemary?" Patricia looked positively, well, positive. I haven't seen her this happy since July 2007, the height of a seller's market.

"No," I glanced through the flyers that seem to breed in my in box, anything interesting for my clients, the Browns? No, they are looking for a "bargain," and have been looking (or I should say, I have been looking) for going on eleven months. This is Sonoma County, California, not Kansas; there are no bargains. The best the Browns can hope for is to find something with a price that doesn't send them immediately into cardiac arrest. But they are young, resilient, and have far too much time to search for perfection.

"She erased her hard drive," Patricia announced happily.

"Erased?" I was still glancing through the flyers. Many price reductions.

"The whole thing, wiped out," Patricia reported.

"How on earth did she do that?"

"Magnets."

I smothered a smile just in time because Rosemary herself, draped in a green sari scarf (she is a bit too robust to wear the full sari, the scarf wouldn't cover enough, so it has to be accompanied by additional articles of clothing. Like I should talk) waltzed by the front desk. She seemed to be taking her spontaneous hard drive cleansing in stride.

"Did you call that nice man who retrieves information on hard drives?" she asked Patricia, who nodded in response.

"Oh, Allison, but of course you should try these," Rosemary pointed to the heavy bracelets still clutching her wrists. "I feel so much more energy, so much more alive!"

"That's because you drained all the energy from your computer," I said.

"Oh, kind of like the Fantastic Four," Patricia piped up.

"No, no, it was an accident," Rosemary said.

"There are no accidents. We all make up our own reality and in fact you all don't really exist at all; you are just a product of my mind." Katherine emerged from the copy room and regarded her competition.

"Who is she listening to now?" I whispered.

"Someone named Patent," Patricia explained.

Did I mention that Katherine and Rosemary are the top producers in our office? They each have a shelf of golden trophies to prove it. They compete for top position in the office every year. I pick up accolades and trophies as well, but I'm always a few dollars short of their stellar activities, so I'm allowed to be friendly with both of them. In fact, I've learned a great deal from each (in terms of sales) and they treat me like a baby sister. Which is good. As long as they don't stuff me into a dryer.

Gaunt Katherine and expansive Rosemary faced off in front of the reception desk like Xena Warrior Princess versus Sheena, Queen of the Jungle.

"So," Katherine tossed the first volley. "How is 239 Grant Ave. coming?"

"Well, I have an open house on Sunday," Rosemary said, pretending it was a good idea.

"Another one?" Katherine raised a thinly plucked eyebrow.

Rosemary eyed her. Katherine waited patiently.

"We had another price reduction," Rosemary admitted.

"Ah," Katherine smiled. "I sold 68 Claudius Way."

"Already?"

"Fifteen-day escrow, the buyers are anxious."

Price reduction versus short escrow, Rosemary was toast. Today, the Warrior Princess was also queen of the jungle.

I slipped out to the computer room to print my contracts.

"How about 90 Honor Place?" I heard Rosemary volley back.

Ouch, that one had gone through three price reductions and the owners were getting desperate. Katherine was not having fun with that one, plus she had foolishly agreed to a reduced commission of 2.5% to secure the listing.

It was war out there. So I cowered in the back and worked as quietly as I could. I updated, downloaded, printed. All those chores that take roughly half your attention, so the other half thinks about ways to make life more complicated than it really needs to be. So I called Carrie.

"I am not having any luck," she complained. "The sisters don't leave us alone, Patrick doesn't talk much when they do, and I don't think he likes me at all."

"Ready to give up?"

"No. I am not giving up. But I need to find a way to get him alone for longer than just a car ride home."

"Get him alone? What is this, a Jane Austen novel? Ask him to have a picnic with you, hike, do one of those cute bicycling adventures where you end up on a windy beach and share your first kiss, something like that. Come on, you have an imagination."

I pulled off my copies and waved to Patricia, who scrutinized the number of pages I held in my hand, but since she was in a magnanimous mood, what with Rosemary's erased hard drive and all, she let me pass.

"A picnic, that's a great idea. Come with me?"

"Come with you? Are you mad? Hi, here is my friend Allison, she's the third wheel and here to look after me."

"Then bring that guy."

"What guy?" I separated my contracts; one set for my files and another set for my transaction coordinator and put her set in her box. I know, I know, by the time you read this, all our transactions will be online, but I still needed something for the clients to actually sign. Not everyone is wired.

"The contractor guy — you can bring him too. I know, wine tasting, we can go wine tasting on Saturday."

"Everyone goes wine tasting."

"Sure, because it's easy, fun, and we live in the Wine Country, duh."

"But does the boy drink more than milk?"

"Come on, Allison, help me out, will you?" she cajoled.

"Okay. Saturday." Since my last outing was to a funeral, I thought, what the hell, help the girl along; maybe talk with Ben about the murder.

Okay, I didn't put it that way when I called up Mr. Stone. A little spin was important. Besides, the contact with Mr. Sullivan of Cooper Milk could be advantageous for both of us; always look for the business angle, especially if you think that the relationship angle may not lead to anything.

I called Ben immediately before I lost my nerve.

"Wait." Ben turned off something loud in the background and was immediately clear. "Your friend needs to get her boyfriend away from his sisters? What is this, *Sense and Sensibility*?"

"Thank you, that's what I said." Wow, he knew more than one Jane Austen title. Maybe there is something to be said for a Stanford education.

"Saturday? Are we all going in one car? I'll drive if you'd like."

"So, you'll be the sober one."

"Not necessarily."

Have you visited the Wine Country? The one in Sonoma County, not the highway strip that cuts through the expensive valley they call Napa. No, I'm talking about funky wineries with names like Toad Hollow and Roshambo, free tastings, and winding roads riddled with potholes and no shoulders so you have to be careful of the bicyclists.

I'm talking heavy clusters of purple and green grapes hanging low under canopies of dusty green leaves. I'm talking rolling hills, appellations like Dry Creek and Alexander Valley. You've seen the pictures; Sonoma County really does look like the very worst of the sentimental photographs and calendar art with titles like "Wine County Autumn" or something silly like that. In fact, I'm surprised Thomas Kinkade hasn't painted vineyards. Maybe the light is too difficult to capture.

I'll tell you why the light is difficult; there is nothing like the golden light in California. Nothing. Even Rosemary will admit that. Even dour Patricia appreciates it. And in the early autumn the light is luminous. It fills the afternoon like a bright chardonnay — one that doesn't taste like horse piss.

I digress. The chardonnays around here have gotten much, much better. Aged in stainless steel tanks instead of oak. Not perfect, but better.

I still prefer red.

Ben, handyman-turned-chauffeur, showed up at my house exactly on time driving a silver Mercedes sedan with tan leather interior, very nice.

"Grandma's. She only drives it on Sunday to go to church," he explained briefly, and I believed him, because sedans are very grandmotherly. Which is why my mother owns one as well, because she's a grandmother. But not because of me. We've been over that.

We traveled to the base of the Dry Creek appellation (which doesn't really mean much, but now you know so you can show off to your friends) and worked our way north. My record for wine tasting is thirteen wineries and tastings in one afternoon. Personal best. (Don't try that at home, but you really can't try it at home because the wineries have to be located pretty close together in order to visit thirteen between 11 and 4). Come out here and see.)

Ben and I traced out a more sedate schedule for this afternoon; after all, we had young people with us.

We put Carrie and Patrick in the back seat. It was very quiet in that back seat on the drive up, but Carrie rallied and worked the conversation to include all of us, so Patrick didn't sound too silent.

Patrick is a handsome boy, but not substantial enough for someone like me.

I need substantial.

Ben Stone, on the other hand, was looking more solid as the day arched overhead.

As I said, we began at the border of the Russian River and Dry Creek appellations and worked our way up Westside Road.

Ben and I worked at leaving Carrie and Patrick alone as much as possible. While they tasted, we wandered through vineyards, or a beautiful garden, or just claimed it took two of us to carry a case of wine back to the car.

We paused at Mill Creek Vineyards, currently producing some great whites depending on the year. So I bought three bottles of the sauvignon blanc (tasting note, if you don't know what kind of white to buy, sauvignon blanc is almost always good, not as tricky as pinot gris, and certainly not as risky as the aforementioned chardonnay and you can get away with an eight-dollar bottle). You're welcome.

Ben and I lingered on tasting room wraparound porch while Carrie and Patrick walked through the tiny garden adjacent to the tasting room and admired the waterwheel (mill, get it?).

"Here, you have something on you," Ben brushed my skirt.

"Thanks." I glanced up at him, and brushed off a leaf from his hair. His hair was thick and curly. I wanted to linger and touch his thick curls, but I resisted.

We stopped off at Pezzi King Winery. I enjoyed a lovely moment at Pezzi King during one of the many Passport events I've attended. Passport is a spring wine tasting event in Dry Creek that is so popular the organizers hold a lottery to distribute tickets. Some years you get lucky, some years you can't attend. I enter the lottery every year.

Here's why people bother with the lottery and the price of the tickets; one year, Pezzi King decorated the winery in a circus theme and paired a gewürztraminer with cotton candy. That's why we keep coming back to that event.

But today we were just wine tasting in the real world on an average Saturday afternoon, so there were no decorations and no party except the party we created ourselves. Here, Ben and I left Carrie and Patrick in the tasting room to find the notes of tobacco and pencil shavings in the cabernet/merlot blend. No, I'm not kidding. No one in Sonoma County kids about wine; well, maybe a little. The wine with cotton candy pairing was certainly amusing. Ben and I walked down to the lower gardens to a secluded pergola. Behind us was a wall of green ivy, before us the valley filled with rows of vines opened up under the blue sky.

We settled onto the benches and admired the view.

"You have beautiful skin. How do you get it so smooth?" He brushed his knuckles across my cheek. I resisted the urge to nuzzle against his hand, but ducked my head, becomingly I hoped, and fortunately there was nothing nearby to knock my head against. Good news.

"Thanks. I owe it all to my Mary Kay consultant."

"Do they still make that stuff?"

"Indeed they do, and how do you keep your hands so smooth?"

I grabbed his hand and flipped it over. For a contractor and handyman, his hands were remarkably unmarked.

"I thought you said your dad complained about your rough hands," I said.

"Used to. I found some salt scrub and some lotion."

"They feel nice," I couldn't help it. I stroked his wide palm. He didn't jerk his hand from mine, so I continued to hold it.

My phone buzzed. It was my mortgage broker.

"I got it." She was jubilant; I felt a little less so.

"That's great." I attempted to feign some interest. Yesterday this would have been fabulous news; I mean, it's business. "You locked it in?"

"Just now. They should be fine. Do you want to call them?"

"Umm," I glanced over at Ben. "You can call them."

"Great, see you at the signing."

I clicked off the phone.

"Good news?" he asked.

"Locked in a difficult loan, I'll close escrow on Monday. So yes, good news."

But the moment I really cared about, the moment between Ben and me, was lost.

We walked over to Dry Creek Vineyard because it's across the street. By this time, Ben begged off a full tasting (not much, by the way; a pour is about one swallow, but the numbers of pours is what you have to watch out for).

"Here, taste this." I handed Ben my glass and his hand lingered on mine as he took it.

"Very fruit-forward," our pourer encouraged.

"Very forward," Ben agreed seriously.

I just tried to breathe evenly.

Dry Creek offers benches nestled up against large trees; Carrie and Patrick needed some lunch so we stayed there and ate, despite the fact that there was no view. It really wasn't my date so I can't really complain.

Carrie had found a real picnic basket and had packed it with completely appropriate items. She calmly pulled out a round loaf of fresh sourdough bread, Gallo salami (not the same family), three different cheeses, one hard, one goat, and one triple-cream Brie. She pulled out tiny knives for the cheeses, a bamboo breadboard, and real glasses. Grapes and a container of chicken salad completed the meal. Patrick bought a bottle of the Dry Creek Fumé Blanc for lunch and Ben bought sparkling water.

I watched Carrie carefully. The meal represented a substantial investment on her part; I knew what she made and it wasn't enough, in my opinion, to support something extravagant like fifteen-dollars-a-pound cheese. But I didn't say anything and just vowed to pay for our lunches together for the rest of my life.

The wine theme did help along the conversation, and Patrick proved to be more knowledgeable than I had initially given him credit for. He had taken the wine business class at Sonoma State and he and Ben indulged in a robust debate on wine marketing.

I won't bore you.

Carrie and I retreated to the gift shop for a few minutes, then to the restroom.

At Quivira Winery, I begged off and sat under one of the pergolas and enjoyed the hot sun. After a few minutes Carrie joined me, leaving Patrick and Ben in the tasting room.

"How is it going?"

"It's going good," she said. "He's talking to me more and Ben is really helping. Thank you."

"That picnic basket is just beautiful." I couldn't help it; I saw similar versions for sale at Dry Creek Winery, $150 for the small ones.

"Oh, thanks. I found it at Goodwill, five bucks, can you believe it? And I made the napkins."

"You know, I underestimate you."

"I know you do," she said smugly.

For our last winery, I insisted on traveling further north on Yoakim Bridge road up to Dutcher Crossing Winery because I wanted to finish the afternoon with the perfect winery moment plus I love the wine and it's hard to find in the stores. One of the wine consultants there is a genius. His wine is a bit on the expensive side (unless you only buy Two Buck Chuck, then everything else is expensive, but this wine is expensive for me and Ben. Not expensive for Mr. Sullivan), but it's worth it.

The tasting room at Dutcher Crossing is furnished with comfortable chairs grouped around a wooden coffee table. Patrick and Carrie snuggled in an oversized armchair and were served wine and nuts.

I, on the other hand, wanted the privacy of the outdoor benches grouped under a pergola nestled against a big outdoor stone fireplace. I carried my glass outside, not really caring who followed me. I guess if you live alone, sometimes the sound of talking and conversation can become tiring.

It was a perfect afternoon — 80 degrees, a brilliant blue sky. There is nothing like the sky here in the fall: the blue sky, the green vines, the green and silver trees flashing in the breeze. It was all good.

I closed my eyes to feel the afternoon surround me. Maybe I can meditate. I know, I keep thinking it would be a good thing to do. Then I seem to always find something else that's more important. Like accidentally smacking Ben with a meat cleaver. Not relaxing.

"Hey." Ben sat on the bench beside me.

"Hey." I didn't open my eyes, but I could feel Ben breathing next to me. For a moment, I just wanted, well, the moment. I live here for a reason, I talk people into buying here for a reason, and it's because it can all be so good.

"Beautiful," he commented.

"Yes, isn't it? I love this place," I said, my eyes still closed. I shouldn't get sun on my face; heard that lecture a million times. I smiled, remembering how a friend of mine described her last trip to the dermatologist. The very young doctor (yes, the doctors now are all in their late 20s) asked Marilyn, and I quote: "Did you ever get sunburned when you were a kid?"

And Marilyn just looked at this young thing in disbelief and declared, "It was the 60's; everyone got sunburned."

Apparently back then kids didn't need sun block because there was still some ozone left to do the job automatically.

Not for me, for you.

In our valley, wine tasting shuts down at 4 p.m., which leaves you with plenty of sunshine left in the afternoon, a happy buzz, and nothing to do. So we drove back north to Healdsburg to just wander around the central town square.

Facing the square is the new (relatively, those who specialize in Healdsburg properties always refer to the hotel as the new hotel) Hotel Healdsburg. The locals protested mightily against a high-end hotel in downtown Healdsburg. But lo, the hotel appeals to a well-heeled crowd and that crowd is now happily spending lots of money in downtown Healdsburg and everyone is happy. Carrie and I investigated shopping options along the street front, and Ben and Patrick obediently trailed behind us.

We passed the restaurant, just opening for drinks.

"Oh, Dry Creek Kitchen, I hear it's good," Carrie said.

"It's very good. Want to go?" Patrick offered.

"Hard to get reservations," I commented.

"I'll talk to them." Patrick ducked into the restaurant and we hung out in the shaded square.

"Isn't he wonderful?" Carrie asked.

"Oh yes," Ben and I assured her.

"Done. We'll have dinner at 7." Patrick came back flushed with triumph, his version of killing a mastodon for his woman. Actually it was pretty impressive; I underestimated the boy.

At dinner I realize that it's good to be Patrick Sullivan. Our service was exemplary; waiters rushed to fill our glasses and cheerfully hunted down a bottle of Palmeri syrah/cabernet blend that Ben insisted I try.

"If you liked the Dutcher Crossing, you should try this. It's the Damskeys' own label." Ben poured a generous amount into my Riedel glass.

I had to agree, it was to die for. Ben did not tell me the cost. He just grinned when I expressed my deepest enthusiasm.

Patrick was also busy during dinner. While I ordered an appetizer of Ahi tuna sashimi with rice noodles and ginger soy dressing, Patrick was introducing Carrie to an elderly couple that knew his grandfather. While Ben ordered the organic baby arugula with Dry Creek figs, Carrie was introduced to two middle-aged women who used to dress as the Cooper Chicken, back in the day. By the time our entrées arrived, Patrick had greeted five people in the restaurant and introduced Carrie to two more couples. To her credit, Carrie became more gracious and interested with each introduction.

Good girl, maybe she can pull this off.

We talked of general things appropriate for dinner. I spent most of my time raving about the wine; Ben was a generous server.

For dinner, I indulged (when do I not?) in the duck breast with five-bean cassoulet and baby bok choy. Ben ordered the Alaskan Coho salmon and the kids both had the Pan-roasted Rosie chicken with black mission figs. There, now you know what's served at one of the poshest restaurants in Sonoma County. Next book I'll take you to French Laundry.

While we ate, another couple approached our table, but this time I thought they were heading for Ben. But he shook his head and they moved away.

"Who was that?" I saw the gesture.

"I thought I recognized them, but I was wrong," he replied easily.

In the car the "kids" were suspiciously quiet, and I resisted the impulse to look into the back seat.

I faced forward and gazed at the road.

"So, ever married?" I asked. It wasn't even a real question, I just felt like making conversation.

"Yup." He kept his eyes on the road; his hands were firmly on the steering wheel.

"Local girl?"

"Yes. She took everything, kept everything, even my name, so I changed it, and just got on with my life."

"That sounds suspiciously ugly," I said.

"Not even suspicious. It was ugly."

"Long time ago?"

"A couple of years."

I sat back, knowing the conversation was finished. Bad marriage, bad ex-wife. Possibly bad, rich, ex-wife. Poor guy, no wonder he didn't own anything; couldn't, she had it all. At least he had his grandmother's house.

Now, the big question: does he hate all women, or just that particular member of our species?

We drove back to our starting point at my house. I considered it neutral ground for the young lovers. I did not have to worry. Carrie bid

us a hasty goodbye, Patrick thanked us, and they both scrambled out of
the back of Ben's car and sprinted for Patrick's, leaving us sitting alone
in the front seats.

"Nice place," Ben ventured.

"Would you like to come in?" I offered. It was Saturday night, after
all.

"No, I'm good. I figured out what's wrong with your young man."

"Oh really?" I crossed my arms under my breasts; it was much
cooler here, closer to the ocean.

"Painfully shy," Ben continued. "His sisters habitually protect him
because of it."

"Why do you think he's so shy?"

"Well, he admitted he didn't really date much, probably because the
family is careful about keeping him away from gold diggers like your
friend Carrie."

"She's not a gold digger," I denied on her behalf, even though I
knew really she was. But I also knew she was beginning to like the guy;
she wouldn't be so frustrated if she didn't like him. Patrick was like a
cat that wouldn't come. I've seen her do this; the further a cat shies
away from her, the more determined she becomes to win him — the
cat, the boyfriend — over.

"There's more to it than that," I defended her.

"Are you sure?"

"Are you sure there's not?" I countered.

Well," he hesitated.

"Aha! You mistrust her because she's beautiful, don't you?" I
wanted to add, "and your ex-wife was beautiful too wasn't she?" But
I'm not an idiot.

"No, no, of course not," he denied.

"Then lay off my friend," I shot back.

"I'm not laying into your friend at all. I'm just telling you what I see." His voice raised a fraction.

"And I'm telling you it's not true, what you see may not be what is reality. Believe me, in my business, I know." My voice rose two, okay maybe three, more fractions.

"Fine then." He brought the decibel level back down to cold, quiet righteousness.

I was cold, our heat has dissipated into the deep night — isn't that poetic? So I opened the car door and slid out.

He rolled down the window and looked up at me. "So you would give up a potentially lethal night of sex over an argument about your friend?"

"Always." I was terse and was in the right. I marched through my own doors into my own home and slammed the doors after me. I waited for the sound of the car to leave before I could take another breath.

"So, how was the goodnight kiss this time?" I had to call Carrie first thing in the morning.

"It was," she was distracted by something. "Good. Don't. Can I call you back?"

Well shit, the girl got him to bed. But that didn't get her out of my plan. There were more than just disgruntled dudes at that warehouse in San Rafael and I intended to take a look. In the daylight, don't worry. But I did need to do more than sit around an open house waiting for something to happen. Apparently I had given up a lethal night of sex and I was pissed.

A little sleuthing around would at least make me feel like I was accomplishing something. I have no idea what. But I did know I needed an accomplice, the Ethel to my Lucy. And since my Ethel is currently a very happy girl, she was the perfect choice. She wasn't very big, but she could work a phone and call 911 in case of an emergency.

I finally got a hold of her at 11. Eleven? What were they doing? I did not ask. "Meet me at the Navaho white house at 4 and we'll go down together. The least I can do is save you the gas," I cajoled.

"Are you sure it's safe?" She was suspicious. I have no idea why.

"Perfectly. Sure."

She didn't ask how my evening finished up with Ben and I didn't tell.

Norton's open house was uneventful. A few people came by, like the neighbors and people just shopping around. One couple lied and told me they had a realtor. No, they did not want to enter a chance to win a gift certificate. No, they weren't really interested in another home like this; they were just looking. At least no one cringed at the sight of the paint. White is a good color.

Carrie arrived promptly at closing time and helped me pick up the open house signs. I, in turn, spent the drive south listening to the new features and benefits of Patrick Sullivan the wonderful. As it should be.

Me? I got plenty of rest and spent too much time ruminating over the insensitive Ben Stone. I really shouldn't go into my own head alone.

The warehouse was empty when we pulled up. I parked the car down the street in another parking lot and we hiked back. It was warm; I had changed into shorts and a practical T-shirt with no identifying logos, just in case. Carrie wore shorts as well. On her they looked sexy.

"What are we looking for?" she asked.

"Evidence."

I always carry a camera in my car. The plan was to walk up to the warehouse windows, snap a few photos of the coke lying around and, voila, we have a case.

"What are we doing here again and why should I care?" Carrie marched along beside me, but she wasn't happy.

"Because it's an adventure and you can say you've done something interesting. Consider it conversation for your upcoming dinner."

And because you owe me, I thought silently, but I wasn't going to burden her with that. We enjoyed a nice time during the afternoon, Ben and me and that, as they say, was that.

As we approached the deserted warehouse, I paused. "We need to be quiet. Quiet like a fish." I quoted a line from the movie *Chicken Run*.

"You are so weird."

A cat mewed and Carrie veered off — "Hey," I called, forgetting to be quiet.

"Don't worry, I still have my finger on the cell phone," she called back. "Here kitty, kitty, kitty, good kitty, who's the pretty kitty?"

I went on ahead to the warehouse and looked for a window. Really, that's what I thought, that I'd take a picture through the dirty window and be finished with the project in less than ten minutes. It wasn't even worth changing outfits. I know, sometimes my naïveté is flabbergasting.

The warehouse had no windows. How inconvenient. Maybe there were windows in the back. I could hear Carrie cajoling the cat as I walked to the back of the warehouse.

There were some chinks in the wood, sloppy workmanship. I pressed my face to one of the larger openings and cupped my hands around my eyes to block the light. At first I saw only blackness, but then as my eyes adjusted I could see a fairly empty room. Some light seeped into the area from another poorly nailed board at the opposite end. No, I couldn't see much at all. There weren't boxes of coke, no doors. Not much at all. Then why did the dudes come here?

I heard the sound of a truck, but I was too intent on my search to pay much attention. This was an industrial park; there were trucks and heavy equipment all over the place.

Before I die I want to consume a large quantity of allergy medicine and operate a piece of heavy equipment. It's one of my goals.

And I may not make it to that goal. I heard a crunch on the gravel to my left, lifted my head to see if it was Carrie and yes, got smacked in the head again for my trouble.

And they hit me on the same sore place. Damn and fuck, it hurt like hell. They probably used the tire iron. I should stop thinking up those kinds of options, because, according to Katherine, when I do, they manifest in my life. Well, they manifest all right, in the form of a blunt instrument assaulting my poor head.

I staggered a bit but didn't really pass out. I just didn't know where a few of my body parts were located, and I couldn't seem to gather them all together to perform a coordinated routine.

I heard a yelp from Carrie and a pitiful meow from the pretty kitty, but I couldn't do much more than be groggily aware that I was being dragged across the asphalt parking lot, which was shredding my shorts as well as my thighs. The good news — the pain actually helped clear my head.

I was really pissed by the time we got inside, but all they did was toss in Carrie behind me and slam a big heavy door cutting off all the light from outside.

"Shit," I heard one say. "It's her again."

"Hey," he nudged me with the toe of his shoe, very rude. "Are you a cop or something?"

I struggled to a sitting position and looked around for Carrie. She was a few feet away, face down, and not moving. I know she's far more fragile than me. I wanted to reach out — to make sure she wasn't dead. But I couldn't move.

"Look at these shoes," I gestured to my bright green Tod's loafers. "Would a cop wear shoes like these?"

My assailants didn't know what to make of that answer, so they kicked me again.

"I told you we should have killed her," said one.

"No killing, we don't kill. We just get out. Here, help me with this," replied the other. I liked him best.

I tried to get up and limp, drag, crawl to Carrie, but before I could, they noticed and rushed over to subdue me. I shrank back down and tried to look cowed but I was still pretty angry. My scrapes hurt like hell and the floor was cold. Carrie. Had they taken her phone? They hadn't taken mine.

There was just enough light seeping around the edges of the warehouse to show me that one of the dudes, the one I did not like as well, was pointing a pistol right at me. Oh great, and he probably grew up playing single-shooter video games and was far better at the real thing than anyone would suspect.

I shrank back further.

"Just stay," he commanded. "Come on, get the stuff and let's go."

"Dude, this place smells like shit."

"It's the varnish; toss it in the dumpster."

"Where?"

"The dumpster outside," he snarled. Our gunman was quickly tiring of his management responsibilities.

The boy gestured with the gun, his cohort found the can, and we were all momentarily blinded by the light as he opened the door and tossed the can with a bang into the dumpster.

"Great, happy? Now get the stuff and we're out of here."

"What about them?" The staff for this operation, Dude Two, found what I too was looking for the bag of coke, or whatever; I'm not familiar with the production and distribution of cocaine, I deal in houses. But it did seem the boy was carrying a rather impressive bag. Despite my mother's innuendos, I don't know that much about drugs. But I was sure that bag represented a great deal of cash. There was a lot of money in those doors. And not because they looked good.

I needed to gain time, any time. I still had unfilled dreams — heavy equipment, another trivial New Century statue, more advice to give Carrie — I wanted to live.

"Is this the part where you explain why you've been following me around and hitting me over the head?" I asked as casually and calmly as I could.

"No man, you just got in the way," the Dude waved the gun and smiled. Great, he was enjoying himself.

"What happened to the doors?"

"Gone," grunted the second dude.

"Why didn't you just remove the coke from the doors and put the doors back where you found them?" I asked. "No one would have known."

The boys stopped what they were doing and looked at me in complete surprise.

"I should shoot you," said our friend with the gun.

I shook my head, working on my advantage. "No, you don't want to do that, the state actually frowns on that."

"Yeah, like we're worried about that." They both laughed.

"Come on." Our man with thousands of dollars' worth of drugs clutched in his arms gestured to our man with the lethal weapon in his hands.

"We have to go. Remember we're meeting him?"

"I should take care of her." The gun hovered over my head. I swallowed, but my throat was so dry that swallowing had no effect at all. So I tried to clear my throat; that didn't help. I thought of standing, towering over him; of course I out weighed him and I could take him, but my head was woozy, and the gun loomed large.

"Come on, leave her. We're just supposed to get out of here." I held my breath.

"Come on!"

My would-be killer took one more thoughtful stare, saluted me with his gun, and dashed out after his friend. Well, I'm glad they were still teaching some manners in school: don't kill. That's a good rule.

Gunshots outside curbed my enthusiasm.

Chapter 10

I dragged myself up to my knees just before the door opened again. The shaft of light caught me full in the face.

"Well, shit. Look who it is." The figure silhouetted in the light sounded somewhat familiar but my poor brain had been dashed around inside my skull a little too often. I wasn't making the connection. If he would just stand still and hold that flashlight up to his face, I could probably recognize him.

"I thought you were just a realtor."

"Surprise." I managed to get on my hands and knees, and of course, kept talking. "You didn't think I'd notice missing doors? That everyone wouldn't notice missing doors?"

"That was a problem," he mused. "But as the acting DA, it wasn't too much of a problem to suppress it. I did pretty well, didn't I?"

He kicked the door closed and it took a few seconds for my eyes to adjust again, but now, in the dim filtered light I could make out his features better. Yes, crap. It was Mark, candidate for DA, father of three, devoted spouse, and sibling. And head bad guy. And my client. How fucking perfect.

"Very well," I agreed. Agree with madmen and men with guns, oh and the mother of the bride. I read that somewhere. Probably not in my positive thinking literature; there is nothing about guns in *Seven Habits of Highly Effective People* "You know, I thought Dad would have more money left in that house," he said conversationally. As if we were sitting in the living room of Mortimer's house.

"You never can tell with parents," I agreed readily. Damn, I had actually kind of liked him. I had liked him more than I liked Hillary. But to Hillary's credit, she hadn't killed anyone recently. I could not say the same for the future DA for Marin.

"It was supposed to be simple."

"Good help is so hard to find," I said sympathetically. Really, it is hard to find good help. Have you tried to find a good housekeeper? But I digress. I was in danger here. I should pay attention.

"So if you're so smart, who killed my Dad?"

"What do you mean? Your door dudes." I was ready, I pushed my weight up onto my hands and then heaved again — determined to stand. But he jumped forward and shoved me back down — hard.

"Nope, they don't know how to work a gun." Mark scratched his head with the small tip of the flashlight, which wasn't a flashlight at all; it was a rather large gun. It was larger than the one the dude I didn't like held, or hadn't liked.

I didn't know about that. It seemed to me they knew more than Mark in that respect. In fact, I hoped Mark knew something about working a gun. The last thing I needed was a botched murder job leaving me paralyzed or stupid, or both. The least he could do was execute a clean kill.

Really that is exactly the kind of stuff that runs through my addled brain.

"It wasn't me. I didn't kill Dad. My cohorts aren't really killers. But they are handy with heavy objects, no? Maybe it was Hillary?" he asked, a little too plaintively considering he was the one holding the firearm.

I recognized the tone; it had been used on me too often during my childhood. If my brothers couldn't think of a good excuse, they just threw out my name, and my mother was instantly distracted.

"Hillary? Do you think she'd kill her own father?"

"Don't underestimate Hillary," he commanded.

"I'm not, I'm not." I protested. "Really, I'm not."

"He was supposed to have more money hidden. Hillary said he bragged about it; he told her. "I have money in the house.""

"He meant he had equity in the house," I said. Oh Jesus, was that what she was looking for, the money in the house? I didn't know if I felt vastly superior to her or sad.

"You're very smart aren't you?" Mark asked.

"Surprised?" I countered.

"Don't underestimate your enemies."

"Don't underestimate your friends." I glanced over at Carrie.

That was her cure to come to her senses and do something spectacular like throw a cat at him or deliver a surprise karate chop. She didn't move. That distracted me even more. She doesn't have a hard head like to do, no siblings on which to toughen up. Her silky brunette hair (natural) fanned out on the filthy cement. I was worried about what the dirt and grit was doing to her skin. I was about to call to her when Mark smacked me with his open palm.

"Pay attention. I'm the one with the gun."

"I'm concerned about my friend," I replied, using my best phone technique. When we performed role-playing at the Monday office meetings, this one never came up. Okay, I'll be the realtor in trouble and you be the madman holding a gun. Okay, what do you say? See? It's a rather uncommon scenario.

"No. I'll probably have to kill her," he said sadly. "I have to kill you too, don't I?"

I took a breath and searched through my troubled mind for an answer to that. How do you negotiate such a thing?

"Not necessarily. I can be bought," I offered. Well, it's almost true; for that moment I could be bought. I might possibly change my mind when I was out of danger.

"No, extortion is messy and distracting."

"Really? Then what about your henchmen? Your dudes?"

"They were," he paused. "Fired."

My stomach tightened and my heart started beating harder. Shit. I had underestimated him by more than a little. I had underestimated him by a mile and a half, with an extra acre hidden by trees with an easement included. I was so screwed. Actually, I was dead. I wondered who to pray to at the last minute. Really there should be some sort of secular last-minute God. You know, like a God for emergencies.

Just when I was getting fond of the dudes. Remember, no open casket, we all ready discussed that.

"Well, since I plan to stay in Marin and I'm head of the investigation, and you and your friend are unimportant..." He swung away from me to the right and aimed the gun at Carrie's inert form.

"No!" I rose up on my knees and lunged forward, aiming for whatever I could hit. I collided with his legs and only managed to push him closer to my friend. He yelped and the gun fired close to my head — loud, very loud. He staggered but did not fall; I didn't have enough strength to really smack him down. I was very sorry about that, you can be sure.

The bullet hit a chip out of the cement.

"You bitch." He regained his balance and turned to me, which, I suppose, was my stupid goal.

"Fine, then you first." He was right over me and I couldn't wiggle backward. It wouldn't do me much good anyway. He raised the gun and — I admit — I closed my eyes. I couldn't bear to watch myself get killed.

I heard a click, then a big slam. The warehouse door burst open and light flooded the room again. This light/dark thing was giving me a headache. I opened my eyes just in time to see Mark fall down.

Oh come on, you wanted him to burst in at the last minute. And so did I. I was thrilled to see him, so I said the first thing that came to my scrambled brain to yell at him.

"What the hell are you doing here?"

"Rescuing you."

"I don't need rescuing. Haven't you seen *Sex in the City*? Carrie, not this Carrie, clearly says, 'I don't need rescuing.'"

"But when a girl has a gun to her head and is about to bite the big one, I think rescuing is needed," he retorted.

"Oh, you think that?"

Ben put his hands on his hips and glared at me. I could feel that look even in the dim light. "I think the bodies in the dumpster outside will help my case along," he said quietly.

I swallowed. Poor little dudes.

He extended his hand and I reluctantly took it. Really, I could get up by myself. I was pretty sure. I wobbled as I stood and he caught me against his side and tightened his grip around my waist.

"Come on, let's get you outside."

"No, no, I'm fine right here. In fact, I'll just sit down. Don't mind me, just go about your business."

"No," he moved me forward, toward the light. Was I supposed to go toward the light? Wasn't there something about not moving toward the light? I couldn't remember. It wasn't up to me anyway.

"You are coming outside. You don't look very good. People really have to stop beating you up."

I took two steps and stopped. I think that sinking to my knees right there in the nice cool warehouse would be a fine idea. Or I could vomit. There seemed to be a myriad of choices, none of them included moving forward. That light was very bright.

"I'll take you by Starbucks if you come outside with me right now," he coaxed.

"Caramel Macchiato?"

"Any strange concoction your heart desires." He propelled me smoothly past Mark, who moved as we walked by. Ben kicked him in the head on the way to leading me outside into the sunshine.

"Sit right over here." He steered me away from a dumpster, which, when I thought about it a number of seconds later, was probably THE dumpster. I gingerly lowered myself onto a couple of empty pallets and lifted my face to the sun. My legs ached from the contact with the cold cement and my scratches burned. I was not in good shape. However, I was alive; that's a good thing.

Ben carried Carrie out, because of course, he could — she's a little thing and looks perfect as the victim, the one who really needs saving. Her brunette hair flowed over Ben's arm like a wash of water. She groaned as the sunlight hit her face.

"Here." he set Carrie down next to me. "I'm going to lock the door and call the police. Stay with her."

I heard him lock the doors, and watched Carrie's eyes flutter against the hard light. I've never been more relieved in my whole life.

"I feel like shit," she said.

"It's okay, you don't look bad," I reassured her. She didn't; a cut on her forehead, scrapes, bruises, a cut on her arm from the flying cement chips. I reached out and brushed away some of the blood. It had been so close. But I did not bring that up; I may never bring it up.

She groaned and tried to move, but I put my hand on her tiny thigh and stopped her.

"If I die," she wheezed. "I want you to have my shoes."

"Thank you, that means a lot to me."

"And if I don't die," she sat up and started to gingerly pat down her hips and thighs, "I'm going to kill you."

I accepted her wrath because it was so pitiful. And I was so happy she was alive and relatively unscathed. I listened for any movement from the warehouse; there was none. That was good.

She found what she wanted and pulled out her cell phone.

"Who are you calling?"

"The cavalry," she said.

There was a cartoon — Dudley Do - Right — in which Dudley saves his sweetheart Nell at the end of every episode. Within twenty minutes of Carrie's call, Patrick Sullivan was here to save the day, no wait, that was Mighty Mouse. Anyway, Patrick pulled into the driveway in his low-slung sports car instead of his trusty steed, but just the same, he scooped up the heroine.

"You should see a doctor." He frowned at her scrapes and bleeding temple.

"Oh no, I...."

She didn't want to say she didn't have insurance, not in front of him, and I wasn't going to say anything that would make things worse.

"I'll be fine." Her voice was shaky and much less self-possessed than when she threatened to kill me. Fair enough, if she wants to be the damsel in distress, that's her prerogative.

Patrick pulled out a blue blanket from the trunk of the roadster and wrapped it around her. The blanket looked like cashmere, and of course Carrie made it look even better. How *can* a woman who has been through hell and back look that good? It was not fair.

"I'll take care of it." He soothed her — he bundled her into the passenger seat, and turned to glare at both Ben and I. The rescue cat mewed; Carrie turned her head around to look for it. I struggled to my feet, picked up the offending object, brought it to her, and dropped it onto her lap.

She grabbed it like a lifeline.

Patrick said nothing more; he drove her away just as the police pulled in. Fair enough.

"He bought the economy model." Ben walked up to me and steadied me with a hand on my elbow. "And wow, cashmere and only 80 degrees outside. Our boy does know how to do it right."

"What would you know about it?" I brushed at my shorts. I didn't even want to know how bad they looked from behind. I needed a blanket to cover the damage. And my arms were starting to sting. A cashmere blanket would be nice. Hell, some sympathy would be nice.

Unfortunately the detective on duty was the very same one I annoyed earlier in the story.

"Nancy, right?" I squinted at her pitifully narrow name tag.

"Yes." She glanced down at my shoes.

There is no justice. Especially since I had to explain just exactly why I was hanging around the scene of a very ugly crime. And the conclusion was that I brought this all on myself. But the cops were happy with the cocaine, once they fished it out of the dumpster. And they were delighted with discovering Mark at the scene of the crime. It seems he is not very popular with city and county staff.

We made our statements. Mark was carted away. Just try explaining this to Hillary, I thought vindictively. As if the worst thing that will happen to him is facing his sister. Maybe it is.

"Are you okay to drive?" Ben had not left my side as we spoke to the police.

I tried to remember just exactly where I had left the car. Oh, yes, down the street because I'm so clever. I glanced at my watch. It was only six o'clock, far too early to have hysterics; I usually try to schedule all hysteria for after 8 p.m.

"Yes," I said reluctantly. Is there an addendum to fill out if one of your sellers turns out to be a murderer? I didn't think so. At least there wasn't one yet.

"Yes," I focused on Ben, who at least was looking at me with sympathy.

"I can follow you home," he offered.

"No, no, that's okay." I'm tough remember? And when the going gets tough, the tough drives herself home.

I showered and applied Sponge Bob Band-Aids on the worst of my cuts. I wrapped myself in a Turkish cotton robe and loaded up my favorite DVD. I was not in the mood for anything but cartoons; I was not in the mood to talk. I was not in the mood.

Except when I saw it was Ben calling, I paused the movie and took the call.

"What are you doing?" he asked.

"Nothing." I was right at my favorite part of *Lilo & Stitch*, where Lilo delivers the line about a pet, a chainsaw, and rediscovery, but I can't quote it directly because Disney would sue my not insubstantial ass if I even mentioned something as extremely copyrighted and protected as a product by Disney. Funny how something that seems so child-friendly and benign could in reality be so nasty and vicious in protecting its own interests.

"His own interests," I said into the phone.

"Whose own interests?"

"Sweet, quiet unassuming Mr. Fischer," I said.

"What are we talking about? Professor Plum in the dining room with the wrench?"

"No, more like Scooby-Doo, and it's Mr. Givens, the kindly groundskeeper who dressed like a ghost at night to keep people away from the buried treasure." "And I would have gotten away with it if it weren't for you kids," we said in unison.

"So you think it's the executive director. But how would he get the mural if Smith was dead? Why kill him at all?"

"I don't know, that was all my brilliance today," I admitted.

"You're doing pretty well," he paused. "Are you up for a drink?"

"Sure." I reluctantly set down the pint of Ben & Jerry's I had been clutching in my left hand. I didn't really want to abandon it yet; there was still some ice cream left at the bottom. But I could finish it up after the drink.

We arranged to meet in downtown River's Bend.

I wasn't really up for anything more. An afternoon spent being repeatedly slammed down on a cement floor leaves a surprising number of bruises. But I'm a trooper. I decided to take one more for the team.

I dressed to kill, taking a page from Carrie's book of seduction. I also owned a red dress, a Diane von Furstenberg look-alike. The fabric wrapped perfectly around my breasts and followed the plunge my bra created. I can create cleavage that is roughly the size and depth of the Grand Canyon. Not. Professional. At. All. I wore matching red pumps.

Ben actually was silent for a full minute when I appeared at the Steamer Lounge. The Steamer is a bar that use to be a barn and before that, it was a bar. It was still decorated with brass railings and limp ferns placed there in 1975 and never moved. Oh, and it was dark. That's an important feature for a bar, dark. It was listed for sale once a few years ago. No takers.

"You look amazing," he finally said.

"Thank you." His expression, one of wonder and — was that lust? It was enough. I needed male feedback that wasn't derision, condescension, or God help me, professional.

Sometimes I get so tired of professional. Sometimes I wish we could all have sex with anyone we wanted.

And there were some people I wanted.

We found a booth. I ordered a Cosmopolitan, he ordered Mazzocco Zinfandel.

"Ben, like *Gentle Ben*," I said.

"You are not supposed to remember that movie," he growled.

I grinned. "Then you need to date very, very young women."

"I don't like very, very young women."

"You have no idea how much that pleases me."

Oh sure, he has nothing. He rents. Because he changed his name, I couldn't find him on any of our lists, MLS, tax records, nothing. He managed to slide off the grid, which is difficult to do. He has a credit card for the business, that's it. Not that I'm giving up, mind you. He's a mystery man with a past. But for now, I was prepared to take him, as it were, at face value.

"Imagine," Ben mused, "here was this huge mural, featuring the wrong man as the central character, and it appears at exactly the wrong time in history and so, for the greater good, the work is slated to be destroyed." He shuddered at the thought. I took another sip of my drink. Vodka is very good for bruises and pain.

"So our friend Mr. Smith decides that it shouldn't be destroyed, because it's art after all, but at the same time, it can't be displayed, so he hides the Guerra, forever."

"Why hide it in California?"

"If it was right before World War Two, California wasn't on the radar, Pearl Harbor hadn't been bombed, no one was looking West, so it was reasonable to believe that no one would think of looking for stolen art here."

"No one on the East coast ever pays attention to California."

He squinted at his wine. "They still drink French wine."

"I know."

"You know a great deal about art," I pointed out.

"I read a lot," he countered back.

He looked at me. I looked at him. We sipped our drinks. No one was going to give an inch, and Ben was not going to hand over any more personal information. Not even the cleavage moved him.

"So," I finally said, "our theory is that in 1940 the war is on the verge of breaking out, the faces in this painting are controversial, and controversy is destroyed, or not allowed in the building in the first place. Smith can't bring himself to destroy the art, but he can try to hide it forever."

"So even at 18, Smith was an idealist and a radical."

"Mom just said he was a lovely man," I mused.

"Then why was he shot? Lovely people don't get shot," Ben pointed out.

"I always hoped just the bad people got shot." But the dudes didn't strike me as necessarily bad, but they had in fact struck me.

"Accident? Revenge? Just because it's a dish best served cold?" Ben sipped his wine and drummed his fingers on the table.

"Could be, or whoever it was finally found the opportunity," I suggested.

"That's a hell of a long time to wait."

"Let's go ask the curator," I suggested.

It's that simple, just ask. Sometimes Inez asks me to speak to new agents and invariably the question comes up: how do you close the sale? What is the magic? How do you do it? And of course the answer is: Just ask. So do you want to sell your house? So do you want to make the sale? Ask, ask, ask, close, that's the Allison Little technique.

Ben did not think it was that simple.

"What are you crazy?" He stopped drumming his fingers. "You can't barge in and say, 'Hi, did you happen to kill Mr. Mortimer Smith?' Besides, if Mortimer was killed, wouldn't the curator or whoever, steal the painting?"

"He couldn't find the painting, remember? Maybe the shooter was so aggravated that Mortimer Smith wouldn't donate the painting, even after all these years, and that he, the shooter, couldn't even find the painting that he just shot Smith in frustration."

But even that didn't make sense and I always make sense.

"You don't shoot a donor," Ben said.

"You do if you need the CRT to kick in," I pointed out. That was true. The million dollars donated to the Lost Art Museum was in the form of a Charitable Remainder Trust. Mr. Smith did indeed donate a million dollars, but the museum wouldn't receive the money until Mr. Smith died. Until then, Mr. Smith had use of the interest off of that money; he just couldn't spend it on anything else. Or anyone else. The children, needless to say, were tough out of luck.

"True, but usually no matter how dire the situation, or how badly you need the money, it doesn't often come down to shooting the donor. Word would get out."

"Okay, then what is your fabulous theory?" I retorted.

"Don't have one." He drained his wine glass. "So I think we should visit the museum."

"Is this a date?"

"Sure," he shrugged, "what the hell."

There was a strange resistance between us. Like he was wearing a negatively charged magnetic bracelet and I was wearing a negatively charged bracelet. Yes, you can thank Rosemary for that metaphor. He touched my hand as we left the bar, but that was all.

It occurred to me as I drove home that I hadn't talked to Hillary — the client — in a couple days. And with the change in status of one of the owners, I needed to know if they still wanted to sell. Clients are skittish, every one of them. One little change in a person's life and they "can't handle anything more" and pull out on a sale, or a purchase contract, or the listing agreement. Apparently the average person can only cope with one project at a time. I think that's why the whole nation shuts down for Christmas, as if it takes the entire month of December to prepare of a single day.

I wondered if Hillary was one of those single-project people, or if she could multitask. Actually, she had one of the better excuses to pull out of the sale. Her father was dead and her brother had just dropped out of an election, and he may be indicted on charges of possession of stolen goods, drugs, and murder. I connected to her voice mail.

"Hillary, I'm just calling to touch base. How are you doing?" That was an understatement. But on voice mail, understatement works best.

Chapter 11

Monday morning was the classic can't-get-out-of-bed-blues Monday. My body ached, my head ached. Hell, my teeth ached. My stupid toenails ached. I had repeated nightmares involving dumpsters and pretty kitties. I was a mess, and my hair wouldn't cooperate, so I called in sick at 7:30 a.m. to avoid talking to any human at all. I left Patricia a message.

Satisfied with my plan, I hunkered down, finished the Ben & Jerry's for breakfast and watched *Ed, Edd n Eddy*. Happy.

Until Hillary found me.

"Hillary," I tried to sound like I was at my desk, not crouched down on the couch in my fluffy robe and slippers. Oh and upbeat. If you greet clients with the right tone — that everything is fine — you can head off the problems they've grown in their heads by sounding like there are no problems in your own head.

"This is just the last straw," she started out. "I just can't believe Mark would do such things, for what?"

"Winning the election?" I offered.

"Well, then it didn't help, did it? He pulled out of the race, you know. All that early advertising lost. It's a good thing Dad is dead."

"Have they discovered…?" I trailed off letting her fill in the blanks.

"The police have no leads and Mark insists that it was his accomplices who killed Dad."

"But we'll never know that for sure."

"In cold blood," Poor Hillary continued. "Isn't that a title of a book? My God, I can't believe he'd kill someone. He says it was an accident, that those other kids were wrestling with the gun and it went off. Poor Mark, it must have been quite a shock."

I remembered the sound, and his cold assessment afterward. I said nothing.

"Never mind, never mind." Hillary gathered her forces. "We'll get through this. I'm in charge. And I say we just sell the damn house. What's the holdup?"

"The bathroom," I said automatically.

"Well, fix it."

"Would you be willing to drop the price?"

"Whatever it takes, it doesn't matter. Mark gets nothing. I'm through with him. Poor Karen." Karen was Mark's long-suffering wife; Hillary pointed Karen out to me at the funeral, but we had not been introduced.

"I'll make the changes," I assured her.

"Good, I'll meet you at the house tomorrow and sign whatever you need."

"What about the art?"

"Give it to that museum, the first one. Just get it all out. You can do that tomorrow as well. God, I can't believe this is happening to me."

Great, I was back pimping art.

I popped three Aleve caplets, changed into a skirt and light sweater, and pulled my hair back into a ponytail. The trick, when someone was purportedly sick but has to drag her sorry ass into the office anyway, was to look the part. I skipped the mascara, an omission that with my coloring makes me look less the picture of health and more at death's door, which is where I'd been recently knocking.

So I still had the listing, I had carte blanche, which is what I usually insist upon anyway. Why wasn't I ecstatic? Why wasn't I jumping up and down for joy?

Well, mainly because I never jump. Go ahead, this is the last chapter, just visualize what I would look like jumping. I'll wait here.

I walked into the office clutching the Ocean View files. I nodded to Patricia who made a moue of sympathy in my direction.

No one was on floor, or at least Patricia was alone at the front desk. I walked to my own office and changed the price of the house and the listing information. And because my name WAS dragged into the papers in connection with the DA candidate being caught selling drugs to finance his campaign, (discovered by local realtor Allison Little and local contractor Ben Stone — I hoped his phone was ringing off the hook so he couldn't get any real work done either) and because the average person loves a famous person even if they don't know why, I had to field ten requests for house listings, and another fifteen from buyers, all of which is very good news. But I knew that come next week, the sellers would evaporate, citing the timing, lifestyle, or a spouse who doesn't want to move. The buyers will disappear almost as soon as they meet me. They really just want to drive around in my car and pretend to be serious about searching for a house. It's a tedious game; I entertain them, they take advantage of me. I did not return any of the "buyer" phone calls that morning.

I made a note to remember the camera tomorrow for new pictures of Ocean View (without the art) and an another note to track down Mark so he could sign the final papers when it came to that. (Little known fact, his is a valid signature, even from prison.) I've never visited the Marin County Jail. Was it decorated more nicely than the Sonoma County Jail?

I plopped down the files on the front desk and left to hunt down our escrow coordinator, Tammy, when Katherine loomed up into my field of vision.

I didn't think I was quite ready for Katherine, but here she was.

"Feel deep appreciation for all your experiences," Katherine intoned. "Feel gratitude and appreciation for everything in the universe."

"Where's Maria? Isn't she supposed to be on floor this afternoon?" I asked back instead.

"She didn't appreciate what she had," Katherine said sadly.

"That's nice, but where is she?"

I liked Katherine better when she was obsessed with attraction. Not like Rosemary's magnets. Katherine's theory revolves around the idea that you magnetize yourself to bring in all the good that is coming to you, as if good things are like tiny metal filings that cling to your sweaty skin. But there probably can only be one magnet theory in the office at one time. We do have a lot of electrical equipment around here.

"But the experience is what makes the life," Katherine insisted.

"I'd like to experience someone on floor to answer the phone." Patricia shot back.

I gathered up the files, ready to retreat. I'd take them directly to Tammy's office just to avoid more conversation with Katherine.

"Me too," Rosemary echoed emerging from her office. "Cracker?" Rosemary thrust out a flat object covered in black spots. "They're flaxseed, very good for your digestive system, working wonders on my cat's allergies." She took a bite and regarded me for a moment. "Maria quit today. She's taking a job at State Farm Insurance."

"What a shame she couldn't reach her potential," Katherine intoned.

I regarded the wafer of cardboard Rosemary offered. "No thanks. I'm due for a Carl's Jr. burger — it's on my rotation diet."

"Your rotation diet?"

"I only eat things that have rounded corners, so they can rotate, like meatballs, burgers, cookies, and pancakes."

Rosemary rolled her eyes and escaped with her flaxseed and trailing was her flowing sari scarf behind her. Katherine grinned and escaped to her office, located at the opposite end of the building.

I'd like to go to Thailand.

So we are selling, we are painting. We are calling back Ben Stone — Rock Solid Service to expedite both projects.

"Hi," I started, as if he didn't know who it was. Caller ID has eliminated the best part of a phone call — the mystery. Who is calling at this hour? And who is it? What will they say? Now there is no warm up, no mystery, so to speak.

"You still think it was the curator in the bedroom with the walking stick?" Ben answered the phone with his question. See, no preliminaries; it's like skipping foreplay.

"I don't know what I think. Perhaps a new career."

"No, you seem pretty good at what you do."

"Thank you. I do need the bathroom painted."

"What color?"

"I don't know, pick something. And we're supposed to take down the art to the Lost Art Museum and give it all to them."

"For the tax write-off."

"You know something? Hillary was so distraught that she didn't even mention the tax write-off."

He paused for a moment, contemplating that idea.

"Are you still angry about my comment about Carrie being a gold digger?"

When was that? A lifetime ago. "No, but she's my friend and those are hard to come by."

"You're right. I'm sorry."

"Apology accepted. Can you help me take the paintings down to the City?"

"Only if you let me take you to dinner afterward."

I paused, pretending I needed to check my calendar. "Okay."

I checked my PDA; one showing that resulted in one single ray of hope. An agent had a client who was interested as long as the bathroom was painted and that odd art wasn't included in the sale.

Oh, we can do that.

I called the agent back and offered up an ambitious finish date; he'd get back to me after discussing it with his clients.

Ben and I met at the house early Tuesday morning. We cautiously circled each other as we each took to our tasks. He disappeared to paint and I gathered up the art and slowly loaded it into the back of the truck. The pieces upstairs were a bit too heavy and awkward to handle. I should have gotten help, but I wanted the bath painted, and I was dressed for heavy work — shorts, sandals, and an old T-shirt from Race for the Cure. No, not the rock group; I'm not that old.

"It probably needs a second coat, but I bet we can get away with it as is for showings." Ben emerged from the bathroom. On him, his paint smeared tee and shorts looked — marvelous.

He regarded me for a moment as if we hadn't been in the house together for over three hours.

"You look good."

I glanced down and bit my lip so that "What? This ratty old thing?" did not pop out unbidden. I already said I hated it when women like Carrie said similar disclaimers, and I wasn't going to do it myself.

"Thank you?"

"No, I mean you look cute all messed up."

He reached out and swept something from my hair.

"Cobweb."

"Thanks."

Hillary and I were scheduled to meet at noon. I changed my outfit so I would be ready; Ben had an errand to do and promised to meet me back at the house at 1 p.m.

That's a whole hour with Hillary, but maybe she wouldn't want to stay that long.

If I'm lucky.

"This is just a disaster! How much more can I take?" She marched through the house and dropped a copy of the *Chronicle* on the dining table. This afternoon she wore a lavender ladies-who-lunch suit with open toed pumps. And yes, the blouse sported a floppy bow. The very thought of floppy bows making a fashion comeback was depressing, but Hillary had more problems than dubious fashion investments.

Me? I had slowly changed into a bright purple silk suit, a long skirt and jacket; I couldn't bear any heavy fabric on my cuts and bruises. Needless to say, no pantyhose, but the Kate Spade high-heel slides, in of course, bright purple, were a perfect match. But I don't think Hillary was impressed.

Hillary flipped over the paper with a snap of her wrist. The second headline read: Marin Candidate – current acting DA involved in Alleged Murder – Pleads Not Guilty. At the bottom of the paper ran an op-ed titled, "The Youth of Marin, Turning to Crime?" The story on

Mark began above the fold which would have been great media exposure if he was still running. But apparently the voters in Marin didn't tolerate accused murderers as their DA. No, it has never come up in Sonoma, so I don't know.

"He says he'll fight it." Hillary tapped her long nails on the newspaper, as if it was the *Chronicle's* fault that Mark was in trouble.

"I see the signs are still up."

"Oh crap, we'll have to do something about that." She wrapped her arms around herself as if it was cold; it was not. The weather was pleasant and warm — the first weeks in September usually are.

I nodded. I had no experience in counseling, but from the looks of her, counseling would not be out of line. Losing a father to violence and a brother to scandal? Plus finding out your expected fortune was not appearing? And I did not even want to bring up what "money in the house" really meant. I think Hillary definitely needed counseling. I probably need counseling too, but we're not discussing me.

"Well,"" she said grudgingly, "this does look better."

I thought the house looked strangely empty without the blast of color of the art. I even missed the weird guy in the bathroom.

She shook her head. "Mark cared about the money from the house, but not as much as I thought he would. Karen did, but she didn't know about Mark's other sources."

"Why did he do it?" I asked, not really expecting an answer.

"I don't know."

"Well, he is your brother."

"Yes, well, you know how it is. You have your own life; you lose touch. We didn't see Dad that much, let alone each other. We all have things to do."

I eyed her. She knew perfectly well what her brother was thinking. She was helping him run his campaign. But maybe she needed to distance herself now. From the looks of it, she and Stephen weren't all that close, and the buzz on the scandal would fade. There was enough news in the world, even in our own individual counties, for this event to quickly become an inside paragraph in *The Bohemian*, the local alternative newspaper. Once Hillary was home, she could ignore some of what was going on this side of the Bay. In a way, that wasn't a bad thing at all.

"You're pretty smart, aren't you?" She abruptly changed the subject.

"Yes," I acknowledged as calmly as I could. It was the same thing Mark accused me of. Those two were more alike than they cared to admit.

I pulled out the new price adjustment addendum for her sign. You don't technically need to attach an addendum; you just need a form for MLS, but with this family, I wanted every decision signed off and acknowledged.

"Do you like having a career?" Hillary suddenly asked.

I stopped fussing with the contracts. Believe it or not, this was a loaded question. Some women search for careers and some have careers thrust upon them. But I didn't want to tell her that. All I have is my career. She was the one with the house, husband, and three perfect girls. Well, I thought of the oldest girl dressed in her punked out Chanel, maybe not so perfect "I like my career, yes," I assured her. I knew from experience that her question wasn't about me at all; it was about my "alternative" lifestyle. I think working is natural, but both my sisters-in-law have the same life as Hillary; that is, they stay home full time. So I'm familiar with the question, and the look. There's a part inside every full-time mother and homemaker who wants to hear that

I'm miserable, because my misery will justify their choice. But they also need to hear that I'm successful and happy because it bodes well for their own future. They want to know that there are still choices out in the world. They want to hear that they could leave the house and hop back into work at a moment's notice.

Ah, but the average stay-at-home mom I talk with has been absent from the work-force for about fifteen years, And fifteen years is a long time to be away from the business world, especially if you haven't kept up. But I never say that. And what else I never say is — Oh, and when you DO return to work, you won't become the VP of PR just right off the bat because a 25-year-old will have the Internet skills and the computer skills and the drive that you, my friend, won't acquire for quite a while. So you'll end up the assistant for a person ten years younger than you. Nope, I don't say anything at all. I just smile and if I'm lucky, I have a drink in my hand when the question is asked.

"I should look into something," Hillary said.

"Don't you have volunteer work?"

"Boards and things." Hillary dismissed those commitments with a wave of her hand. She signed the papers where I pointed and handed me the pen.

"Thank you for taking care of the art," she said simply.

Her sincere tone startled me so much I didn't respond immediately.

"You're welcome," I finally blurted.

She left soon after, giving me a reprieve of about half an hour before Ben showed up. We had an appointment with Mr. Fischer at 2:30 p.m.

Ben arrived exactly on time, hair damp, blue polo shirt decorated with a crest I didn't recognize, but I didn't spend much time worrying about it because I was more distracted by how the shirt color brought out the deep blue of his eyes.

We'll pause a moment while I contemplate the futility of my infatuation. Thank you, now we can drive to San Francisco.

The Lost Art Museum did need a new building. A building far, far away from the original location, if that was possible. The current home to Lost Art bordered the Tenderloin. The building was a tired, blackened structure leaning against a dilapidated long-term hotel on the left, and illuminated by a fairly new McDonald's restaurant on the right.

Mr. Fischer, I can't remember if he is a doctor Fischer or not, sorry, buzzed us in. The lobby was dimly lit, and the linoleum floor was discolored by yellow stains and deep dark gouges. I pressed the up button for the ancient elevator but after a minute, nothing happened.

Ben nodded toward a door to the far right. I followed him and we climbed the narrow cement stairs.

A large, surly man stomped down past us.

"Fourth floor. Get the paintings," he mumbled. Ben thanked him; I pressed up against the wall to get out of the man's way.

"Can a million dollars even fix this?" I asked.

Ben passed me and took the stairs two at a time.

"The museum is in a new location. These are just the business offices — and Fischer's apartment."

I paused for a moment on the third floor landing. "He lives here?"

"For now." Ben called down from the floor above me. "Coming?"

"Yes." I felt as surly as the handyman who just passed us. I'd be unhappy too if I had to climb these stairs every day.

Fischer's office wasn't much better than the lobby. My heel caught on the threadbare carpet but I recovered quickly. From his office window we enjoyed a full view of the homeless lining the streets. Lost indeed.

"I read about that Mark Smith in the paper, just a tragedy." Mr. Fischer rose from behind his desk and offered his hand. We had no choice, but I hung back so Ben had to suffer through the man's dead fish handshake first.

Mr. Fischer made tsk-ing noises and shook his head. He gestured to a set of split leather chairs facing his desk. I took the smoother of the two. My legs still hurt, but the silk skirt protected the cuts well enough.

Ben did not sit down.

"So are you pleased you get the Guerra?" I asked innocently, I hoped.

"This is a great addition to the museum." Fischer smiled, but it had the effect of a death mask, or one of Smith's angry paintings.

I settled a little lower into the chair as if the cushions could protect me.

"What do you know about the painting?" Ben asked.

"I don't. My father knew some of the history about it, and encouraged me to acquire it, if possible," Fischer explained, his death-mask smile still in place.

"Your father was the expert," Ben confirmed.

"My father," Fischer trailed off. Something fell in another room and it startled Fischer. "Excuse me." He rushed out a side door, not the one that led to the hall, but another door, probably to a back storage room.

"What is that about?" I turned to Ben. There was something about Ben's expression that made me stop. He wasn't pleased; his eyes were dark, like he was carrying on an internal dialogue. I hoped it wasn't about me. I know, it's always about me, but this time, really, from that look? I really did not want to be on the receiving end of that look.

"No! I will not!" A howl went up from the next room and suddenly the door blasted open. If it had been a Gilberto door, it would have cracked the plaster wall.

Mr. Fischer the elder panted in the doorway. He was thin and stooped, much like I imagined Mortimer Smith had looked: wiry and thin. Both these men had lived through some of the worst history the world had endured. (God, had I heard that line from Carrie? Since she began these lectures with Patrick, she came up with all sorts of odd references). I suppose that living through a depression that segued into war after war either gave people strength, or it killed them. I have also found that the experience of such history did not, in general, impart a raucous sense of humor to the individual. With the possible exception of my grandmother.

I saw that lack of humor in Mr. Fischer's face. No laugh lines, just deep grooves etched on each side of his mouth, like suffering puppet. Ben moved just slightly, but placed his bulk between the old man and me.

"I'm sure he's harmless," I whispered. I craned my neck to look around Ben.

"Don't be so sure," Ben murmured back.

"Father!" Fischer the younger barreled up behind his father and almost pushed the man further into the room instead of pulling him away, which I'm sure was his intent.

"The damn Guerra! It was the death of me!" he bellowed. "And a million dollars! What the fuck was that! Throwing in it our faces! And this one took it!" The father threw back his hand and smacked Fisher in the chest.

"The man ruined us and you took the blood money!"

"Dad, Father," Fischer hovered behind his parent, doing little more than wringing his hands. "The museum needed the money, you know that. How much better to use Smith's so his own children don't get it. See? See how that works?" Fischer pleaded. But his father was not listening, or maybe he hadn't even heard his child.

"You sold yourself to that lying, cheating bastard! He was supposed to destroy it, that's what we did to commie, subversive junk like that. An expert! Ha! He was no expert. He was a common thief!"

"Dad."

Ben moved slightly so I could see, but I was still well hidden behind him. I didn't dare move. I did not want to attract Mr. Fischer the elder's attention; he was tiny and possibly harmless, unless he had a gun.

A gun. I froze, really froze. Oh my god.

"The bastard escaped, and I took the blame! Me! And I would have done what was asked, I would have destroyed it, and now you bring it into the house!"

The old man was foaming at the mouth. Spittle sprinkled the air before him, giving physical weight to his words and his anger.

"Dad, your heart," Fischer pleaded.

"Fuck my heart. I don't have a heart. You ripped it out the day you took that money!"

I drew back. Ben pushed the corner of my chair and ever so gently inched me and the chair further away from the scene.

"Dad," Fischer moved around to face his father. He was pleading, but his father wasn't hearing his son at all, he was listening to his own ranting inside his head. A vein began to throb against his thin skin.

"But Dad, you went to Stanford, you got that degree, you were an expert," Fischer reminded him.

Stanford, what was it with Stanford all of a sudden? There are other schools in California.

"GI bill," the man shot out. "I earned it."

"How You Going to Deep Them Down on the Farm," Ben sang softly.

"Smith earned nothing! Nothing!" the old man staggered into the room. Fischer ducked around his father, hovering, fluttering, but not touching the man, as if he could herd his father into complacency. I suspect it worked in the past, but it wasn't working now.

"Fischer," Ben started. "Is there anything?"

"He'll be fine," Fischer insisted. "I have some pills from the doctor."

"No pills! You and that fucking doctor always trying to make me do things!" he roared.

I was paralyzed by the effect of such anger from the man. Not that I couldn't knock him down. I could, but just the energy from him was enough to make me cringe. All those years. He could be lethal with the right equipment. I thought of the dude; armed, he was the master of the universe.

"But he got it in the end! " Fischer announced with relish. "Shot by the pistol they gave me to shoot Germans. He deserved it!" The vein throbbed; his face was turning red. I'm not a doctor (we covered that in the beginning remember?), but the elderly man did not look healthy.

"He deserved it!"

"Dad," Fischer was desperate now, he hovered around his father, trying to find the right way to fend him off, or move him away, or anything, something. But the man was immovable. No amount of soft patting and cajoling was moving him.

Fischer finally made up his mind and lunged for his father, but Fischer the elder eluded his son. He stepped back, his eyes rolled back, and he hit the floor with a muffled thud.

"Oh," was all Fischer could express.

I let out a breath I hadn't realized I'd been holding.

"Ambulance?" Ben pulled out his phone.

"Yes, that's what they use, or the fire department. Just ask for something," I said absently. This was where I walked in, dead old guy on the floor. Heart attack for real.

Fischer hunkered down and lifted his father's thin hand.

"He heard about the million dollars, asked me who donated it," Fischer addressed his father, not us. "What was the harm in telling an old man? He didn't know anyone. No one important." Fischer amended. "Then he quizzed me about the art and if Mortimer was giving any art to the museum and I said no, and he disappeared."

"Who disappeared?" Ben finished talking to the dispatcher and closed his phone.

"My father. I didn't notice it because I had a board meeting that day and at the time Dad could still drive pretty well. Right afterward I took his license away."

"Drove where?" Ben asked.

"I think he drove to Smith's house. He said it was to get the painting back."

Ben and I looked at each other, thinking the same thing — and I would have gotten away with it if it weren't for you kids.

"You saw, you heard," Fischer continued. "He and Smith worked together with Rockefeller. The Guerra was too controversial and the board of directors ordered that it be destroyed. My father refused, and was fired, and subsequently drafted. Smith then offered to destroy it and was rewarded with a position out here in California, probably to get him out of the way. But it turns out he hadn't destroyed it all."

Fischer moved his father's hand to rest on his chest.

"So when the money came in, he finally had Smith's location. And, he was convinced, the painting's location."

"But Smith didn't tell him where it was after all," I said.

"When I came home that evening Dad was so agitated that I gave him some of my sleeping pills. It wasn't until the papers the next morning, the sudden death, that I thought of Dad."

"Where did he get a gun?"

"He's always had that gun. Used to take it out and show me. He talked about traitors and Germans even back then."

"Not very stable," Ben commented.

"My father? No," Fischer conceded.

"No, those old guns." Ben said. " You can actually pull the trigger and nothing happens, then five seconds later the gun goes off."

"Well, that makes it a little hard to predict," I said.

"Are you going to prosecute?" Fischer the younger stood, his eyes still fixed on his father's form. He started twisting his fingers together again. The sound of a siren wailed in the distance. We all paused, but the sirens didn't come any closer. False alarm.

Ben shook his head. "We've done so much to get this capital campaign off the ground, a scandal, no matter how old, won't help." He paused and regarded the elderly man on the floor. "Won't help anyone."

"Are you on this board?" I asked.

"He's a major donor," Fischer added. Well, since we were all blurting out information, I was happy to hear more about Ben.

"Really? Tell me more." But I wasn't that sincere, information about Ben could wait. I needed to process this incident a bit more. An accident. I suppose the shooting was really an accident. The gun could have been "fired" and not gone off, then the two wrestled and surprise, the gun did fire, seconds later than the intended time. Considering Mr. Smith's infamous lack of coordination, I'm surprised the bullet hit him at all. But it had. And now our terrible villain was dead too. Hillary already had to deal with a brother in jail and a scandal in the family and three burgeoning teenage girls. She had enough.

So the dudes would be blamed. Mortimer Smith, a victim of a robbery. I felt badly about that. Even if I still had the bumps and bruises from their most recent assault.

"I don't think that prosecuting would do much good for anyone," Ben finally said. "What do you think?" he turned to me.

I studied him for a minute. He was working very hard to look guileless. If I went along with him, he'd owe me. That would work for me, this handsome man being somewhat in my debt, or realistically, not even in my debt. This knowledge would make me marginally less in his debt.

"Okay, Mortimer Smith can be the victim of a robbery and our poor dead dudes can be the bad guys. I suppose it doesn't matter," I acquiesced.

In a sick, convoluted way — it was fair. I sighed and nodded. I didn't even want to say the words out loud. The whole thing wasn't really equitable, but it was finished.

The firemen came — all cute, thank you, I looked. They carefully took poor Mr. Fischer away. Heart attack. I'll be nice and not make a comment about how living a lifetime dominated by resentment and simmering jealousy makes a heart more vulnerable than an Olympic size pool full of ice cream, because you probably figured that out for yourself.

Fischer had to leave with his father. We followed him down the stairs and out to the street.

"So the new museum will be located where?" I watched Fischer get into the ambulance with his father. Why are parents so difficult? At least my mother hadn't accidentally shot someone. At least I think she hasn't. Bridge can get pretty intense.

"Over by the Yerba Buena Center, we're already building. It will be small."

"But with compliant restrooms," I put in. The ambulance pulled away. The fire truck pulled away and made an illegal U-turn in the street. I resisted waving to the pretty, pretty firefighters.

"Yes, the restrooms are a thing of beauty. You'll have to see them," Ben said.

I let that invitation pass; I'd follow up later. "So you're a major donor, are you?"

"Actually, it was my wife's idea. We gave a nice amount just once and that put us on the books forever. You know how it is."

No, I didn't know how it was. But I did know that Ben still owed me dinner. Actually, I owed him dinner.

We stepped outside, the truck was empty, and we had a shaky signature on the receipt in our hands for Hillary who, by April, would remember that she really did want that tax deduction after all.

"Perfect." Ben held his face up to the sun. "It's always so perfect here in September."

"Well? What do we do now? We could go to Nordstrom. There's a sale on shoes." He didn't strike me as the shoe shopping kind of guy, but I thought I'd try anyway.

"No, shopping. That's a winter activity. Let's go to the beach. I need to clear my head after that."

I sighed, the beach. I was not dressed for the beach.

Ocean Beach was populated with hardy locals and a few tourists lucky enough to land in San Francisco at exactly the right season. The breeze was still strong, but the sky was clear blue, the water was gray-blue and the crashing waves blocked out any city sounds.

I always want to pretend that the weather is like this year round — you know, to perpetuate the California myth. The reality is that in June and July, the coast is usually completely covered in fog, accompanied by a brisk wind and mournful foghorns. This surprises most people. Just a heads-up for you. Come here in October; it's lovely.

Our day in September wasn't bad either.

"Come on." Ben helped me out of the truck and lifted me just slightly so my full weight wasn't on my bare feet. We hustled over the rough, hard parking lot to the soft beach.

I left my purse, my shoes, and my phone in the truck. I glanced at his belt. He had left his phone in the truck as well.

That should be some sort of leading indicator. I wonder if Carrie had read an article about it, "Does He Leave His Phone in the Car? And Other Ways to Tell if He's Interested." Maybe I need more magazine subscriptions.

The beach, the sand, and cool air did feel good. I held up the hem of my skirt to keep saltwater off the silk. Ben didn't do anything immature like dash me with water, or chase me, or any of those picturesque beach activities couples in love indulge in. We strolled at an easy pace on the wet, packed sand. We didn't hold hands. We didn't even speak.

It seemed there was a lot of death in the last weeks. I think I needed a break after this. Maybe go away for a while.

"What are you thinking?" He finally asked.

"Where do you want to go to dinner?" It would be our last dinner together. That thought hit me like a death too.

"Where do you want to go?"

"Peruvian? Fusion? Thai/Asian?" I suggested. I wanted to take him to something romantic, some restaurant that had low lights and soft music and bizarre modern couplings of food. I wanted a dining room with candlelight. I look better in candlelight.

"How about Mel's? It's on the way out."

"Mel's?" I squawked.

Needless to say, Mel's does not offer candlelight.

We stopped at the original Mel's Diner on Lombard. Mel's is a true 50's diner featuring authentic-looking, linoleum -topped tables with chrome legs, booths, napkin holders, and tiny jukeboxes featuring musical selections from the 50's.

We slid into the red vinyl booth and gazed at the black and white photos of *American Graffiti* stars before Ron Howard lost all his hair.

We ordered burgers and shakes because Mel's does not offer Asian fusion dishes. Mel's offers extra fries.

"So tell me about the Lost Art Museum. You built their restrooms?"

"Yes." He took three of my fries.

"Or, you donated the cash to have them built." I took five of his fries.

"Same difference." He took two fries back.

"No, it's not the same difference." I stopped his hand from taking more fries before it was my turn. "You aren't poor at all, are you?"

"Maybe not as poor as you think." He slid one fry away and I let him.

"And your ex-wife didn't take absolutely everything, did she?"

"Maybe not absolutely everything." He dipped three fries into a puddle of ketchup.

"Maybe not everything," I echoed.

It could be considered romantic, if it weren't for the bright overhead lights and the fact that I almost got stuck in the ladies' room because unlike the new ones at the Lost Art Museum, the single restroom at Mel's didn't have to be compliant.

When Ben drove up to my house, the seven o'clock sky was still bright and cloudless. I did not want to end the evening. At all. So I lingered in the driveway. I fussed with my shoes, I adjusted my purse. I was running out of delaying tactics when Ben finally jumped out of the truck and circled around to my side. I waited for him to approach, because that's what the heroines do in the movies, even in a Jane Austen movie. Minus the truck.

Ben did indeed approach. He stood in front of me. Then with no word at all, pulled my head to his mouth. His hand was sure as he guided my waiting lips to his…sounds like a romance novel, doesn't it? And since I don't read them, that's all I know. Anyway, he finally kissed me and I don't know how Cooper Boy kisses, but Ben Stone is indeed rock solid.

We kissed for a few minutes, or forever, I'm not sure which, before his attention wandered to my most prominent feature.

He had to step back to rub his palm over the extensive territories that are my breasts.

"Jesus, woman."

"Is that a hammer in your pocket or are you just glad to see me?" was my answer.

His hand was still exploring my wide breasts, and he didn't answer the question for another minute. We kissed again, for a long time — the old fashioned, full tongue kind of kissing.

"You are like a woman and a half," he whispered against my lips.

"Thanks, I think."

He pulled back but didn't release my breast (one at a time, no one can take both with only one hand, are you kidding?)

"You are my teenage wet dream," he sighed. "It was all I could do to keep my hands off you the first time we met. You are everything a woman should be, times ten."

"Finally, you say the right things."

"I've only seen women like you in films," he admitted, still focused on my breasts.

"Just in films?"

"Well, once live at Mitchell Brothers."

"Liked them, then?" I asked. Oh come on, you have to ask. Women have to hear the words, get confirmation. That's why we make such great realtors; we always want everything in writing. We're a natural for the business.

"No," he said, startling me out of my smug assessment of me and the sisterhood in general.

"No?"

"I liked the whole package." He stepped back and executed a full frontal fondle. "But I will follow these anywhere."

"You can follow me inside."

So he did.

And I did have a happy ending.

Printed in the United States
206186BV00004B/9/P